La Familia:

Carl Weber Presents

La Familia:

Carl Weber Presents

Paradise Gomez

www.urbanbooks.net

Urban Books, LLC
97 N18th Street
Wyandanch, NY 11798

ISBN 13: 978-1-60162-555-7
ISBN 10: 1-60162-555-3

First Trade Paperback Printing March 2014
Printed in the United States of America

10 9 8 7 6 5 4 3 2 1

Distributed by Kensington Publishing Corp.
Submit Wholesale Orders to:
Kensington Publishing Corp.
C/O Penguin Group (USA) Inc.
Attention: Order Processing
405 Murray Hill Parkway
East Rutherford, NJ 07073-2316
Phone: 1-800-526-0275
Fax: 1-800-227-9604

Chapter One

Mouse

"Fuck that bitch up! Fuck that bitch up!" Sammy shouted at me as I went blow to blow with Denise in the middle of the street.

The crowd surrounding our fight was hyped and shit. Bitches and niggas were yelling and animated like they were watching a Mike Tyson fight on the block. Bitch shoulda charged muthafuckas to watch this ass whooping I was giving this bitch. But this was the Bronx, Edenwald projects—survival of the fittest out here, and I was a bitch who knew how to survive because I had no choice. I'd been through hell growing up and this bitch wasn't just going to disrespect me in front of my peers like I was some clown-ass bitch, so I had to give her the fundamentals in a quick beat down.

I caught Denise with a few hard rights to her face and made her stumble, but she refused to go down. She was no match for me. It was a one-on-one fight so far. None of our girls jumped in yet; they all sat on the sidelines screaming and huffing. I knew my best friend, Sammy, was ready to go tag team on this bitch and get her hits in too. She couldn't stand Denise either, and was ready to pull her hair out by the roots. I was already trying. I had that bitch's weave wrapped tightly around my fist and yanked her ass in every direction. I pulled and then caught her with a few more hits to her black-ass face.

When she finally fell on her back, I went fuckin' in on this dumb bitch!

"Yeah, Mouse, fuck that stupid bitch up! She ain't shit!" Sammy screamed, excited that I put that bitch on her back.

"Edenwald projects, bitch. EBV, bitch. Edenwald Blood Vixens!" I shouted, letting these haters know where we were from and who we represented.

Denise instantly went into the fetal position and tried to cover her face, but it was too late. I already had half that bitch's cheap weave pulled out and in my hand, and caught the side of her face multiple of times. It felt so good punching that bitch while she was down, it was making my pussy wet—almost better than some good dick. I already felt her shit swelling up. I wanted to kill this bitch, but she wasn't worth catching no murder charge; just me embarrassing this bitch in front of her peers was proud enough.

Denise was always a shit talker in the hood. She never knew how to keep her fuckin' mouth shut and wanted to spread rumors behind a bitch's back, saying out loud to people that I was fucking her man and gave him an STD, gonorrhea at that. And she thought she was too cute with her split ends, nasty weave, and no ass. The bitch was whack.

So this bitch came at me on some disrespect shit with accusations about me fuckin' her man, Danny. Now I admit Danny was a cutie with his long cornrows, hazel eyes, and chiseled physique, looking like Terrence Howard somewhat. However, Denise had it twisted; he wanted to fuck me. I wasn't even interested in that nigga, and he was a fuckin' whore. Danny would put his dick into anything wet with a pulse. He had a reputation already for fuckin' with multiple women and being a playboy. I personally felt the nigga was a walking STD. And I wasn't fuckin' with him at all. I loved my health. Too bad I couldn't say the same about Denise.

But anyway, I was in the projects kicking it with my bitches, Sammy and Tina, and here came Denise marching my way with three of her friends and this nasty scowl trained at me. This was a dumb, bird-looking bitch.

"You fucked my man and gave him gonorrhea, you nasty-ass bitch!" Denise had shouted at me.

She had jumped in my face with her hands and shit. I wasn't going to take accusations like that, especially when it wasn't true.

"Bitch, you the fuckin' nasty one, and get ya facts straight. I don't want that nigga, and I ain't never fucked that nigga!" I had shouted heatedly.

"Bitch, you fuckin' nasty. You nasty, bitch. You nasty, stay the fuck away from Danny before I fuck you up," she had ranted.

We continued to exchanged harsh words, and it don't take much to set me off, especially when you come at me about some dumb shit that I ain't do and want to try to humiliate me. So I swung first. She ain't see it coming and we started tearing into each other like savages.

I already had the advantage. My hair was real and already styled into a ponytail, and hers wasn't. It was a bad weave, loose and down to her shoulders, easy to grab and pull the fuck back—mistake one. Her second mistake—nah, actually her first mistake—she came at the wrong bitch, 'cause I was known to fuck bitches up on the block—me and Sammy. My hands should have been licensed because I used to box when I was younger. I had training. I started when I was ten and it lasted until I was fifteen. My gang, music, and the streets became more important to me. Denise was a puppy trying to go against a lion, something sad to watch. The first two hits opened her face up like a breezy day. The third, I saw the fear in her eyes. I had power and speed. She was just a loud bark without any bite.

"Get the fuck off me, bitch! Get her off me!" Denise screamed with me on top of her, her body against the pavement.

This bitch's face started to feel like wet tissue against my fists. I started kicking her face in with my sneakers; I wanted her to feel my wrath and everything. I wanted to make her regret that she even came to me with that bullshit.

"I'm Mouse, bitch! Don't you ever fuck wit' me!" I yelled.

My fists and feet rained down on that bitch like a thunderstorm. She couldn't get up. She cried out; the lion had the puppy in its teeth. But then I felt myself being attacked from behind. It wasn't a fair fight anymore. It's like that in the Bronx. You see your friend losing badly, so then you jump in to help, and Denise's girls decided to jump in when they saw the bitch getting her face and teeth smashed in against the concrete. I felt my ponytail being yanked and I caught a blow to the side of my face. But it didn't deter me from still pounding on Denise. I had friends too. Sammy and Tina didn't let the unbalance go on for too long. They intervened, and then a full-blown fight ensued right in the projects. It was nothing new though.

The crowd around us became more glorified. It was four against three, and we still had the advantage. Sammy and Tina were nothing to play with. They were already itching to get into a fight, and when they tried to jump me, shit done set off. Denise's girls weren't a match for Sammy. Right away, she dropped two to the ground and she and Tina jumped on the next bitch. There were weaves and torn clothing everywhere. Tits were being exposed and the niggas watching the brawl were excited and drooling like they never saw breasts before—so fuckin' pathetic. I was still working on Denise, though; she was done for, out for the count, and her weak-ass friends were about to be the same way. I already proved my point. Sammy and Tina had to pull me off that bitch.

"C'mon, Mouse, let's go!" Sammy shouted.

I was so heated. I wanted to scar that bitch for life. But I didn't have my razor on me, because if I did, I definitely would have cut her face and left a disgusting mark for her to personally remember me by.

"Dumb bitch!" I shouted.

My final hit was the tip of my sneaker crashing into the side of her face, causing blood to spew from her mouth, and her face and body to twitch violently like she was having a seizure.

"Damn!" the crowd hollered in awe.

We took off running, once again, being the victors in the brawl. The Edenwald Blood Vixens were nothing nice to play with. We ran deep, and our reputation was fierce in New York, especially in the Bronx. You fucked with any one of us, and you were going to get fucked up, cut or, worse, killed. Yeah, we were some pretty bitches, but on the inside, we were pit bulls in skirts.

We called ourselves the Edenwald Blood Vixens, EBV for short, because, one, we gonna always represent where we come from—our home, Edenwald projects in the Bronx, New York. And we were part of a notorious blood set that wasn't fucked with, and Vixens, because a Vixen is a female fox, or a spiteful or quarrelsome woman, and that's what we were, what we represented. That combination described us so accurately.

We left for Tina's apartment on the other side of the projects, on the north side. Among us, Tina had the more stable home. She lived with her mother, who had a city job working for the MTA and making bank. It was just them two, and Tina's moms was rarely home. If Ms. Green wasn't working, she was spending time with her boyfriend in Brooklyn or gambling in Atlantic City. So it pretty much felt like Tina had her own place, and whenever she had her own place, then Sammy and me had our own place. When times became rough with our parents, Tina would let us crash at her crib until things calmed down in our homes.

Tina was a great friend. The three of us were like sisters. Yeah, we rocked with other bitches, our gangs had straight love for us, but Sammy was my best friend, my ride or die sister, and Tina was right along with us. The two or three of us were always together.

Tina's place was quiet, like always. I was in the bathroom licking my wounds, but there weren't any wounds to lick. Denise barely got a hit off me, maybe a scratch here or there, but beside that, I was fine. I stared at myself in the mirror. There was a reason these bitches hated and niggas wanted to fuck me so badly. Not to boast, but I was a bad bitch. I knew I looked good with my angelic features, high cheekbones, and petite figure. It was one explanation for why my friends called me Mouse. I was only five feet three inches, with shiny raven-black hair that flowed freely, and it was my real hair, no weave. But despite my beautiful and innocent appearance, I was one ferocious bitch when it came to fighting. I didn't take shit from anyone, and if you started it, I was surely going to finish it.

Lil Wayne and Drake were blaring in the background and I could already smell the weed burning from the living room; it was haze and I couldn't wait to put my lips to the blunt. Sammy was no joke when it came to rolling up a joint, and I needed to smoke. It had been a stressful day and smoking and laughing with my girls was something I needed.

I walked into the living room and Sammy and Tina were lounging on the couch and already on like their third pull. I loved chilling at Tina's place. She had all the amenities a bitch like me could get used to: large flat-screen TV in the living room, plush couches and chairs to relax in, a high-end stereo system and surround-sound entertainment system to enjoy, and an extensive DVD and CD displayed on the shelves for us to see. If Tina weren't my friend, yeah, a bitch would hate right now.

"Damn, y'all bitches couldn't wait for a bitch?" I joked.

Sammy took a deep pull from the burning haze, exhaled, and then responded, "Bitch, you shoulda stopped tryin' to look cute in the bathroom mirror. You okay anyway; that bitch ain't even put a fuckin' hand on you."

"Why bitches be so fuckin' dumb and shit?" Tina chimed.

"They don't know how we get down, right, Sammy?" I replied, slapping Sammy five.

"Damn sure don't," she responded.

She passed me the blunt and I took a few pulls, feeling the weed seeping into my system and already soothing me. I sat next to Sammy, took another pull, and passed the blunt to Tina. I lounged, listening to Lil Wayne's voice chime through the speakers in the room:

Yeah, I tell her, 'now go on, pop that pussy for me'
haters can't see me but them bitches still looking for me

I nodded, feeling Lil Wayne was one of the best rappers in the world. I kinda had a crush on him, loving his swag. He made me want to tighten up my own rhymes and become his first lady; fuck that bitch Nikki Minaj. I truly felt Sammy and I were better than her. I loved rap. And despite rap/hip-hop started before we all were born, we grew up on it and fell in love with music. I was a huge fan of the old school: Kurtis Blow, Slick Rick, the Sugarhill Gang, Fab 5 Freddy, Busy Bee Starski, Grandmaster Flash and the Furious Five, Ice-T, Doug E. Fresh, LL Cool J, and so many more.

I started to rhyme at twelve years old. Coming from the Bronx, the birthplace of hip-hop, we had visions of becoming superstars in the game. I remembered my first rhyme at twelve: "My name is Mouse, I love the boys and get shit poppin' on the rouse, and I'm pretty fine, so smile, got all the boys loving me like Mattel. BX is where I'm from, Edenwald is my home, so I'm lethal wit' it, ain't no traps catching this mouse, cuz I'm slick wit' it, got my own cheese, no need to scurry around, on stage like Broadway, I am the show, got my own traps for these dumb, black cats, how they gonna try an' eat me, bitch, I ain't nuthin' nice to digest."

It was cute when I was twelve, but now things done changed and I'd been through a lot more drama and pain. My rhymes were sexier and harder, more methodical and catchy. And now I had a partner, Sammy, and we called ourselves Vixen Chaos. We felt that name described us perfectly, 'cause we were vixens wherever we went and we could easily create chaos on the scene. We'd been doing our thang in the clubs for one year now, trying to make a name for ourselves on these New York streets and get put on. We had a small buzz out there, but it wasn't anything life changing that had us ready to move out of the projects and live a rock-star lifestyle.

They say fame and success take time, but we were ready now. We put in our dues, we felt. I mean, growing up in the Bronx projects was already a rite of passage. We weren't fake and what we rhymed about was real and what we'd actually been through, not like some of these lame rappers in the game making up fraudulent street credibility. It was a laugh to me. The world needed to know our stories, and our talents needed to be displayed. I was a gift ready to be opened.

Sammy and I grew up together. I'd known her since I was eight years old. Back in the days our mothers used to be best friends. Like us today, they did everything together, even got high and smoked crack. So while they were getting high in the apartment, Sammy and I would be playing in the hallway, maybe the rooftop, and getting into all kinds of mischief. We were learning about life's hard lessons on our own without too much parental guidance interfering.

Sammy grew up to be too beautiful. We were both eye candy in this asshole of a place called the projects. I mean, the Bronx is my heart, but I always knew there was more out there for us. We thought in a different way from our peers. Don't get it twisted, we were fuckin' hood as fuck, got it poppin' and whatnot, but I had big dreams of becoming somebody important and having respect that reached beyond the projects. Sammy was with me too.

This place took my mother away from me when I was ten years old. She had overdosed on a bad drug and died in the stairway of a project building in Soundview. She had a crack pipe in her hand when she passed. Her death troubled me. But I learned how to move on.

Sammy and I did everything together since we met ten years ago. We were like two peas in a pod. Shit, we were so close that people thought we either were sisters or lesbians—so far from the truth. However, we both lost our virginities together with the Johnson brothers at fourteen on the building rooftop. I was with the older brother, Mike, and she was with Cashes, and there we were, the both of us on our backs next to each other on tattered blankets against the hard gravel with our legs spread, Mike forcing his nice-sized dick into me, causing me to cringe, and Cashes trying to work his shit inside

Sammy. It really hurt at first, but we got through losing our virginities together because we supported each other.

We stole cars, sold drugs, shoplifted, got into numerous fights with hating-ass bitches and niggas, ran from police, and got arrested together. If it happened to me, it happened to Sammy, and vice versa. We constantly fought to protect our territory and reputation, and remained loyal to each other. I think the only thing we truly feared the most was losing each other.

Me, I would die and kill for Sammy. She was my best friend, my ride or die bitch. When I looked at me, I saw her.

Chapter Two

Sammy

Tonight was the night Mouse and me were set to perform at Latin Quarters in Harlem. It was rap night at the club, where numerous rappers, or MCs as some like to call themselves, got on stage either as individuals or in a group, and showed the crowd their skills in five minutes or less. The event was hosted every second Saturday of the month, and some of the best of the best, and even the worst, got on that live stage and did their best to entertain the crowd. And if you weren't nice, then the crowd would let you know within a heartbeat. They were brutal. It was like our own ghetto Apollo.

Tonight would be our first time performing at the club instead of being spectators. We had our act and rhymes together. I was more the salacious one in the group, while Mouse was the Left Eye of TLC, and together we were Vixen Chaos. We tried to be different, not falling into that same cliché that other female rappers do. Yeah, we rhymed about the streets and sex, 'cause the streets was what we knew and sex was what I was good at, but we tried to put some humor into our rhymes along with realness. Like Biggie, we were storytellers. I wanted to tell my story, because my story was deep. I wanted to be a voice out there. I wanted to be heard and my story was told via rap.

Growing up was hard for me. My mother was a whore and she was HIV positive. Shit like that scared me. My biggest fear was becoming like my mother, burnt out from being in the streets too long and becoming sick. That slow death was the worst for me. I mean, slowly, I could see my mother deteriorating day by day. She was a heavy drinker, a nympho, and a chain smoker, so of course her immune system was shutting down. Her health was nonexistent. I mean, every day it was one thing or the other with my mother. Her life had caught up to her and it caught up to her in the worst way. Catching that monster was a stigma on you. Back in the days, my mother, Dana, used to be a beautiful woman; she had a lot going on for her, and many said I favored her in so many ways. But I didn't want any of her traits. I wanted to become my own woman. I wanted to use my talents, which were rapping, singing, and my looks, to bring me out of the projects. I needed to become that success story. I needed to break this curse of being trapped in this place and shut the haters up.

I stared at my outfit for the evening hanging on the back of the closet. It was a quiet night in my room and in the projects for once—no gunshots and no violence. Yesterday's incident with Mouse and Denise was being talked about heavily. But there were always fights and shootings in the projects, and for the moment, the topic of the day was our brawl; but then tomorrow, it would be something else that caught the project's attention.

I sat near my bedroom window, with the dark kinda inviting, and stared at my home, one of the most notorious projects in New York, from the sixth floor and thought about my rhyme for tonight. Living in Edenwald was a muthafucka, but it was home, and would always be home. I done experienced the good, the bad, and the ugly, and I survived the ugly.

Edenwald was located in the northeast section of the Bronx, north of Baychester, south of Wakefield, east of Bronxwood, and west of Boston Road and "the Valley," a sub-neighborhood of Eastchester. Edenwald project was the largest housing development in the Bronx and home to the forty-seventh precinct, one of the most active precincts in the city. With forty buildings from three to fourteen stories tall, it had about 2,000 apartments housing 5,000 people. Yeah, with all them muthafuckas stacked up over each other, you were going to have some shit and deal with all kinds of trouble. I mean, it was the Bronx, and the Bronx was an infamous borough, known for everything from being the birthplace of hip-hop to breeding some of the most notorious gangsters that New York has ever seen. Pistol Pete, Larry David, and John Gotti. Yeah, Gotti is from the Bronx. But the Bronx to me was much more; it was a place of culture and diversity. We have the Yankees, the most dominant baseball team in the world, and we have our history, the people.

Where I lived, the crime rate was heavy and the drugs were prevalent. Everybody wanted to escape their poverty. The drug dealers did it by selling drugs and making money, the fiends escaped their hell by getting high, the residents did it by working every day and maintaining, and I escaped by music, and yeah, sex. But we each had our own little way of zoning out from our harsh reality, even if it was only for a moment.

Tonight, performing at the Latin Quarters was going to be our escape, me and Mouse. I was nervous, because it was going to be a huge crowd and there was no telling who was going to be in the house. The Latin Quarters was known for having A&Rs from different music labels coming through to check on the talent, trying to decipher who was nice enough to take it to the next level and have a big hit. I definitely wanted to catch a bigwig's attention via my talent and my sex appeal.

I looked at the time and removed myself from the window. It was almost seven p.m. The show started at nine p.m. I wanted to get there early and check out the scene. When it came to my career I didn't do the CP time.

I decided to call Mouse. Her phone rang a few times before she decided to pick up.

"Hello."

"Mouse, you gettin' ready?" I hollered through the phone.

"Yeah, 'bout to," she replied nonchalantly.

"What you wearing tonight?" I asked.

She sighed. "I don't know."

"Yo, we gotta be on point tonight, so we gotta be lookin' sharp. I think someone from Def Jam might come through to peep the show."

"You serious?"

"That's what I heard. You know Search be knowing everything that be going on. He like know everybody and shit."

"I know."

Search was a homeboy of ours. He wanted to become the next Russell Simmons in the music game. Search was affable and sharp when it came to his business. He definitely had the gift of gab and wanted to manage us. He already saw the potential in us and always said that we were destined to become superstars. Search was the first person who believed in us. We grew up together in the same building. He lived below me with his aunt on the fifth floor. He was okay looking, bald head, dark skin, but he wasn't my type at all. He was on the chubby side with glasses and smooth features, but he was such a cool-ass dude. Everybody called him Search because he was always searching for something, either via hustling, a come up, something to do, pussy, or just a bitch to be his.

"Anyway, Search talkin' 'bout come early so he can introduce us to a few people," I said.

"Okay, okay. We there, Sammy," Mouse said, sounding a bit jovial now.

"I'ma start gettin' dressed now, so meet me in front of my building in like an hour, Mouse."

"No doubt. One."

"One," I replied.

I hung up. I was always the punctual one. Mouse would be late to her own funeral. I knew she wanted this music career to happen too, but sometimes Mouse could get trapped into other dumb shit that would be irrelevant to our come up, like niggas. Don't get it twisted, I love dick too; but if it came in the way of my money and career, then I didn't need it in my life. Mouse, on the other hand, even though she was a bad bitch, she was a gullible bitch, too. She was thirsty for that attention, but I'm not saying my girl was a ho, because she wasn't; but when it came to looking for love, Mouse could become open like a book. I was bit more unyielding when it came to looking for love. Love hurts, love is damaging. Love is a dangerous emotion. It can lead you off track, sidetrack you, and have you feeling sick and unwanted. Love could make you feel alone and used up. Love was a muthafucka! Love is a hater! That's why I wasn't so quick to find it.

Yeah, I'd been in love twice, and the two niggas I loved done broke my heart and damaged me in so many ways that, I admit, I would run away from it. My first boyfriend, the boy I fell head over heels in love with, was Cashes. We were fourteen; he was a corner nigga, a bad boy, and the one who took my virginity. Cashes was a sweetheart when he wanted to be, but there were times when he would act as if I didn't even exist, especially when he got around his friends. It felt like he could easily love me alone, in private, but when we were around each other in public places, it was a different story. He would become aloof toward me.

Cashes sold drugs, and he would take me shopping on Fordham Road or Third Avenue and buy me whatever I wanted. It was one of the perks of dating a hustler. I would come home with shopping bags full of expensive things. And the sex was good. He had my heart in a vise grip. I only wanted to be with him. I thought I was Cashes' queen. I believed he was a good dude and only loved me. But a year later I found out the hard way that Cashes was a fuckin' dog. Besides me, he had many other girlfriends he took on shopping sprees on Fordham Road and spent money on. And I wasn't the only girl he was sexing. He got two bitches pregnant at the same time, and one was a friend of mines. I was just another notch on his belt. He got the pussy; he took my virginity. His was the first dick I sucked. He was the first man I ever loved and the first boy to break my heart like a priceless vase shattering against concrete. I was fucked up for months behind him.

The second heartbreak in my life was Marcus. He was Puerto Rican and black, and a real cutie. I met him when I was sixteen. I was finally over Cashes, reason being he had gotten locked up for drugs and was sentenced to five years upstate.

Marcus had long, beautiful hair that reached to his shoulders, and smooth brown skin that seemed to glisten and melt like ice underneath the sun. His eyes were green, and his physique was amazing. It looked like he was born with a six pack and nice arms. I'd met Marcus at a house party in Westchester, the suburbs. His conversation was nice and I was definitely attracted to him. He wasn't a thug, but very well educated. He was a senior in some affluent private school and on his way to college trying to become an engineer. He talked different from the other niggas I grew up with. He knew big words and knew how to use them fluently in his sentences. He knew about things that I was unfamiliar with, like politics and history. He spoke three languages and played the piano. Being around Marcus made me want to better myself. I mean I started reading books because of him and looking up big words in the dictionary to improve my vocabulary, which became a plus when I started rhyming. I wanted to become the female Nas.

A week after meeting, we fucked in his bedroom, and the dick was so good. He grew up having both parents in his household. He was privileged. Marcus was going places. He was on his way into doing bigger things and I wanted to go along with him and do big things myself. He was my boo and l truly loved him. I wanted to always be around him. But there was one problem: his mother. She hated me. I wasn't from their world. I was from the ghetto; they were from the suburbs. I went to public school; her son was always in private schools. Marcus talked proper English; I used Ebonics and had a checkered past with the streets. I wasn't good for her only son. I was considered a bad influence. The bitch once told me, "Stay the fuck away from my son. I don't need him to get you pregnant. He won't ever be a baby daddy to ghetto trash like you. He has a lot going for him, and you are only poison in his life."

Oh, I wanted to go off on that uppity bitch. But the only reason why I kept my composure was because I loved Marcus and didn't want to disrespect him at all. As long as he loved me, then I was good. Shit, I was ready to be spiteful and get pregnant by her son on purpose, and then there wouldn't be any getting rid of me. I would permanently be in her son's life. But I just couldn't do it to Marcus. He was always good to me and had a very bright future ahead of him. If he wanted kids by me, I was ready to give him some. But we weren't ready and I wasn't rushing to push a child from my womb.

We dated for a few months, and I was in love with this man. Then a week before my seventh birthday, the unthinkable happened: Marcus got another bitch pregnant. Once again, I thought I was the only one in his life, but I was clearly mistaken. While he was doing me, he was also doing his ex-girlfriend, Cindy. She was the girl his mother was happy to see him with. She was pristine, came from a good home, with both parents being lawyers, she was educated and had a full scholarship to attend Spelman in the fall. I was just something for him to sow his wild oats.

I became crushed, almost suicidal. Mouse was there for me. She comforted me through those hard times when I just wanted to be alone and die. And I always did the same for her. On my birthday, Mouse just received her income tax check and she took me to Coney Island for a day of fun, just us. We spent the day bouncing from ride to ride, eating junk food, playing the games that you knew were rigged, and just momentarily escaping from our crazy worlds. Sometimes I think if it weren't for her, I don't know where I would be. But that was a year ago, the last time I was in love with someone.

The one thing me and Mouse were fortunate about so far was that we weren't any baby mamas to anyone. Shit, we done had plenty of dicks run up inside of us, sometimes raw, too, coming inside our tight, wet boxes, but never any babies followed after a good nut. Thank God. We were both young and free from the diaper changing and baby feeding that so many girls our age were trapped into. We were a rarity in the projects: two bitches as fine as us and we didn't have any kids. That's why niggas were on us. They wanted to be the first to get us pregnant and have bragging rights in the hood. Yeah, to pop a baby in either one of us sent out a statement: they got us.

With it getting late, I hurried and got dressed. I was home alone, which was great. I didn't have to deal with my mother's shit. She was still in the streets doing her, after everything she'd been through; nothing was slowing that woman down.

I got dressed in a pair of tight jeans that highlighted my luscious curves and nice round booty, a patterned tie-front top that showed off my flat stomach and pierced belly button, and some wedged heels. With my sensuous hair flowing down to my shoulders and my makeup on point, I was looking like a goddess. I was ready to strut around on that stage with my goodies showing and illustrate my talents for these niggas and bitches.

Before I left the apartment I called Mouse to see if she was ready.

"Yes, I'm ready," she said.

She wasn't.

"Meet me outside, Mouse, and hurry up," I hollered.

"Okay, Sammy. Damn!"

I sighed. It was already ten minutes after eight. The club and show started around nine. It was going to be cab ride down there. The trains were going to be too slow and too far of a walk. I exited my apartment and walked toward the elevator. I could hear my neighbor, Mrs. Dinkins, arguing with her husband of ten years. It was a regular. The next apartment down you could smell the heavy weed smoke lingering and spilling into the hallway. Ray was Jamaican and was always getting high and always trying to talk to me.

The narrow hallway was covered in graphite and smelled of weed. And when I stepped in the elevator, it smelled of fresh urine. Like always, the elevator became someone's personal bathroom. Fuckin' nasty!

It was still early spring, early April, warm and balmy. I walked through the courtyard that was littered with broken glass, discarded cigarettes butts, liquor bottles, and weed remnants. The hustlers were on the boulevard either rolling dice or selling drugs. The residents were inside nursing their kids or nursing a nice drink after a long day.

I hurried toward Mouse's building. On my way there, I came across Kay. She lazily swaggered across the courtyard toward me. She was dressed in a pair of dirty black jeans, a spaghetti-strap blouse, and house shoes. Her hair was matted and uncombed, her lips were dry and terribly chapped, and her eyes were sunken deeply into her head, indicating her heavy drug use: crack, meth, heroin, something. She was grotesquely skinny and fucked up.

Kay was in her mid-thirties and a hot mess. Back in the days they say she used to be the shit. She had a body like mines and the fellows were all over her like white on rice. She was the prize to get in the projects, but that was years ago. Now, it was hard to look at her directly. She made you want to turn your head from her and run the other way.

"Sammy, Sammy." Kay called out my name with a smile. "Sammy, let me hold five dollars."

"I don't have it," I said.

"What, I'ma pay you back, Sammy, you know it. I just need a favor from you," she pleaded.

"I don't have it, Kay," I reiterated.

"Damn, Sammy, I thought you was my homegirl," she said, scratching in areas that looked like they were going to fall apart. She looked at me and smiled again. "You lookin' all fine tonight. Where you goin'?" Kay was fidgety, and her eyes were all over the place, indicating her need to get high.

"I'm performing at Latin Quarters tonight."

"Ya still rhyming I see."

I nodded.

"You always had talent."

"Thanks, Kay."

There was nothing more to talk about. Kay couldn't get what she wanted from me, so she hurried off to harass the next fool. Kay was something that I didn't want to become. She got caught up with the wrong man, fell in love with him, and he got her hooked on that shit. Every day she was losing herself deeper and deeper, probably to the point of no return. It was scary. It was because of love Kay ended up that way.

I didn't have time to dwell on her. Mouse and I had someplace to be. The cab was already on its way to pick us up and take us into Harlem. I hurried toward her building. It was already eight-thirty and it looked like us being punctual was going out the window. When I got in front of her building, I dialed Mouse from my cell phone. It went straight to voice mail.

"What the fuck, Mouse," I cursed.

I dialed again. This time it rang. She picked up after the forth ring. "Hello?"

"Mouse, what the fuck! Are you ready?" I hollered.

"Damn, Sammy, I'm coming down now," she hollered back.

I hung up and sighed with frustration. We were going to be late. But knowing black people, the show was going to start on CP time. I already knew that Search was looking for us out front. I had to call his phone and let him know that we were running a little late.

"Sammy, hurry up, it's already gettin' packed out here," he said.

"We there, Search."

Mouse came walking out her building with a smile, like we weren't late already. But she looked good though. She was clad in a pair of tight jeans like me, only mines were black, and hers were blue. She sported a pair of fresh white Nikes and wore a tight black T-shirt that accentuated her tits, and on the front of it read GIRLS' NIGHT.

It was definitely going to be our night. Mouse was ready to do her thing. We were looking spectacular. We looked like we belonged on tour with Beyoncé, Alicia Keys, Rihanna, or somebody making noise in the music game.

"Damn, look at you, lookin' like a million dollar diva," Mouse said jovially.

I twirled around in my heels and showed off my outfit. I was looking like a star. But we didn't have time to marvel on our appearances. We had somewhere to be and fast. Like clockwork, the gypsy cab arrived on time and we climbed into the back seat. The trip to the club took twenty minutes and cost us twenty dollars. It wasn't like we were banking like that. That twenty could have gone to more useful expenses.

When we pulled up to Latin Quarters, the line outside was long. It was mostly niggas outside with their sagging jeans, and hood attire. The minute we stepped out of the cab, the wolves were on us. Like on cue, they saw the tight jeans, the heels, and our succulent curves, and the calls followed along with the corny pickup lines.

"Yo, ma, let me holla at you fo' a minute."

"Damn, can I roll wit' y'all?"

"Hey, sweetheart, what's your name? You wit' somebody? I ain't tryin' to intervene . . ."

"Yo, y'all got a man?"

Thirsty niggas, like they never saw pussy. Scratch that, like they never saw two beautiful women before. We weren't interested at all. We came to do a show, and they were paying to watch. I started looking for Search. It was already nine-thirty and we weren't about to start waiting in that line.

"You see Search?" Mouse asked.

"Nah, not yet."

The crowd outside the club was swelling like a bee sting. It was a good thing that it was nice outside, because we would have been looking stupid lingering outside in the cold. We walked toward the front entrance and security outside was tight. Two beefy bouncers who stood over six feet tall and weighed a ton each were making sure niggas weren't getting in with any weapons and maintaining order outside. When they saw us approaching, they remained deadpan.

"We're performing tonight," I said to them.

"Who y'all?" the one with the Rick Ross beard asked. He looked us up and down and didn't seem impressed at all.

If I thought he was cute, he would have hurt my feelings.

"Vixen Chaos," I said.

"Y'all with Search, right?" the second bouncer asked.

Now he was a cutie, with dark skin like Wesley Snipes, and a bald head, tattoos like a thug, and built like the Rock. I loved big men with nice arms and a swelling chest. And he was my type. I locked eyes with him and replied with, "Yes, we with Search." I couldn't help but smile. He didn't smile back or hinted that he was interested in me. Was these two niggas gay?

"Sammy, Mouse," I heard someone call out.

I turned to where it came from and there he was, Search, smiling hard like a proud father seeing his daughter for the first time. Search came our way, moving through the thick crowd. Around his neck was a black and gold VIP pass. He had on a pair of old-school gazelle glasses and sported a black-and-white Adidas tracksuit; and his sneakers were nice, the black and white shell tops, talking about retro.

He hugged us both, praised our outfits, and then sassed us for being a half hour late. I blamed it on Mouse. She refuted. But we didn't have time for petty bickering. Search put two VIP passes around our necks and escorted us into the building. He was one of the sponsors for tonight's show. He had pull and made sure we were taken care of.

The crowd inside was thick and the lights dimmed. The rap music was blaring. The DJ was playing Kanye West and Jay-Z: "Otis." I loved this song, and I loved these two rappers. Instantly I started dancing to it and reciting the lyrics. "'Photo shoot fresh, looking like wealth I'm 'bout to call the paparazzi on myself.'"

Jay-Z was my nigga. Already I had the boys' attention in the club as I danced in my high heels, showing off like usual and spitting lyrics out like the beast on the mic that I was. We continued to follow Search. The club was mostly niggas, but you had a few bitches sprinkled around. It was rap night, and not too many fly bitches came out to catch the show. But the ladies were out and so were the sharks.

Search led us behind the stage; it was off-limits to nonperformers and whatnot. You had to know somebody to be somebody. And I had to admit Search was definitely becoming somebody. He was hungry. He was ready to commit and tear into fame and success. I was the same way.

"Hey, Craig," Search said, tapping this tall and long-limbed man on his shoulder.

He turned around and looked at Search. By his reaction he was excited to see our friend. The man Search called Craig wasn't cute at all, but by his demeanor in the place I knew he was someone of importance, especially if Search was trying to introduce us to him.

"Search, what's happening, man?" he greeted him back.

"These are the two ladies I wanted you to meet, Sammy and Mouse. They go by Vixen Chaos," Search said.

Craig smiled at us. By his expression he already liked what he saw. He fixated his eyes on me. I played it cool. He rocked a nappy afro, no facial hair at all, and was high yellow like butter—ugh! He definitely wasn't my type at all. But it was about business. I wasn't trying to fuck him.

"Vixen Chaos, now that's a unique name," Craig said.

"We're two unique females," I returned.

"I can't wait to see y'all perform. Search speaks very highly of y'all, saying y'all are the new Salt-n-Pepa duo."

To compare us to Salt-n-Pepa, wow. I was mostly doing all of the talking. Mouse was playing the background, looking cute, peeping the scenery. Craig was an A&R for Def Jam records and despite his whack looks, just shaking hands and talking to him made me tingle. He could make it happen for us. So far, I liked his personality, but would he like us after our performance?

"We can't wait to show you what we can do," was the only thing I could say.

Search started to do most of the talking for us. He was putting us on a pedestal. We weren't going to make Search look bad. This was really our first big show. There was a crowd of about a hundred-plus ready to either cheer or boo us.

The performances started around ten p.m. We were scheduled to perform fifth, which was good for us. We didn't want to be first and you damn sure don't want to be the last act on stage; by then, after so many acts, the crowd starts to dwindle and lose interest and then you start looking at a scattered crowd of drunks and tired people ready to leave.

The first to go on was this group who called themselves Series. They were a trio from Brooklyn and their rapping was hardcore. They moved around on stage with their sagging jeans, dreadlocks, and Timberlands, screaming "Brooklyn! Brooklyn!"

The next act was a duo from Newark, New Jersey who called themselves Poison DeVoe. Now these niggas was nice and cute—tall, fine, and black like night. Their style was on point and they rocked that stage like Kanye West and Jay-Z were on the stage themselves. They did this rhyme called "True Niggas." I was truly impressed. I also noticed Search and Craig had their eye on them.

The next two acts before us were mediocre; they really didn't stand out too much. One was from Queens and the other, A Gangsta Story he liked to call himself, was from Brooklyn too. The only things I heard from these two were a lot of screaming on the mic and cursing. Their lyrics were whack to me and I wasn't the only one feeling that way. Their audience wasn't feeling them either. Of course, their time on stage was cut short.

When they were done, the host of the evening jumped on stage and clowned them. He was too funny. "I guess not everyone is meant to be rap stars. Hope they didn't quit their day jobs for this shit."

I laughed. He was a funny dude. If a performer or group was whack then he would have something sly and foul to say about them. If they were nice he definitely let it be known. He was raw and a cute guy. The crowd was ready for some more, and we were next. I had butterflies in my stomach. Mouse and I weren't new to performing, but when it came to trying to get a record deal and having an A&R present, it was nerve-racking.

I looked at Mouse and she looked at me. We both were thinking the same thing: *this is it.*

"Y'all ladies ready?" Search asked.

Mouse and I nodded simultaneously. Here we were, two Dominican females from the Bronx projects trying to make big things happen. You could hear the crowd of over a hundred people behind the walls. The DJ was taking it back to the old school; he was playing Mobb Deep, "Shook Ones." A classic.

"A'ight! A'ight! Cut that, cut that. You keep playin' that joint and some people might end up gettin' shot tonight," the host shouted humorously.

The music came to an end. There was laughter. The host, who called himself True, was once again on stage and ready to announce the next act.

"Yo, yo, we got our next group comin' to the stage, and these ladies are somethin' special. We got our first female rap group about to come on. Shit, I'ma keeps it real, my niggas, they are fine, and if they can rap as good as they look, shit . . . we in trouble," he proclaimed spiritedly.

I took a deep breath. Search was encouraging us. Like always, he was all smiles and there for us. Like a boxer before a fight, I started to warm up by punching the air, doing a few combinations like I was Floyd Mayweather about to get into the ring.

"Yo, yo, here they are, Vixen Chaos!" the host shouted out.

I emerged first. Mouse was right behind me. Instantly, from our looks and attire alone, we had the crowd's attention, especially the men's. Yeah, we were eye candy, but being beautiful and luscious just wasn't enough. They expected talent from us.

The DJ began to play our beat. He put on the instrumental to Nas's "One Mic." I was in love with this song. I gripped the microphone like it was welded to my hand and moved around on stage freely in my wedged heels. The nervousness I felt earlier faded. I was hyped. I locked eyes with the crowd, opened my mouth, and said, "Let me come out wit' the intro. Fellas, this for y'all grimy niggas that don't know what us ladies be going through wit' y'all," I shouted roughly through the mic. "So Vixen Chaos is now on stage, and to let y'all know, we're more than big tits, a smile, 'n' a phat ass. The Bronx, Edenwald projects is in the house. Bronx, where you at?"

There was lots of screaming and shouting. The Bronx was definitely in the house tonight.

They were feeling my intro. Now it was time to go in and show them my talents. I started to spit. "You keep falling victim to things that really don't matter, addicted to the person who keeps shattering your laughter, hooked on a love that's tainted like acid, it's blasphemy how you stay chasin' after an unwilling happening, in your heart, you know that love ain't happening, their charm got you delusional, your yearned got you seeing illusions, you thirst for that first, wanna win the race 'cause last ain't the right place, so ya ready to devour that lie, hang on to that un-need high, the wrong turns got you doin' U-turns, and it's a one-way street, clinging to an dumb interest, face to face with disaster, you wanna call it natural, but it ain't usual, tryin' to see the sun through the clouds forming, the thunder should have been a strong warning, choose to remain under the dark sky, watching as the downpour drowned your craving sunshine."

Mouse came in on cue and started to spit her rhyme. "You're such a trouble li'l angel, drama queen they made you be, feathers ruffled, your soul tearing 'cause the weight of their love is too bearing. You didn't know you would fall a victim to such his cool, his love crept onto you like an unwanted cold, the way he talked to you made you sway like leaves dancing in the wind, his words warmed your heart like a nice spring day, the attractive smile turned ya frown around, his touch made you feel wanted, the right talk really made you feel so hunted, that sought-after chick like you was an R&B hit. Believed his love completed you, but his lies only depleted you, the drama damn near defeated you, got caught up in his intricate system. Damn, you then finally realized you only became a victim to his enduring system."

I then went on to singing the hook and my voice boomed through the mic like Beyoncé, shocking everyone like, "Oh shit, this bitch can sing, too."

"We Vixen Chaos and we don't play them games, so see us rise from the bottom to the top like a building frame and stay there, 'cause we like clouds, we won't ever fall, like stars, stay above, shine better when that darkness fall, we beauty and brains, say no more, putting clown-ass niggas in their place, 'cause bitch 'n' fake-ass niggas wear more makeup than us, see us coming into the game is like niggas gettin' mad when I close my legs, 'cause they can't eat no more, so recognize who we be, two thorough-ass bitches from Edenwald," Mouse and I said as one.

Everyone loved us. They were cheering and screaming and I was on cloud nine. We exited the stage feeling so good. I couldn't stop smiling. Search approached us and was exhilarated. He hugged me and Mouse. Craig gave us two thumbs up. By his look, I could tell that he was impressed with our rhymes and performance.

It was over with and we rocked the house. I mean, we were getting so much love from left and right that it felt like I just won a Grammy. The duration of the night was spent mingling with Craig and Search. Craig was ready to put us on and I was ready to pass go. Search was the businessman. He knew how to talk to these corporate muthafuckas. He went to school and everything. I just wanted to make it happen and take things further.

The only thing that upset my night was when I looked over and saw Mouse chatting with Rico outside the club. He was posted up on the hood of his gleaming 650i coupe with the chrome rims and tinted windows, and looking like the hustler he was. Rico was from our hood and about trouble. For some strange reason, I felt he was going to be bad news for us. There was Mouse, smiling and laughing, showing her interest in this thug after we had a successful performance.

Search and Craig wanted to go out for drinks in the city; I was ready to do whatever. I wanted to pick Craig's brain all night. It was still early and the night had only just begun. Mouse walked over to us and I told her what the plan was, to continue to chill with Craig and Search, but by the look on her face I could already tell that she had something else in mind.

"I might go chill with Rico for a minute," she said.

"Chill wit' Rico?" I was dumbfounded. "Are you serious?"

"I'm sayin', Sammy, he cool peoples. He really liked our show a lot and wanna talk."

"Talk about what, Mouse? Rico ain't nothin' but a thug," I refuted.

"He just wanna chill," Mouse argued.

I didn't want to become frustrated in front of everyone, especially with Search and Craig around. It was a nice night, but Mouse wanted to ruin it by chasing Rico. I could have choked her.

"You can go ahead and talk to Search and Craig, tell them I had to run. You was always good wit' networking anyway," she suggested.

"Mouse, c'mon. You can't be serious."

But by the look she gave me, I knew she was dead serious. I sighed with frustration. Mouse wasn't about to change her mind. Rico was still posted by his ride, waiting for Mouse to come back his way. He gave me a head nod, but I didn't acknowledge him at all.

"I'm not gonna be too long, Sammy. Go handle that business for us and I'll give you a call tomorrow," she said.

She walked away from me and climbed into the passenger seat of Rico's flashy ride. I just wanted to punch him in his face. I watched them pull off, looking helpless that I couldn't get Mouse to come take care of important matters. I turned and there was Search standing there, looking lost himself. I had to go over there and give him some excuse why Mouse decided to run off with a thug instead of networking with an A&R from Def Jam. I swear, she was my best friend, but sometimes her priorities were totally fucked up.

Chapter Three

Mouse

The sun was at its peak when I finally made it home. Rico pulled up in front of my building and parked. The radio was playing HOT 97, but it was on commercials. We both were exhausted. I had a really busy day and busy night. But I had a good time with Rico. After we left the club, he took me to Philadelphia with him, and I had a great time at this club in South Philly. He had to take care of business out there with some associates of his. While I was on the dance floor doing it up, Rico disappeared into one of the backrooms in the club to handle his business. I wasn't naïve to what he was about. Rico was a drug dealer, becoming big time. However, he was an exciting guy, charming and attractive: the bad boy and the heart-throb in the hood. His chiseled physique was something to drool over. He was tall, six feet one inch, with brown skin and a thick goatee. His onyx eyes were piercing and the respect he had was appealing.

I lingered in his car for a moment. The leather interior was soothing and the coconut smell was freshening. It was my first time being in a BMW. It was an impressive car. I wasn't ready to leave his side. It was a beautiful afternoon and I felt there was so much more to do. I wasn't getting much sleep, being so active from fighting, to performing, and hanging out with Rico, but I wasn't tired. Being next to Rico gave me energy.

Rico removed his shirt and tossed it in the back seat. He was in a wife beater. His cut physique became exposed. His arms were so muscular and defined, and his tattoos manifested the way he lived: gangland, drugs, thugs, and "C.R.E.A.M. (Cash Rules Everything Around Me)." His diamond-link chain with the monstrous Tech Nine pendent that was diamond cut hung low to his abs. I didn't want to gaze at him too hard. Yeah, I was interested in him, but I didn't want to look thirsty and shit.

"I had a good time wit' you, Mouse," he said, smiling.

"I did too."

"You and Sammy did y'all thang the other night. You got talent, yo, fo' real. I mean, y'all were the best group to perform, real talk. You got skills."

I smiled. "Thanks."

"I ain't wanna bring you back home right away, but I got other moves to make," he said.

"I understand. It's cool."

"But ya beautiful, Mouse."

I smiled heavily. "Thanks."

"How come you ain't got no man?"

"Don't be havin' the time. And I'm picky wit' mines. Besides, I work part time and I'm tryin' to make this music thing happen wit' Sammy," I said to him.

"See, I like that though, you about ya business. You ain't like these others bitches around here that ain't doin' shit. You and Sammy, y'all about somethin'. I respect that," he complimented me.

I loved the praise. He was making me blush.

"How come you ain't got a girl in ya life?" I asked.

"Ain't had the right shorty hold me down yet. I'm picky myself, ya feel me?"

"I feel you."

He stared at me again. I could see the hunger for me in his eyes. I wanted to taste his lips again. They were so full, so enticing. I was ready to jump on him, but I kept my composure. In Philly, we almost got it popping after we left the club, tongue kissing heavily in his ride, with his hand between my thighs massaging my pussy through my jeans. I was becoming hot and bothered. I was ready to fuck him right there, but it didn't happen.

We continued to talk. The projects were still sleeping. It was quiet because it was Sunday morning. People were either in church, or coming over a hangover.

Rico looked at me; his eyes became fixated on my thighs and hips. I knew what he was looking at. My figure was looking great in the jeans I wore. We hadn't fucked yet, but it was obvious he was thinking about some pussy, hypnotized off my body. I was thick, juicy, and in shape.

"When I'm gonna see you again?" he asked.

"Whenever. You got my number."

"Yeah, I do, and I'm gonna definitely use it."

"You do that."

"Can I get another kiss before you leave?" he asked with a smile.

"That can definitely happen."

We leaned toward each other and pressed our lips together fervently, locking our mouths tight like magnets. Our mouths hungrily devoured each other's lips as our tongues battled for dominance. I would suck every now and then on his tongue, easily pulling his wet muscle into my playground. I felt his hand cupping my breast and his other hand pressed against my thigh. My pussy throbbed. I loved the taste of his breath against mines and I loved the way he touched me, heatedly, yearning for me and my goodies. It'd been a minute since I had sex. I wasn't fuckin' niggas like that. They were chasing for my treasures, but the treasure chest wasn't going to open easily for anyone. I had some good pussy, 'cause I'd been told that by everyone who had the chance to slide into me, and when some niggas get a taste of it, they don't know how to act afterward. They become possessive and wanna stalk you. That's why you gotta be careful who you give your cookies to. Next thing you know, you got the Cookie Monster coming after you looking crazy and fiendish.

I already knew Rico was going to get some though. He had me open. He was smart, ambitious, and funny. I mean, even though he was Puerto Rican and thuggish, this man was impressive. He was a hustler, but he could talk that Harvard shit. I was attracted to his intelligence. Street smarts and book smarts were making my pussy wet.

We continued kissing and groping each other in the front seat of his 650i. I would occasionally give into his needs and probe my long, sinuous muscle into his mouth, coiling it several times around his own. I had him hard. The bulge in his jeans was notable. I wondered how big his dick was. With his swag alone, I knew the dick had to be good. But I had to get my mind out of the gutter and make my exit. This nigga had me ready to take my jeans and panties off in the front seat and ride that dick in broad daylight.

I pulled away from him, panting and feeling horny.

"That was nice," I said.

"Yeah, you got a nigga feeling crazy nice right now," he replied.

"I do, huh?"

He nodded.

We talked briefly again and I had to go. I stepped out of Rico's car with a pleasant smile on my face. With it being a beautiful day, I wasn't ready to sleep yet. I was high off of life, having a great time in Philly and with him. Rico waited for me to walk into the lobby until he pulled away. I watched him drive off. They said he was dangerous, but he was such a gentleman. I never been out of New York and he took me two states away from home. I definitely wanted to see him again.

The minute I stepped into the elevator my phone went off. I looked at the caller ID and it was Sammy calling. I figured she was worried. I was having such a good time that I forgot to give her a call.

I answered and the first thing Sammy said to me was, "Damn, bitch, you forgot about me. I hope you had a great time wit' that nigga."

"I'm so sorry, Sammy," I apologized.

"Where did he take you? At least give me that since you ducked out on Search and me last night," she said.

I was reluctant in telling her the truth, but Sammy was my friend and we didn't hide anything from each other. "He took me to Philly," I said.

"Philly?" she hollered into the phone.

"Yeah, Philly."

I already knew she was really upset and would be against me and Rico hooking up. I tried changing the subject by asking, "So, what happened? What did y'all talk about?"

"If you would have been there then you would have known what went down, Mouse. That was so fucked up how you did us," she proclaimed.

"Well, I'm sorry, Sammy. I can make it up to you."

"You better, Mouse. I really want this music thing to happen in our lives, so we gotta be on our grind."

"I feel you."

"Search set up some studio time for us Tuesday night. He's gonna pay for our sessions. You good wit' that?" she asked.

"Yeah, I'm good."

Sammy and Search wanted to start working on our demo and an underground album. I was excited. Search wanted to market and promote us. He had these extraordinary plans for Vixen Chaos. Search had a vision for us, but first we had to create a buzz out there on the streets, create a strong following for ourselves. Doing shows in places like the Bronx, Harlem, and Yonkers was nice, but we needed something tangible to put in people's hands for them to play in their cars or on their iPhones. Search was the brains and we were the talent. He always said we needed to get into the studio and start recording. I was down.

"Don't let love blind you, Mouse," she warned.

"Who said anything about being in love?" I replied, becoming a bit irritated. "We just hung out and talked. It ain't like he brand new to us, Sammy. Rico is cool peoples."

"I know you, Mouse."

I sucked my teeth. I didn't want to hear her fuckin' preaching right now. "Sammy, stop tryin' to set up a wedding date and shit. Maybe I just wanna fuck the nigga and keep it moving. You know I ain't had any dick in a minute," I proclaimed.

She laughed. "You crazy, girl. You and me both. But all I'm sayin' is just be careful wit' Rico. You already know he 'bout that life and he can be trouble."

In more ways than one, I thought. I was thinking about all the nasty things I wanted to do with Rico's fine ass. But I didn't let Sammy know about it. I was already being criticized by her.

"Rico's about his business, Sammy. Like us," I replied.

"And let's stay about our business. So Tuesday night, we up in the studio wit' Search and his peoples. A'ight?"

"I'm there."

"I love you, Mouse," she said genially.

"And I love you too, Sammy," I returned.

We both said our good-byes. Even though Sammy could get on my nerves, sometimes acting like she was the big sister when we were the same age, I still loved her. I knew she was only watching my back. Now that was friendship, when they tell you something you need to hear instead of something you want to hear. Sammy was never the one to sugarcoat anything. Real recognized real, and that's why we were so fuckin' close.

I walked into my apartment after talking with Sammy. Yeah, she was tight that I went with Rico last night, but I had a thing for him. I wasn't trying to marry the nigga, but I had a feeling that things with him might work out. Now I'm not saying it was love at first sight, but there was some sparks between us.

With it being late morning, almost early afternoon, my apartment was dark. The shades were drawn and not an ounce of sunlight percolated into the living room. My father was sleeping on the couch when I walked in. He was on his back. He had an empty bottle of Mad Dog 40/40 in one hand and an expired cigarette in the next hand. Once again he had drunk himself to sleep. He was shirtless with his gang tattoos and war scars showing. Even though my father was in his late thirties, he still had it going on, physique and looks wise. These young bitches in Edenwald all had crushes on my father. Back in the days he was the man, balling, making bank, and doing big things.

However, we both lived a rough life; my father lived a very hard life growing up, especially coming from the Dominican Republic. My father, Hector, who went by the street name Ozone, was a serious OG in the hood. He ran with the Latin Kings back in the days and moved up in the ranks quickly. He was an enforcer for the notorious gang. He did everything for them, from murders, moving drugs, beatings, and extortions. My father's name rang out heavily in the streets. He had been to hell and back so many times, the devil had a personal timeshare for him there.

For the past two years, my father had been keeping a low profile. He'd been trying to keep out of trouble. Since he was ten, trouble was the only thing he knew. I never knew my grandparents; they still lived in the Dominican Republic and never came to the States to visit me, and I never went there.

When my father was fourteen, he was a terror out there and he had gotten into serious trouble on the island. His parents had gotten him a visa and sent him to America to escape death or prosecution. He came to live with his aunt. But living in the States didn't change his ways. He became worse in America, being in and out of jail since he was fifteen, and then he met my mother when he was seventeen and they had me two years later.

He came home for good three years ago and was now on parole. Hector became tired of the streets, going in and out of jail since he was ten years old—first in the Dominican Republic and then in America—dealing with the shootings, stabbings, and murders. My father done seen it all. His respect preceded him and I was his baby girl, his only child. But most times, I didn't feel like it. My father was a personal hell in my life.

I pretty much raised myself when he wasn't around. When my mother died our lives became more gripping and hard, but we survived. The streets were in our blood. I followed in my father's footsteps by joining my own gang, the Edenwald Blood Vixens, and soon I was getting arrested and becoming a menace to society. Music was the only positive thing right now I had going on in my life. But to keep it real, I was also lonely. Yeah, I had Sammy in my life, but I was looking for some intimacy and love in my life, too. Rapping wasn't going to keep me warm and scratch my throbbing pussy at night. I wanted my cake and to eat it, too. Why not have the best of both worlds: my career in music and a good man in my life?

I wasn't trying to wake up my father. I wanted to let him sleep because I didn't want to hear his mouth and endure his abuse. He was also mentally unstable, pretty much crazy. He was on medication. The streets, the killings, and prison fucked him up pretty bad. The nigga was unpredictable. When he got drunk, it got worse. It was when he would put his hands on me and forget that I was his little girl.

I went straight into my bedroom and undressed. The place was quiet. Usually my father would have his peoples and bitches come over, smoking, drinking or playing cards. Our apartment was the hangout spot. My father wasn't in the streets anymore killing and doing grimy shit, but he still had his ways about him and he was still somebody you didn't want to fuck with.

As always, the first thing I went for was my stereo system. I turned it on and put in Kanye West and Jay-Z's album, the two rap icons in the game. TV wasn't my thing like that, I guess because we only had one TV in the apartment and it was in the living room, and the living room was always occupied with niggas. So when I was home, I would stay reclusive in my bedroom with the door shut and music playing loudly.

I walked around my bedroom in my panties and bra and rolled up a phat blunt, some kush, and got high near my window. The sun was peaking in the sky and the courtyard below my window was gradually coming alive with the local residents. I took a few pulls and stared at nasty-ass Kay strutting through the courtyard, searching for her next high by sucking someone's dick. I shook my head in disgust. She looked like a fuckin' broomstick with clothes. It wasn't going to be my future.

I continued to smoke my joint, listening to my rap music. This time I had 2Pac playing, and as I heard him rhyme, I was coming up with a few lyrics of my own to spit next time. I quickly grabbed for my notebook and pen on the bed and began jotting down some lyrics. Living here, there was always something to write or rhyme about. When I started to write, Rico came into my head. I started thinking about him heavily and smiled. I just left him only a few hours ago, but I wanted to see him again. I was tempted to give him a call but I didn't want to look desperate.

I exhaled out the window and my attention stayed fixated on the courtyard below my window. I watched the young hustlers emerge from their apartments to linger around on the benches to serve the daily fiends wandering around, and to drink, smoke, roll dice, and waste their day hanging out.

Yup, it was Kurt, Manny, D-dot, Feach, and Floyd. They were the neighborhood bad boys, drug dealers, playboy, gangsters, and killers. They were my niggas, though, young, exciting, and fresh, and just didn't give a fuck. If you came at them, you better be heavily armed and ready to die, and if they came at you, you done fucked up.

I eyed Feach the most though. We had a thing a while back, like six months ago. I fucked him. He was the last nigga to get this sweet pussy. And the dick was good. I liked him, but he wasn't ready for a relationship. Feach was crazy like my father. He was two steps away from incarceration or death. Feach was a trigger-happy goon. He was very violent and temperamental, but also very handsome, and looking like Fabulous in his sagging jeans, Timberlands, and long cornrows.

Everyone was rolling dice and I watched. The hustlers had the area on lockdown. If they didn't know you, then you wouldn't dare to pass by them, risking a serious beat down for interrupting their dice game or narcotics sales.

After smoking, and being up for a very long time, I felt my eyes getting heavy. I retreated to my bed and the minute my face touched my pillow, it was lights out.

I woke up a few hours later to Jose de Rico, "Rayos de Sol," blaring from the other room:

> *Quiero rayos de sol Tumbados en la arena*
> *Y ver como se pone tu piel dorada y morena*

I instantly knew that my father was awake and he probably had company. I got out of bed and looked out the window. It was dark. I glanced at the time and it was almost midnight.

"Damn," I uttered.

I had slept for twelve hours straight. I was so tired. I reached for my phone and saw the missed calls. Two were from Sammy, the next was from an unknown number, the other one was from Tina, and the final was from Rico. I smiled when I saw Rico's number on the screen. I was ready to call him back.

With me being up at midnight, I was ready to hit the streets and do something. My home felt like trouble to me. Rico had tried to call me around nine p.m. and I wondered if it was too late to hit him back. As I was contemplating my next move, I heard a loud knock at my bedroom door. Before I could say to come in, the door swung open and there was my father standing in the doorway. He was shirtless with a cigarette dangling from his lips and, as was customary, a bottle of alcohol in his hand. I cursed myself for forgetting to lock my door.

"*Despertar dormilon*," he said in Spanish.

"I am up," I replied.

"Come join the party, Mouse," he said.

"I'm okay."

I could hear loud chatter coming from the living room. It was a full house in our small apartment. I smelled the lingering cigarette smoke and heard the Spanish music blaring like we were at a concert hall. My father's cronies always made me feel uncomfortable.

My father looked at me. He was already drunk and it wasn't going to take long until something bad happened. Either he would be fighting with me or with one of his guests in the other room. He stepped farther into my room with his saucy eyes locked on me. It felt like the devil himself was in my bedroom.

"Papa, ya drunk," I said.

"I'm not fuckin' drunk! Where were you last night?" he hollered.

I moved back toward the window. He took a swig from the bottle and glared at me. This wasn't going to be pretty at all.

"I went out wit' Sammy," I said calmly. I didn't want to anger him.

"That little friend bitch of yours that is always gettin' you into trouble. *Ustedes dos son putitas,*" he shouted.

How can a father call his own daughter a whore?

"She's not a whore and neither am I," I argued.

"You are a fuckin' whore! You think I don't know, Mouse. I still have people in the streets."

"Papa, get out!"

He rushed toward me and smacked me across the face. I toppled over the chair in my room and hit the floor. My father towered over me, scowling.

"You don't fuckin' tell me what to do. *I manejar las cosas aqui.*"

He suddenly became furious, shouting at me that he ran things in this apartment. My eyes became flooded with tears. I stayed glued to the floor. I was still in my underwear and embarrassed. It was the liquor controlling him.

It was the only time he became so abusive and mean to me. When he was sober, it felt like we were the best father and daughter team of the year. He would talk to me. He would love me. He would protect me. But that alcohol made him schizophrenic. It turned him into a fuckin' monster.

"Get up, you little bitch!" he screamed.

I refused to get up so he could strike me back down. Here I was, one of the baddest bitches in my gang and in my hood, having respect from block to block, but here, in my own home, I felt like a coward. I was scared.

"Get up!" he screamed again.

He hit me again. The blow struck me on my cheek. He was strong. He was dangerous. I continued to cry.

"Papa, stop it!" I yelled.

"You're my daughter! You do what the fuck I say. Ya not grown, you little bitch! This is my home and you keep ya fuckin' legs closed. You better not end up fuckin' pregnant or I'll kill you and cut that bastard baby out ya belly!" he said harshly.

Where was this suddenly coming from? Who was he talking to? I wanted to know. It scared me to death. My father was crazy, and even though it was the alcohol talking, I knew there might have been some truth to his words.

That ominous feeling grew deeper around me. I felt paralyzed for a moment. I just wanted him to leave. *Please God, let him leave or have him leave me alone. Please.*

"I can really hurt you, Mouse. You know that right?" he exclaimed.

I knew he could.

"Why would you wanna fuck wit' me? Huh? Why?"

I was silent, frozen with fear.

"Answer me, bitch!"

Please God, let him go away. Please!

It was the only time I would pray to God.

I felt him coming much closer to me. I never felt so vulnerable in my life, like I was small prey about to be captured in a predator's sharp teeth and devoured ferociously. He had his fist clenched. The other hand wouldn't let go of that liquor bottle. Tonight, his choice was Russian vodka. He continued scowling at me.

"Hector, what the fuck you doin'!" I heard someone say. "That's your daughter, *puta.*"

I looked up and saw Rodriguez standing in the doorway of my bedroom with a displeased look at my father. Hector spun around and growled, "*Puta,* don't tell me what to fuckin' do in my own home."

Rodriquez stared at me. His look showed that he was concerned. I wanted him to . . . shit, I was begging with my eyes for him to intervene. When he stepped farther into my bedroom and looked at Hector with his hard eyes, I felt my prayers had been answered. Rodriquez and my father went way back, since childhood crime partners in the Dominican Republic. And Rodriquez was one of the very few who wasn't scared of my father. He had known me since I was a baby. He was my godfather.

"Hector, you need to chill. That's your little girl, man, and my fuckin' goddaughter," Rodriquez shouted.

"She disrespected me. She's a fuckin' whore," Hector exclaimed.

"Mouse is no whore, yo," Rodriquez argued. "Ya drunk, nigga."

"I ain't fuckin' drunk."

"Mouse, get dressed. I got this," Rodriquez said to me.

He didn't have to tell me twice. I jumped up from the floor and grabbed my clothes from the chair. But Hector refuted. He shot a murderous look at me and screamed, "Bitch, don't you go anywhere!"

Rodriquez chimed in. "She's leaving for the night, Hector. And I'm serious!"

While the two argued, I threw on my jeans and shirt, and then my sneakers. My father tried to come at me, but Rodriquez came in between us. He was like my shield. He told me, "Just get out of here, Mouse. I got this."

I hurried from my bedroom. I could hear them going at it. They started screaming at each other in Spanish. Like I said, Rodriquez was only one of a few who wasn't scared of my father. He was crazy too, and had a treacherous past.

The living room was filled with men smoking and drinking. They were lounging everywhere. When they saw me, I held their attention like I was a lamb running through a lion's den. Their looks manifested their strong hunger for me. It didn't matter that I was Hector's daughter; these horny-ass muthafuckas still wanted to fuck me.

I made my way up to the building rooftop. When things became too stressful and hectic at home, it was one of the places I escaped to. Lucky for me it was a nice and warm night. I walked toward the end and collapsed against the gravel underneath my feet. I gazed up at the stars and wished I were one of them. The ones showing in New York were so bright to me and were always seen from everywhere on this earth. No matter where you were, from America to China, the stars were always there. It made me want to reach out and grab one and palm it in my hand. I just wanted to get away, go somewhere far. If I could only fly, I would do it every night and probably never come back here. But I would bring Sammy with me for sure.

Chapter Four

Mouse

I ended up staying the night at Tina's place. Fortunately for me, her mother was working the night shift and she allowed me to crash on her couch. I slept like a newborn. Tina's place was so cozy and tranquil that you would forget she lived in the projects too. It made me want a home like this. I yearned for the stability and love that Tina had with her moms. Being at Tina's place was like having a slice of heaven while being in the projects. From having cable TV to food in the fridge and peace of mind while you slept, shit, I would kill for that.

The only reason I didn't go over to Sammy's was because her place was like mines: hell. With her mother being sick, and having niggas in and out, I would have gone crazy.

I rose up and sat upright on the couch. It was afternoon again and the sun was percolating through the windows, indicating that it was another beautiful day. I remained on the couch for a moment. I was thinking about some things. I had more lyrics swimming around in my head. I was ready to hear a beat and start spitting. Last night's episode with my father wasn't the first time, and if I continued to stay there, it sure wasn't going to be the last. I had to get away, and the only way I saw getting away was via music or Rico.

Tina came into the living room with a smile. "You okay?" she asked.

"Yeah, I'm good."

She already knew about the rough night with my father. The incident was nothing new to her and it wasn't the first time I had to crash at her place because of my father's drinking and abuse. It was becoming like a second home to me.

"You hungry? You want some breakfast?" she asked.

I was starving. I hadn't eaten anything solid in two days. I nodded. Tina was a great cook. With her mother always working or going to Atlantic City, she learned things on her own, like Sammy and me.

While she was in the kitchen preparing breakfast, I went into the bathroom to shower and wash up. I had to be at work in two hours. It was only a part-time job at a video/music store on Jerome Avenue. My cousin hooked me up with the job, knowing my passion for music; he figured it would be a good start to work around something that I loved. The manager was cool and I sometimes got away with a lot of things, like coming in late, leaving early, or sometimes not coming to work at all. But I would call in. They said the manager was scared of my daddy and it was the only reason he hadn't fired me yet.

I took a long, hot shower. I just wanted to wash my pain away. The water cascaded on me like a tropical waterfall and it was so soothing. In my apartment, sometimes the hot water didn't work. I exhaled and soaped my body from head to toe. When I stepped out, I could smell Tina's cooking. I couldn't wait to eat. I toweled off, got dressed for work, and went into the kitchen for breakfast.

While eating eggs and French toast, Tina and I talked. I told her about Rico. We all grew up together. My time and talk with Tina was refreshing. The only one missing was Sammy, but I didn't want to call her because the first thing she would have gone into was how I dissed her and Search for Rico. I just needed a break.

When I left Tina's apartment I had the urge to call Rico back. He was constantly on my mind. It felt like I was going to explode if I didn't hear his voice again or see him sometime soon. The minute I stepped off the elevator and into the lobby, my fingers were dialing his number. With the cell phone pressed to my ear, it rang a few times, and when I thought I was going to get his voice mail, his voice chimed through the phone.

"Hey, beautiful," he answered.

I immediately smiled. "Hey."

"It's 'bout time you called me back," he said coolly.

"I had a rough night, but I'm okay now."

"What happened?" he asked with concern.

"It's somethin' I don't want to talk about right now."

"I understand. So when I'm gonna get to see you again?" he asked.

"I don't know. Anytime."

"Anytime, huh? So how about today?"

"Today's good. Oh, but I'm workin' this afternoon," I mentioned.

"What time you get off?"

"At six this evening."

"So how 'bout this, I'll come get you after work and we can chill. I wanna do somethin' wit' you," he said.

"Really?"

"Yeah. I've been thinking about you a lot."

"You have?" I said excitedly.

"Yup. You've been on my mind and we gotta link up."

"I'm definitely down."

"So text me the address to ya job and I'll come scoop you up around six, a'ight?"

I was smiling so heavily that it felt like I was a permanent smiley face. "I can do that," I replied.

"A'ight, beautiful. You do that, and I'll see you in a few hours. We can go do somethin' special," said Rico coolly.

When he hung up I felt like doing cartwheels around the projects. I couldn't wait until my shift ended. I walked toward the train station with such a huge smile that I felt nothing could ruin my day. I had forgotten about last night's incident with my father and wanted to put that behind me. I had to move on. It was critical for me to become a success and find love in my life.

I arrived early to work and was like high off of life. The manager, Damien Green, greeted me with his usual smile.

"Hey, Mouse."

"Hey, Damien," I greeted him with my own matching smile.

He was such a nice guy. I rarely saw him angry or upset with anyone. Some of the employees thought he was a pushover, but we had it easy. The job at the record shop was simple: assist the customers who walked inside the place, know your music and certain genres, not just rap and R&B, but others too, and stay jovial. I mean, we didn't have to wear any uniforms, or work in a hot and sweaty-ass kitchen, because the store was air conditioned; and we got to listen to music on the job or watch videos on the flat screen mounted on the wall in the store. And the pay was okay: eight dollars an hour part time. I was only eighteen and was able to live off that, temporarily anyway.

I quickly got on my job and started stocking the new CDs that just recently came in. Damien was working the cash register and Sophia was working the floor with me. It was a slow afternoon, so we spent the day talking and assisting the few customers who came into the store. My mind stayed on Rico. I was ready to write a rhyme about him. I wanted six p.m. to hurry up and come. I could only imagine what he had planned for us.

The duration of the day I spent in the back room going through open boxes of albums and videos, sorting everything out in alphabetical order. It was a tedious task, but I didn't mind it. I was listening to Drake's new album and sipping on a Slurpee. It was an hour from my shift ending and I couldn't wait.

As I was going through the boxes, my cell phone rang. It was Sammy.

"Hey, girl," I answered.

"You at work?" she asked.

"Yeah."

"What time you get off today?" Sammy asked.

"At six," I said.

"Let's go out and do somethin' tonight," she suggested.

"I can't."

"Why not?" she asked.

"I already made plans."

"Plans? With who?"

I didn't want to tell her about Rico picking me up. But I hated lying to Sammy.

"I ain't gonna sugarcoat it, Sammy. Rico's picking me up after work," I said.

"Oh, he is," she replied, sounding edgy about it.

"Yeah," I replied.

She was silent. I didn't want to make it feel like I was dissing her. So I said, "But we're still on for the studio tomorrow, right?"

"Yeah, it's still on," she said dryly.

"So after we do our thang in the studio, we can go hang out, probably go cause some trouble in Times Square," I suggested.

"You already know how we do, Mouse. They gonna chase us out of there like they did last time." She laughed.

"It was your fault," I chimed.

"My fault. You were the one who smacked that bitch in the face right in public."

"You started to argue wit' that dumb bitch first. But I had ya back. And she shouldn't have gotten in my face like that. That bitch lucky she ain't get cut that fuckin' night."

"I know right. She was a dumb, bird-lookin' bitch. But you know ya crazy, Mouse," Sammy said humorously.

"And you crazy right behind me."

We both laughed.

"So tomorrow then," said Sammy.

"Tomorrow," I returned.

"And don't be late, Mouse. You already know how you are."

"Please, I'm always on time."

"For what?"

"For us."

"A'ight, yeah, whatever. Talk to you, bye," said Sammy.

She hung up. I was happy she didn't stress about me going out with Rico tonight. I probably would have to curse my best friend out if she did. Shit, I needed some male attention. I needed to do something different. And I think Sammy needed the same thing: some good dick in her life. It'd been a minute for the both of us. Lately, it'd been me with my crew and Sammy. And if I wasn't with Sammy, then we were doing a show or I was home fighting off my father. Shit, people started to think that we were lesbians and fucking each other. None of that; I was strictly dickly.

I steadily watched the clock, and when six p.m. came around I was ready to run out the doors. But there was one problem. I hadn't heard from Rico yet. When it became six-fifteen p.m., my jovial spirit started to fade and I was starting to think that he stood me up. I called his phone twice, but it went straight to voice mail. My smile transformed into a frown. I didn't want to go straight home and deal with my father. If Rico didn't show up, then I was going to take Sammy up on her offer.

"Fuck him!" I cursed to myself.

It was still a beautiful day. I told Damien I was leaving and would see him tomorrow.

"You okay?" Damien asked.

I guessed he noticed the sudden frown on my face. "Yeah, I'm okay," I replied matter-of-factly.

"See you tomorrow then, Mouse. Enjoy the rest of the day."

I nodded. I thought I would, but it seemed like plans done changed all of a sudden. I exited the store. I wasn't even outside a second yet, and there was Rico pulling to the curb in his gleaming 650i. I watched him park and didn't know if I should smile or continue my frown and curse him out. I was ready to curse him out, though. He was a half hour late. No phone calls, no texts, what the fuck?

Rico stepped out his ride looking like a million bucks. He was looking so good in a pair of dark jeans that sagged off his behind somewhat, a white V-neck that highlighted his strapping physique, with a gleaming, long white gold chain around his neck and wearing a different pendant, an encrusted diamond cross. He sported a pair of fresh, bright white Nikes that were the color of pure snow, a flashy Rolex, and in his ear was a diamond earring that was almost the size of a bolder. His cornrows were freshly done and spiraled down to his shoulders like little ropes.

I took a deep breath. Damn, he looked so good.

He smiled at me. "Hey, beautiful, sorry I'm late," he said.

"Damn, no phone call or texts," I barked. I couldn't hold it in.

"My phone died and I left my other battery at the house," he explained.

I thought he was lying, but then he showed me his phone. It was dead, or maybe he just turned it off to make it seem that way.

"I'm a busy dude. Phone always ringing about business or somethin' else," he said. "But better late than never, right?"

"I guess so."

He pulled me into his arms and hugged me tightly. His hug felt so good. I just wanted to melt in his arms. And he smelled so good, too. It was such a turn-on for me, a nice-smelling and well-dressed man. I felt the power of his arms wrapped around me. When he finally released me, I exhaled. He looked at me and smiled. It was contagious and I smiled too.

"So this is where you work at, huh," he said, looking at the record shop.

"Yup!"

"Nice. How long have you been working here?"

"About a year now. I always try to keep a job."

"A woman about her business, that's what's up, beautiful," he said.

I would blush every time he would call me beautiful. Rico would gaze at me and not flinch when that word came out. I loved that he was tall and would tower over me. His eyes were pleasing against me.

I was ready to leave. It had been a long day. Rico looked me up and down. I wasn't dressed my best and started to become insecure because I was clad in a pair of faded jeans, a T-shirt, and sneakers—definitely not the proper attire to go out on a date with.

"You know I just got off of work, that's why I'm dressed like this," I said to him.

He smiled. "Don't even worry about that. You still look nice, but I got you. C'mon, let's get out of here."

He ushered me toward his car and I climbed inside. Once again, I felt like a queen in a Roman chariot. Rico was poised behind the wheel, looking like an emperor. He started the ignition and pulled off.

"Where are you taking me?" I asked.

"It's a surprise," he replied. "You like surprises?"

"Sometimes."

"Well, this one ya gonna like," he said. "You trust me?"

I nodded. "I trust you." My words were followed by a smile.

He smiled back. My heart started to race whenever he was near. I felt this electricity flowing through me, ready to spark love inside of me whenever he spoke to me. I felt something so sensational when he touched and hugged me. I lounged in the leather seat and relaxed as the car moved through the Bronx and then into Manhattan like it was gliding on ice. Rico had an R&B CD playing, by Jagged Edge. I closed my eyes and nodded to the track. The song "Promise" was a loving song. Listening to the lyrics put me into a pleasing trance:

> *If you need a love, I got the love that you need*
> *Ain't no way they can take that from me*

With Rico, I felt like we functioned like a well-oiled machine together, intellectually, spiritually, emotionally, and physically.

He drove me to the shopping area on Fifth Avenue, a major thoroughfare in the center of the borough of Manhattan in New York City. Between Forty-ninth Street and Sixtieth Street is lined with prestigious boutiques and flagship stores, and is consistently ranked among the most expensive shopping streets in the world. From left to right, I gazed at some of the world's luxury boutiques:

Louis Vuitton, Tiffany & Co., Gucci, Adidas, Prada, Bottega Veneta, Armani, Fendi, Versace, Cartier, Tommy Hilfiger, Lord & Taylor, Saks Fifth Avenue, and so many more.

I'd never been in any of these stores; they were too rich for my blood. And Sammy and I never hung in the city like that, unless it was Times Square or at a club doing a show. And we did our shopping on Jerome Avenue, or Third Avenue and 149th Street, where we got bargain discounts by shoplifting or having the hookup. Shopping on Fifth Avenue was only a dream for us.

With it getting late in the day, the sun was still shining and the area was still bustling with shoppers and people milling about. I was confused for a moment. Rico parked his ride in the costly parking garage.

"Why are we here?" I asked.

"I'm taking you shopping," replied Rico.

"Shopping?" I replied in bewilderment.

"Yeah, if ya gonna roll wit' me for the evening, then my woman gonna have to look good," he said.

Two things he said had me smiling greatly: that he acknowledged me as his woman, and that he was taking me shopping on Fifth Avenue to look good. What woman could argue with that? I was ready to leap out his car and glide down Fifth Avenue and hit up every boutique and luxury store I came across. I needed new clothes and shoes, too.

I got out of Rico's car feeling like it was Christmas Day. I already had what I wanted to get in my mind. I walked with Rico side by side and the first store we went into was Envy Fashion. It was a store with some really nice trends. The setup was extreme: high-end fashion displayed everywhere on mannequins; there was no clearance or bargain section; the clothes were neatly displayed: and leggy female employees were ready to assist you at the snap of a finger. Like a fat kid in a bakery, I wanted to grab everything in my sight and devour it all. The clothes were pricey, but Rico didn't care. He pulled out a huge wad of hundreds and fifties and said to me, "You know money ain't a thing for me. Get what you want, I got you."

Those were the magical words that I wanted to hear. Jackpot! I was ready to pick out the best things money could buy and have bitches in Edenwald start hating on me fo' sure. Rico put $1,500 in my hands to shop and I was ready to take off like a horse at the starting gate. He stepped out of the store to make a phone call. I raised my eyebrow in suspicion at him about making a phone call when he said to me earlier that his phone was dead. I didn't want to argue about it. There were plenty of goodies in the store to pick up and forget about his lie.

I went picking through everything, from jeans, skirts, dresses, sexy tops, and chic T-shirts. Everything that I tried on was so sexy on me, making me eye candy for the men. I had a blond, anorexic-looking woman helping me. She was cool and knew all about fashion, but the bitch needed to eat a sandwich. I spent an hour in the store, racking up stylish clothing. When I went to the cashier to pay for it all, the bill came up to $989 at Envy Fashion.

I exited the store and Rico was still standing outside, talking on his cell phone. He was a busy man. I walked toward him with two shopping bags in my hands and a warm smile. He curtailed his conversation on the phone, looked at me, and asked, "You got everything you want?"

"Yup. Thank you, baby," I replied, giving him a kiss on the lips.

We went walking farther down the busy and noisy Fifth Avenue. The next thing I wanted to get was some shoes. I walked into this trendy shoe store called High Life Shoes, and their selections of shoes were amazing. Like the last store I left, they were also pricey and their décor breathtaking. I was in shoe heaven.

I picked out two pair of nice and expensive shoes: a pair of studded cop pumps and these pink stilettos that would make me look phenomenal when I stepped out my building. Both pair of shoes was going to go perfectly with the outfit I just bought.

We left there and continued to walk around Manhattan. I picked up a few trinkets and accessories until the sun started to set. I felt like a diva with Rico. With five shopping bags in my hands, and hanging out with my newfound man, he took me out of my harsh reality and made me feel so special. Even though it was temporary, it felt good to escape.

Two hours later, we were walking back to the parking garage chatting and holding hands like we were the "it" couple. And here was me, a young hood bitch from the projects, shopping on Fifth Avenue. Us being boyfriend and girlfriend, was this it? Earlier, he acknowledged me as his woman. Was I really? Before we walked into the parking garage, I needed to know. I wanted confirmation from him. It wasn't cool to assume anything.

I gazed at Rico and asked, "Am I ya woman fo' real?"

Yeah, it'd only been a few days of me being with him. But we grew up together in Edenwald and I liked him a lot. Rico did his thing, and I did my thing. He was well known and respected. He reminded me of my father with his cool and intriguing demeanor. We always ran into each other at parties, events, or when there was trouble around. The bitches loved him, but he sometimes could become so reclusive. Everyone knew what he was about, but not everyone was in his business. It was one of his traits that I was attracted to. He wasn't a loudmouth and a showoff.

Rico stopped walking when I asked him that question. He gazed back at me. Then he said, "Real talk, Mouse, I had a thing for you since back in the days."

It was news to me. I was shocked to hear him say that about me. It made me think, *what makes me so special and why has he never tried to holla at me?* Every other nigga in the project did.

"You did? Why you never pushed up on me?" I asked.

"Ya pops an OG, and I got respect fo' him. You feel me? The nigga's a legend. Latin Kings did they thang," he said. "But I always thought you were different from them other girls. You stood out and shit."

I smiled once again. Rico always had me smiling or blushing. His words were like a soothing harmony to my ears. The evening was going perfectly. Rico was doing everything right so far. I longed to be in a monogamous relationship, did he?

"So where do we go from here?" I asked.

He didn't say anything to me at first. Rico looked at me; he then pulled me closer and pressed his lips against mines. We started to tongue kiss heatedly. His breath mixing with mine was pleasurable. I felt like I was in seventh heaven for a moment. The kiss between us was lasting. He then pulled his lips away from mines and said, "That's how I feel about you."

I was smiling to the highest degree on the outside and inwardly. What was next? The night only just began. I climbed into the passenger seat of his 650i coupe and was ready to be whisked away into a deeper paradise with him. But first I wanted to peel away the old clothes I had on and worked in all day, and wear one of the stylish outfits I recently bought.

Rico was thinking the same thing. He said to me, "I wanna see you in somethin' new tonight."

"But where I'm gonna change clothes at?" I wasn't going back to my father's house.

"You can change at my place," he suggested.

Did he say his place? I had to think about it. Was this a scheme to get himself some pussy? I mean, I was ready to give him some, but I didn't want to be forced into having sex with him because he bought me some nice and expensive things. It wasn't going to become that type of party.

Rico noticed my dubious expression and added, "It ain't even gotta be like that, Mouse. I got respect fo' you, so don't go thinkin' some negative shit about me."

It made me feel a little better.

"You still stay in Edenwald, right?" I asked.

"Sometimes, but I mostly handle my business out there. I learned a long time ago never shit where you eat."

"So where do you eat at?"

He grinned. "I eat someplace really nice."

"It's nice, huh?"

"Yeah, really nice," he added. "I know ya gonna like it there."

It was reassuring to hear. "So you really think that, huh?"

"I have and want nothing but the best, including you, in my life," he proclaimed.

I chuckled. "Now that was cute."

"It was, right," he quipped back.

I grinned and said to him teasingly, "I'm ready to try on some new outfits for you. I want you to be the first to see me in them. Maybe I can put on a special show for you."

I was suddenly becoming flirtatious. We locked eyes and Rico smiled.

"I can't wait," he replied.

Rico started the car and we drove off back to his place somewhere. I assumed it was in the Bronx, but I think it was Mount Vernon. However, I trusted him. He was a friend first. We continued talking. I explained to him the situation with me and my father. I came clean with Rico about my father's drinking and the abuse toward me. I rarely told anyone about my troubling home. Sammy knew, of course. But I kept that part of my life concealed. I didn't want anyone judging me or my father. But if Rico was going to become my man, then he had to know what he was getting into. He had to know everything about me.

Before we exited his car, Rico gazed at me profoundly and said sincerely, "You know I got all the respect in the world for ya pops. Like I said earlier, he's an OG. But real talk, if he ever put his hands on you again, I'll fuck him up for you. Ya my woman now and I ain't tryin' to have anyone disrespect you at all."

Hearing them words come from him made me feel like I was in the arms of Christ Himself. It's what every woman wanted: that loving man to love and protect them from any harm, and spoil us. I was ready to suck his dick in the front seat of his coupe.

Rico didn't stay too far from the Bronx. He stayed in a two-story, suburban home on a quiet block in Mount Vernon. It was quite a distance from Edenwald, but close enough to handle his daily business. He parked in the driveway and we climbed out. I grabbed my shopping bags out of the trunk and walked toward his place, eager to see how he was living. It must have felt nice not living in the grimy projects anymore, and even though he was still in Westchester and wasn't too far from me, it felt like paradise in my eyes. The streets were clean, all the lawns manicured, and the block quiet on a warm spring night. There weren't any niggas gambling in front of the buildings, no loud music playing, no people arguing, and no garbage scattered everywhere. It was a whole new world out of the BX.

Once we were inside, Rico turned on the lights to his place and showed me his comfortable, three-bedroom kingdom. It was definitely a bachelor's pad. The place was sparsely furnished with leather furniture, a giant sixty-inch plasma flat screen in the middle of the living room, and parquet flooring for the décor. Manifested on his living room walls were portraits of notorious gangsters he idolized, some real life and some fictional, men like Tony Montana, aka Scarface, John Gotti, Frank Lucas, and Bumpy Johnson, Lucky Luciano, the cast of *The Sopranos* and the characters from *Goodfellas,* and Al Capone.

"I see you have a thing for gangsters," I said.

"I'm a gangster myself. You gotta respect the heritage," he replied.

"I guess," I replied mildly.

Despite the notorious mugs and hard scowling that stared at you from the walls, it was a nice place, and I wouldn't mind resting my head there from time to time.

"You want somethin' to drink?" he asked me.

"What you got?"

"Liquor, beer, juice, all the good stuff. Ya choice," he replied.

I didn't mind having a taste of the good stuff. I told him to get me a beer. We could save drinking liquor for later on tonight. Rico went into the kitchen while I took a seat on his couch and went through my shopping bags. I pulled out the outfits that I bought. Damn, I had good taste. I couldn't wait to try them on. Rico came into the room holding two Coronas and handed me one.

"Which one do you want me to try on first?" I asked him.

He pointed to the one on my right.

I smiled. "Good pick. Where can I change at?"

"In the bedroom. It's the second door to your right." He pointed.

I walked off with the bags in my hands. I was so eager to try everything on and put on a sexy show for Rico. I didn't close the bedroom door, but left it ajar when I started getting undressed. The first piece I put on was this desert tan draped billow dress and my pink stilettos. I walked out the bedroom for Rico to see me in it and the reaction on his face already spoke volumes. It was obvious that he loved what he saw.

"Damn," he uttered. "You look really good."

"I assume you like it," I said.

"I love it."

I did a little twirl for him in my heels and put on a small show like I was on the catwalk. I looked and felt great. It was time to try on the other outfits. I strutted back to the bedroom knowing Rico's eyes were glued to my backside. The next outfit I put on was a two-piece low-cut halter and matching body short set. It was for the summer time. I put on my other heels and walked out the bedroom to show off my body in this scanty but classy attire. This time Rico had music playing: R. Kelly's "Naked." I grinned. He grinned.

Suddenly, I feel the need to pull you close to me,
But I don't know if it's what you want, baby.

"You tryin' to start somethin' up?" I asked teasingly.

"No, just feel like listening to some music, and I love this song," he replied with a smug stare.

"Um huh. Okay."

"Damn, but you look really good in that outfit, Mouse, shit!" His eyes were fixated on every part of my body. The way my defined legs stretched out in the heels made me look like a supermodel. Once again, I put on a show for him. I teased him by shaking my backside and dancing seductively for him while he lounged on the couch. He grinned heavily and took a swig from his beer.

"You ready to see the next one?" I asked.

"I'm ready to have you," he replied with a lecherous grin.

I grinned. "You think I ain't hear that."

"I know you did."

I couldn't help but smile and feel salacious around him. The way his dark onyx eyes pierced into me made my body tingle with this disobedient thrill. I went into the bedroom to put on the third outfit: a pair of tight Seven jeans that highlighted my young and curvy hips, and a pink short-sleeved tie top with the midriff showing, along with my pink stilettos again.

Rico was speechless yet again. I could tell that he was getting really hard. He kept shifting around in his seat, trying to adjust his crotch area. He was transfixed by my sexy attire. R. Kelly's soothing and alluring voice filled the room:

I'm gettin' head up off yo' sweat perfume
And I'm ready, to explore, every part of you

This time Rico stood up to get a closer look at me. He kept his eyes on me. His grin was becoming mischievous. His naughty look was ready to have him display some ill behavior. And the song wasn't making anything better. Rico reached out to me to pull me closer. He wanted me in his arms, but I took a step back from his grasp and pushed him away lightheartedly.

"I'm not done modeling for you yet," I said pleasantly.

"How many more you have to try on?" he asked.

"Two more."

He sighed and dropped against the couch. His hormones were raging. I was enticing him to the point where he was hurting. I went back into the bedroom and changed into a two-in-one skirt dress. It was pink. Yeah, I love pink. But the outfit, this sexy, broomstick-style piece could be worn as a full-length skirt or a tea-length dress. I showed it off to Rico, but I could tell he only wanted to see me out of it and naked.

I saved the best for last. I came out the bedroom clad in sexy lingerie. It was a pink open-cup baby doll featuring a hot-pink chiffon fly-away halter with functioning satin bowtie and a matching open-crotch thong. It was a fuchsia color, along with my pink stilettos yet again.

Rico couldn't contain himself. "Damn!" he hollered.

My body was looking right in the chic lingerie. I straddled him on the couch and started to kiss on him passionately.

"Thank you for everything today, baby," I whispered in his ear soothingly.

"Baby, ya welcome."

His hands started to explore my body. He cupped my ass and was ready to peel away my attire and have his way with me. I wanted him to. I was just as horny. For days, the tension between us had built like a sweltering, smoldering fire. It was slow burning that became raging with flames. Rico's embrace was tight; he wrapped his arms around me completely, sliding his hands up and down my spine.

We kissed heatedly and it cemented in my mind that there was no turning back. I was about to give him this good pussy. Rico pulled me closer to him. I felt his erection between my legs. It felt so impressive. I wanted to see it in the flesh. I went grabbing for his dick and he was peeling away the lingerie set from my body. When my dark and hard nipples became exposed, he quickly pressed his lips against them and started to suck on them like they were candy. I moaned and gyrated against his lap.

I started stroking his dick in my hand. It was impressive. It was so hard and thick, long, but not too long. I wanted to feel his hard flesh inside of me. We moved around on the couch touching, stroking, fondling, kissing, and rubbing against one another and then we ended up on the floor somehow. I lay on my back against the floor and stretched out, opening my legs and closing my eyes. Behind my closed eyelids, I felt his fingers gently against my thighs, caressing my skin, touching my soul. He pressed the weight of his body into mine and moved between my legs.

He was naked and ready to take this pussy. We were two passionate, lust-filled animals in heat writhing on the floor. He moaned as I reached for his hard tool again and felt the evidence of his passion for me. He was only inches away from the entrance to my soul.

Our strong kisses fed our hunger for one another. With my legs spread for him, he awaited my moment of reckoning. My slippery and sweet juices were flowing freely. When he kissed me in certain places, it sent waves of pleasures throughout my entire body. He kissed me and fucked me with his fingers simultaneously.

"Ooooh, yes, finger that pussy. Ooooh, yes!" I cooed.

He cupped my ass in his hands and pulled me closer to him. Rico was so strong and so passionate with it. He was definitely ready to give me that thug loving. I wanted to feel every inch of him deep inside of me. But I owed him a favor. Before his erection entered the core of my soul, I moved quickly to take advantage of the situation. I pushed him off of me and climbed on top of him. I held his big, stiff dick in my soft hands. I then began to softly and gently lick the head. I licked it like a soft-serve cone and expertly used the tip of my tongue in his slit.

I wanted to show off my head skills. Not too many niggas got to enjoy it, because I wasn't the one to give out blow jobs to everyone. It was my treat to the man I loved.

I could count on my hands how many niggas I gave a blow job to since I started fucking. With Rico, there wasn't any hesitation. I began swirling my tongue around the head, getting it wet and slippery with my spit, stroking him to his full hardness with my hand.

Hearing Rico moan while I stroked and touched him fervently in his private area made me extra horny. I could feel the veins in his dick throbbing. I took his entire length into my mouth in one stroke. I went farther down on him, deep-throating Rico with a nice technique of mine. When he was totally consumed by my throat, the nigga was breathless. My lips, my tongue, my mouth, and hands were all working jointly to suck my man off with the right pleasure, giving him some sloppy, wet, and sensuous head.

I pulled my lips away from the dick and uttered, "Baby, I need you inside me now."

It'd been months, too long, since I had some dick run up in me. Rico positioned himself between my awaiting thighs and with no condom on, but straight raw, he penetrated me slowly. I could feel him becoming lost in so much pleasure, with my pink folds massaging him nicely. I grasped him, almost feeling like I was a virgin again. As he thrust himself inside of me, once again, he cupped my ass and pulled me closer to him. His loud grunts and moans while fucking me indicated he was loving the pussy. My sweet juices coated his raging hard-on. He was so deep inside of me that there was this feeling of joy and tranquility and love flooding my very soul when our bodies were intertwined. Our legs became a tangled mess and our heartbeats began to sync up.

"Ooooh, fuck me! Fuck me, baby," I cried out.

And he sure did.

His hands roamed by body. His kisses devouring me and with his steady pounding inside of me, I came like whoa! My body lit up like a Christmas tree. And then his orgasm hit hard too. It was more than just the physical sensation of pleasure that overtook him, it felt like we could never be separated. I could feel his sperm making its way inside of me. Rico had left his mark inside of me. I could feel his seed surely growing. He panted and then collapsed on top of me, our bodies somewhat sweaty. I cradled him and comforted him in my sweet and loving embrace.

I was in love with him.

I never wanted to let him go.

"I really enjoyed that, Rico. I'm so lovin' you right now, baby," I whispered to him, and then I felt myself drifting off into a peaceful slumber while lying in his arms.

Chapter Five

Sammy

I climbed out of Search's green Durango under the canopy of stars and glistening city streetlights with a cigarette between my lips and new lyrics swimming around in my head. Clad in a pair of tight blue jeans and heels, with a little cleavage showing from the cowl halter top I wore, I felt like I personified rap diva and oozed sex appeal. I wanted to be sexy and have all eyes on me. Yeah, I was nice lyrically, but this was also a business and sex sells, always. First impression was a lasting impression, and I wanted to leave these people I was about to meet via Search with a very high impression of me.

I was eager to get into the studio and record something. I had so much to say, so much truth and knowledge to spill via the microphone, that it felt I was about to detonate like a time bomb. The frustration was building inside of me so much that if I didn't release it in the studio, somebody was gonna end up hurt tonight. And I really didn't want to get locked up. I had so much on my mind. This was my therapy, my session on the couch.

It was a beautiful and warm night, the kind of night where you wanted to chill with a burning blunt between your lips and sip on a cup of alcohol, it didn't matter what kind, but to be just chilling with your peoples in the projects while probably on a park bench, talking shit to each other, listening to a few tracks and letting the time fade by while you got faded with a nice high.

But lingering around in the projects and chilling with my peoples could wait. Business came first and I got high while on the go. It wasn't every day that I got a chance to record in an elite Manhattan studio and the cost wasn't on me. It was an opportunity that I wasn't going to pass up. Search was looking out for us. He was putting his money where his mouth was. I had respect for him and wasn't going to take him for granted. But I couldn't say the same thing about Mouse. She was still a no-show and it was really upsetting me.

Here I was in the heart of New York, Midtown Manhattan, home to some of the city's most iconic buildings like the Empire State Building, Chrysler Building, and United Nations, and containing the world-famous commercial zones such as Rockefeller Center, Broadway, and Times Square, on a balmy night, and about to head into this studio where hits were made over the years, and my girl wasn't by my side. Was she serious?

I gazed up at the fifteen-story brick building. It was a beautiful thing to see. Manhattan was always a fun town. We made it a fun town. I wanted to own this town. I wanted the glitz and glamour. I wanted to go on thousand-dollar shopping sprees and have my face plastered across billboards that stretched for miles long. I wanted to ride around in the fancy cars and live in the most lavish homes. When was it going to be my turn? Right now, because it started here, networking and working my ass off. This was my chance and I wasn't going to fuck it up.

Before I walked into the building, I lit my cigarette and took a few deep pulls. I needed the nicotine rush because Mouse was heavily on my mind and wasn't here yet. While on the way to the city I tried calling her for the umpteenth time, but she wasn't answering her fucking phone tonight. She had to be caught up with Rico somewhere to miss out on our studio time. I told her countless times that we had an appointment tonight, and afterward we probably could get to hang out in Times Square. She couldn't have forgotten about it already.

I decided to leave her a voice mail. So after the beep, I hollered into the phone, "Mouse, where the fuck are you? Search and I just arrived at the studio in Midtown and I've been calling ya damn phone all evening. When you get this message, give me a call back right away. Don't be fuckin' this shit up for us over some dick."

I had to be blunt and raw with her. There wasn't any other way to say it.

"You reached Mouse?" Search asked me.

"No, she didn't pick up," I said.

"She knows this is important," Search replied with frustration.

If Mouse fucked up this opportunity of a lifetime to chill with some hood nigga, then it was going to be World War Three between us. I continued to smoke my Newport while loitering around the front entrance to the building. It was nine p.m. I was itching to get into this studio and start doing my thing. I wanted to be the female Biggie and 2Pac in the rap game. I truly felt that some of these female rappers today were whack; only a few I gave respect to. I wanted to bring something different to the game. Yeah, I knew that's what they all said, but I felt I was different. Coming from the Bronx was my story, and warring every day from gang banging, drugs, and stealing to survive was my street credibility, and I was sexy with it. I had respect for bitches like Nicki Minaj, with her coming out of South Jamaica, Queens, but they weren't fucking with the Bronx and I think I looked ten times better than her. No, it wasn't hate, it was only the truth.

I waited for Mouse to show up for ten minutes, but she was still a no-show. I extinguished my cigarette by dousing it against the building and flicked it away into the street. Yeah, that was hood of me, but nobody was perfect. I looked at Search and said, "Fuck it, let's just go do this and get somethin' done."

"What's wrong with that girl?" he asked.

"Fuckin' wit' these lame-ass niggas," I replied.

We walked into the building. My heels click-clacked against the floor. We stopped at the security desk and Search signed in for the both of us. The security guard waved us through and we headed toward the elevator. I stepped inside behind Search and he pushed for the tenth floor. Once we started to ascend, I couldn't stop thinking about Mouse. Either she was going to be really late or not show up at all. And if she didn't show up at all, I was going to be pissed the fuck off. Her phone was going straight to voice mail. She had to be with Rico. It was the only explanation I could think of. Search was also concerned; he was just a little cool with his temper. I was ready to erupt like a volcano. We were a duo, Vixen Chaos; without Mouse taking this serious then this wasn't going to work.

Search had put up money for us to be here tonight, his own fuckin' dime. He looked at me like I had the answers to Mouse's absence. I didn't. I was in the dark like he was. As we rode upward in the lift, Search asked, "What's up with Mouse? Is she serious about this or what, Sammy? I paid five hundred for a two-hour session with Macky for tonight. Time is money." He suddenly had an attitude. I didn't blame him.

"She wit' Rico," I blurted out.

"Rico?" he replied with a puzzled look. "When she started hanging out with that thug?"

"You already know how Mouse is, Search. She gets around a certain nigga and thinks she's in love and then everything else important goes out the window. I'm sick of it, too," I proclaimed strongly.

"That's what I'm afraid of," he replied.

I sighed heavily. I was afraid of blowing this. We finally stopped and stepped onto the tenth floor. The hallway already indicated something significant dealing with the music business; gold and platinum albums lined the hallway and portraits of famous rappers and R&B stars were seen. I hoped that my face would be on that wall someday. I followed Search and we went into a room marked Studio B. Search didn't have to knock. We just walked in this dimly lit engineer room that oozed a certain harmony to it.

Everything in it looked expensive, even the high-back swivel chairs. There was one person in the room. He was seated behind one of the giant audio mixers, which was lit up in a multitude of lights, and nodding to a beat. It was the isolated control room where hits were made. When he noticed us standing in the room behind him, he jumped from his chair and greeted Search with some dap and a hug.

"Search, what's up," he greeted him.

"Macky, it's been a minute," replied Search.

"I know." Macky's attention went from Search to me. He eyed me heavily and I could tell by his expression that he liked what he saw. "Is this the one you've been telling me about?"

"She is."

He came over and shook my hand like a gentleman with his eyes fixated on my beauty and attire. "Well, if she can rhyme as good as she looks, then I think we have a platinum-selling record," he praised. "But I've been hearing a lot about you through Search. I can't wait to hear what y'all have for me tonight."

I smiled and blushed. "I can't wait to show it off."

He then looked around and asked, "Weren't you suppose to come with two?"

"Yeah, we were," said Search.

"So, where is she?"

Search and I were clueless. I was stuck. What to do now? I already had my rhymes written down and some I was ready to freestyle. Mouse wasn't going to stop the show from running. The producer, Macky, he was ready to get behind the mixer and get to work. I found out that he'd been a music engineer for years, and worked with a few Bronx legends. He'd been on the map since the late nineties and his reputation in the music biz was awesome.

"She's on her way," I said.

"A'ight, as long as she isn't too late. Search, you know I'm a busy man, and I have another group coming in around midnight," he said.

"I understand, Macky. We ain't come to the city for nothing. She's definitely on her way," Search said.

Macky nodded and sat back down in his chair and started messing around with the mixer again. Macky was cool and nice looking, some eye candy for me with his long dreads, dark skin, and lean physique. I loved a man who was about his business. Search and I were praying that Mouse was on her way. I excused myself from the room for a moment and dialed Mouse's number for the umpteenth time tonight while standing in the hallway. Her phone was ringing; I was praying that she would pick up this time. When I was about to give up hope, I heard Mouse's voice on the other end.

"Hello," she answered coolly like she wasn't a half hour late.

"Mouse, where the fuck are you?" I shouted. "You were supposed to be in the studio with me to record these tracks and you are a half hour late."

"I know, Sammy, I didn't forget. We on our way there now," she said.

"We?" I heard music playing in the background and what sounded like wind blowing. She was in a moving car. It didn't take a rocket scientist to know who was driving. "Who's we?" I asked. I just wanted to hear what she was going to say to me.

"I'm wit' Rico," Mouse replied affably.

I hated to hear that. Since they hooked up a few days ago, it was always about Rico. What the fuck! I was some-place different and around company, and even though they were both in the next room, I didn't curse Mouse out the way I wanted to. There was no telling who might be around listening. I didn't want Macky and everyone else to think that we were some loud and hood rat bitches who came with drama. We were already on CP time (color people time) with him. I wanted to look professional. Mouse and I were representing Search and so far we were making him look really bad when he invested so much into us—time and money.

Keeping my cool, I said to Mouse, "Just hurry up and get here."

"I'm comin'," she replied dryly.

I hung up and felt so embarrassed. I released a heavy sigh and walked back into Studio B. Macky and Search looked at me. They were nodding to a beat and when I walked in, Macky asked, "Everything cool?"

"Yeah."

"She's still a no-show, huh," said Macky.

"She's coming," I repeated like a broken record skipping.

I was sick of hearing it myself. Fuck! Macky shrugged and spun around in his swivel chair to face the mixer again. You already knew he was a producer who lived in the studio. He pushed a few buttons and manifested his magic to me and Search. The studio came alive with this breathtaking beat. It had a luscious groove with a ticklish piano melody. I instantly wanted to grab the mic and go into the studio and start rhyming like I was a bitch possessed. I wanted to flow off this beat with such command and power. I found myself nodding to it and opened.

"Ooooh, I love this beat. Is this for us?" I asked him excitedly.

Macky chuckled. He already told me my answer. He replied with, "I don't think you can afford this beat."

"Oh, really," I snapped back.

I was ready to flow. I was ready to show him something. I was never scared to rhyme in front of anyone, successful or not. When it came to showing off my talent, my skills, I was a fucking showoff. You never know who is who. I wanted the fuckin' world to hear me.

As the beat played, my head nodded. I started off with a little harmony from my soul. I wanted to give Macky a little taste that I could sing, too. His look toward me displayed he was already impressed. My sound was soothing, my vocals could shoot high like a rocket soaring.

"I hate you. Ooooh. I hate you. Ooooh, 'cause I love you, I love you. I tried so hard to understand you, I tried so hard to be his one, that woman by his side from dusk to dawn, but I hate you, I hate you," I sang.

"A'ight, I like it so far," Macky replied with a smile.

He hadn't heard anything yet. I stopped impressing him with my singing and went into my lyrics.

"I hate you, 'cause as soon as he came through that damn door, I screamed it, 'I hate you,' but my eyes still show my love, but this nigga's action had my heart so damn torn, his untamed look had me so worn, I stood like a deep chill, frozen, tryin' to find warmth from his cold, I stood the distance, cried every minute, embraced every hitting, got even his niggas asking, 'how can he do you so wrong,' but they just wanted to run up in it, I becomin' that bitch standing in the night 'n' tryin' to see her dawn, but dusk stay forming, the tears fell, 'n' my mind dwelled, staring at this nigga, I started to feel like a drying well. Closed my eyes, tried to shut out my mind, I still felt him come near, reach out like he AT&T, nigga I just wanted to disappear, but his touch made me wither here and there, and this nigga's apologies were nothin' rare, done heard it all before, you 'n' ass more than ya rear, say what, heard it all before, 'I'm sorry' entrenched into my soul, shit was repeated after every unlawful affair he done been through untold. The fuckin' nerve of him, comin into this fuckin' home after all my missed calls. Yeah, nigga, I hate you, 'cause I loved you, I hate you, 'cause I tried so hard to understand you, I tried so hard to be his one, that woman by his side from dust to dawn," I rhymed.

The hyped look on Macky's face said it all to me. I didn't have to ask if he liked it. He just came out and said, "Yo, that shit was nice. Damn, you got skills, love. You can sing and rhyme tight. You're like a Mary J. Blige and MC Lyte wrapped up into one."

I smiled heavily. To hear them words come from Macky, the man, the producer who'd been around so much musical talent over the years, meant a lot to me. I knew he wasn't just saying it to impress me. He was saying it because he saw talent when he saw it.

"So, can I have this beat now?" I asked jokingly.

He laughed. "Nah, we got something special for you."

Search was smiling too. Without Mouse around, I was still making it happen. She was just that final piece to our puzzle. As a duo, we were unstoppable and so much more talented. But I couldn't be the only one thirsty for this shit. She had to step it up and come hard for this success also. She was my best friend, my ride or die bitch, and we vowed to come up together.

"I told you that she was nice," Search chimed.

"Yeah, she is. Sammy, you have lyrics for real and harmony and soul," Macky proclaimed.

"I just wanna make this happen for us," I replied.

"You will."

We continued to talk and wait. I kicked a few other rhymes for Macky to hear and each one came harder than the next. It was like when I started spitting, I became a different person. I was possessed. I demanded that respect. My voice boomed like thunder in the sky and my sassiness was nothing to play with. I could come at you on some sexy and sensual shit, or I could come at you like a fuckin' pit bull in a skirt, raw, ready to bark and bite. I was from the Bronx, and hardcore like no other.

Forty minutes had passed since we arrived and this bitch finally decided to show up. While I was chatting with Search and Macky, my cell phone rang and it was Mouse calling. I almost didn't want to answer it, I was so heated. I already had an attitude because precious time had by now been wasted.

"We downstairs. Where y'all at? We wanna come up," she hollered into the phone like everything was all good.

"No, I'm comin' down to get you. We need to talk about somethin'," I said calmly.

"Okay, hurry up," she replied.

Oh, did this bitch tell me to hurry up!

I held my sharp tongue because it wouldn't be cool to curse her out and act hood and ghetto in front of Macky. He already indicated earlier that he didn't like or want any outside drama or beef in his studio. You either kept it business and professional or you didn't come to his studio at all. Macky was a peaceful man. I had to respect that. I removed myself from the swivel chair, saying to the two men in the room, "Mouse is finally downstairs. I'm gonna go talk to her for a minute and be right back up."

The look on their faces was like mines; they were angry and frustrated. Search especially was annoyed. He paid $500 of his hard-earned money in advance for two hours, and we still didn't get anything done. Oh, Mouse was going to have some explaining to do to all of us.

I removed myself from the studio room and walked toward the elevator thinking about what I was going to say to my best friend once I got downstairs. There were so many choice words to shout out. I was ready to make a scene with Mouse. I walked outside with a scowl across my face and saw Mouse with Rico. She was dressed in a brown seamless leopard jacquard dress and these brown heels, and bejeweled in some pricey items. She was dressed like she was about to hit the club, or the strip club. Mouse didn't come to record a few tracks; she came to swing around a stripper pole. And there was Rico, styling in a wife beater, trying to flex his physique and showing off the multitude of tattoos on his arms, wearing a Yankees fitted and sporting a fourteen-karat white gold diamond chain necklace with the matching bracelet.

I glared at Mouse and approached her with contempt. Search and Macky weren't around for me to keep cool, so I went in on Mouse.

"Seriously, Mouse, now you decide to fuckin' show up when you were supposed to be here like an hour ago, and you come wit' this fuckin' clown!" I exclaimed.

Rico smirked. "Hey to you too, Sammy."

"Whatever!"

"First off, Sammy, don't be callin' my fuckin' man a clown, and second, why the fuck you trippin' fo'? We here now," Mouse retorted.

I wanted to punch them both in the face. These two were so fuckin' ignorant. "You fuckin' up, Mouse," I shouted.

"Whatever, Sammy, where the fuck is Search? 'Cause maybe I need to talk to him, because I can't damn sure talk to you right now," she chided.

"Search is pissed off at you too. He already paid five hundred dollars for a late studio session."

"Fuck it, if ya tryin' to act fucked up like this, then maybe this session don't fuckin' need to happen. Better late than never, right."

I shook my head. This wasn't Mouse. We both were always about our business. She had to be high, or Rico was brainwashing her. This wasn't love, especially not after a few days. We went way back with Rico, but I never saw Mouse become this fucking boorish.

"You high, Mouse?" I asked.

"I'm fuckin' good, Sammy," she replied dryly.

I sighed heavily.

"And anyway, I wanted to tell you some good news," Mouse said to me.

I scowled heavier. What good news could she possibly tell me now? And she was serious, too. "Good news," I replied with a dumbfounded stare toward her.

"Rico is willing to finance us to help further our careers. He ready to look out for us, Sammy," she said.

"What?"

"I'm sayin', he got the money and we got the talent. A great combination, right? We can go places if we start fuckin' wit' Rico."

This bitch had some nerve. "And what about Search?"

She sucked her teeth and replied with, "Fuck Search. The only reason he's backing us or sweatin' us like that is because he just tryin' to get some pussy, from either you or me."

"Mouse, are you serious?"

"Sammy, Rico is paid and he got connects. Believe me, *vamos a hacer esto*, Sammy," she stated.

I wasn't with it. I wasn't going to abandon Search at all. Mouse had it twisted. "*Joder que,*" I spat back, which meant, "Fuck that!"

Mouse frowned.

I continued with, "I ain't abandoning Search. He's the one who's about his business. That *puta* right there is just about gettin' some pussy. Open ya fuckin' eyes, Mouse."

"Sammy, how you gonna try and play me like that?" Rico chimed in. "How far we go back?"

"I don't give a fuck how far we go back, Rico. This is my livelihood you fuckin' wit'," I shouted.

"And I'm tryin' to help y'all," he returned.

"We don't need ya help, Rico," I clearly let be known.

I didn't want to hear anything from him. I just wanted to talk to Mouse. It seemed like everything that was supposed to happen tonight was going down the drain.

"You can speak fo' yourself, Sammy," argued Mouse.

My temper was starting to flare. Here we were, wasting precious time arguing about bullshit, when we could have been upstairs making hits with this well-known producer. I had my fists clenched and restrained myself from going off, either on Mouse or Rico.

"Mouse, I'm tired of arguing; do you still wanna do this or what? Because Search and Macky are waiting for us upstairs," I asked.

If she wasn't coming up, then fuck it. I was still going to go into that booth and do my thang. Like I said before, we were a duo, but Mouse wasn't going to stop the show from happening. She looked at Rico, like she needed to get his approval. I couldn't believe it. He shrugged and said to her, "Y'all might as well get somethin' done, and we can talk 'bout that other thing later."

"Fuck it, let's do this, then," Mouse said.

Finally, I said to myself. But for some reason, it just didn't feel right. I was agitated and frustrated. Mouse was fuckin' brainwashed, and we already lost one hour of recording time. But something had to be salvaged before the night ended. My mood had changed drastically and I was ready to kill someone. I had to release my frustration somehow, and it had to be in the studio. I was ready to catch fire and burn these lyrics that were heating up in my head like a wildfire.

Mouse and Rico followed me into the building. We rode the elevator to the tenth floor silently. You could feel the tension among all of us. Damn, I didn't want to bring this drama into Macky's studio, but I also didn't want to miss out on working with him.

We all walked into the studio. Macky had another hot beat playing. Search glared at Mouse. He had no words for her. He cut his eyes at Rico and sighed. Macky stood up to greet the two newcomers who came into the room.

"You must be Mouse, the second extraordinary half to this platinum group," said Macky nicely.

"I am," she replied with a smile.

I could tell that he was impressed by her beauty, too. He checked her up and down while Rico was around. The way Rico looked at Macky showed he was not impressed by his flirtation and words to Mouse. I loved it. Fuck him!

"And you are?" Macky asked Rico.

"I'm Rico, her man," he sternly let be known.

"A'ight, no disrespect to you, my dude," said Macky kindly.

"None taken," Rico replied with a deadpan stare.

"Search, I'm sorry that I'm late," Mouse apologized.

"We'll talk later. Let's just get something done tonight," Search replied coolly.

Rico took a seat on the couch and chilled, while Mouse and I needed to get our groove and chemistry together. We needed to do this despite our bickering earlier and the tension that was stirring between us. Mouse got aquatinted with Macky and the studio equipment fast, and it didn't take long for us to step into the booth to create our magic.

Macky put on this beat for us to listen to. It was wonderful. The melody was crooning, but the drums and snares came alive like DMX was about to perform. Mouse was loving it too. She nodded to the beat and we both were ready to go. Search and Macky were outside the soundproof glass nodding also. They were ready to hear something hot.

Once we were in the booth and hearing the beat flowing through the room like a tropical waterfall, that rainbow came in the room and the conflict Mouse and I had earlier seemed to fade and we focused on the one thing we loved best: our music. It was our time to shine again. Mouse stepped toward the mic with the pop filter and started to spit her lyrics first to "One Down."

"It's one down, like you shot down, look around, who's the punk now, got you in the sixty-nine, you lookin' pregnant wit' that bitch in ya system, giving birth to another pussy, who the boo, throw my arms around you to blanket the bitch in you, Edenwald Blood Vixens comin' through to kick the shit out of you, it's divine, we don't play them games, we don't deal wit' lames, Sammy and Mouse, a more lethal combination than Mickey 'n' Mallory, fuck it, keep talkin' and watch the .380 pop, separate ya soul, ya spirit is shifting, 'n' watch what gets done to you, natural-born killers comin' through, this ain't the cinema, ya bad mouth done put ya life on the line, death is gonna be real fo' you, I'm that bitch to sit on ya face, have you eat this pussy 'n' then shit on you, drown between my thighs, bleed you like a period. Yeah, muthafucka, you don't leave this position until you clean ya plate, dance on you while you lick between my legs, my name is Mouse, 'n' you ain't gotta do nothin' but love this girl, 'cause I be like fuck, y'all niggas, so don't get it confused when you look at me, Mickey ain't got shit on me, I'm the big bad wolf, so nigga don't fuckin' raise up or you get chomp the fuck down and have ya niggas screaming, but running on E," Mouse hollered heatedly into the microphone with a profound scowl.

I was hyped. I spit my verse after hers with fever and we were so excited. We could go on and on, but we had to keep within the sixteen bars. I saw Macky nodding his head in approval. It made us hyped up even more. Search was smiling in the background, looking like a proud father. Rico remained nonchalant. After we recorded "One Down" we only had enough time to record "Pussy Poppin'." It was a sexual, raw, and funny track with lyrics like, "Yeah, a bitch is pussy poppin', got his big dick inside us dancing like Puffy in a video, as my lips pop, lock, 'n' block around his hard flesh like we on *American Bandstand*, he got my ass goin' crazy, my hips movin' from right to left, front to back, my tits pressed against the S against his chest, my clit swelling to his fresh, he's so fine, extra credit when he fucks me from behind, scratching that itch, his movement inside me feelin' slick, but cancel the Rick, he was my ex, small-dick nigga I care to forget. Fuckin' this wide nigga on his beat, like a few drums banging between my knees, we two stepping to cum, you and me, he got my pussy poppin', he got my lips pop, lock, 'n' blocking."

Macky was laughing at the raunchiness and loved it. It was fun to be different and humorous on a track. There were no boundaries to us. We said what's on our mind and didn't need any censorship.

After our session, I went outside to smoke a cigarette on the small balcony that overlooked the city. We could have gotten more done tonight if Mouse didn't come so late. But it wasn't any use crying over spilled milk. I took a few pulls from my cigarette and exhaled. It was such a beautiful night that I wanted to linger outside on the balcony for a long moment and look up at the stars all night. The noise of the bustling city kept my ears busy and the smell of success had me ready to take a leap of faith. You had to love New York: the city where dreams are made.

"Hey, girl, can I join you?" I heard Mouse ask me from behind.

I turned around. She stood there with a rueful look at me. I couldn't say no. "Yeah," I said to her.

She came and stood next to me. The glare of the city was in our eyes. Mouse seemed calm and cool; her attitude was gone. I shared my cigarette with her and stared at the towering skyscrapers in front of us. I puffed out the smoke and sighed. We were quiet for a moment, puffing and passing. The warm April night was refreshing with May almost two weeks away.

"I'm sorry about earlier, Sammy," Mouse, out of the blue, apologized, breaking the silence between us. "I know I fucked up. I don't know what came over me."

I knew what came over her: Rico. But I kept my mouth shut. There wasn't any reason to bring that drama back up. I took a few pulls from the cigarette and said to her, "We cool, no love lost here."

She smiled. "We did our thing back there, right?"

"Yeah, we did," I replied.

"We gonna do this, Sammy. I know it. And I love you, 'cause no matter what, you never give up on me. Your friendship is all I have right now and I'm not trying to mess that up wit' you," she proclaimed.

They were true and genuine words coming from her. Her eyes were sincere and it looked like she was ready to break down.

"Mouse, you are more to me than my best friend. You are my sister, and we gonna live out our dreams together.

You know the only reason I'm hard on you is because I love you."

"I know."

We hugged each and smiled. All was forgiven.

A moment of silence passed. I broke it by saying to Mouse, "Look at us now. We slowly comin' up fo' sure. We in a Manhattan studio recording wit' Macky, the nigga that used to fuck wit' Rockafella and Smack Records. You gotta admit, Search is definitely lookin' out for us."

"Yeah, he is, but I still want you to think about what I said about Rico. He's willing to invest heavily into us, Sammy, and my baby got bank, too," she said with certainty.

I heard what she said, but I was somewhat doubtful about Rico coming onboard to finance us. He had the cash, there was no doubting that, but did he have the brains for this kind of business? It was going to be drug money behind us, too. It was a risk dealing with him. I didn't know. I wanted to change the subject. I asked Mouse, "We still down to hang out in Times Square after this?"

Her dubious look back at me already told me her answer. "I would love to, but Rico made plans with me to take me somewhere nice to eat."

"Oh, really, where y'all going?"

"Some fancy restaurant in downtown Manhattan. I can't even pronounce the name of it. But I know it's expensive. My baby is treating me like his queen," she said excitedly.

I wanted to be happy for her. Hey, maybe she did find love, but I doubted it. I wasn't gonna continue to burst her bubble. My only concern was that he didn't distract her from our business. It was obvious he took her shopping, because Mouse was looking like a diva in her new wardrobe and jewelry. He was showering my friend with praises and gifts and Mouse was eating it up like crazy.

"I'm happy for you," I said halfheartedly.

"Thank you."

There wasn't much else to say. We continued to smoke and loitered on the slim balcony, being ten stories over the city. I gazed down below; the people looked like ants from my high position. From the bottom to the top, yeah, that was gonna be us, transformed from poverty to prosperity. We had too much talent to stay at the bottom. I could taste my dreams and transformed them into reality.

Chapter Six

Sammy

I gripped the 9 mm tightly with seventeen rounds locked into the clip and took a pull from the burning blunt that was passed to me from the back seat. The haze had my eyes seeded. The moving car was filled with weed smoke and Rick Ross's and Meek Mills's lyrics blaring. I was seated in the passenger seat and ready to take action. My crew had my back and I had their back. The gun was ready to speak volumes to our foes. EBV was ready to make a violent statement tonight. They fucked with the wrong bitches this time. This was the part of my life that I wanted to escape from, keep a secret, or separate from my musical dreams, or tried to anyway. But I expressed my lifestyle via my rhymes and singing. I wasn't one of these studio gangsters who pretended to be hardcore to create an image to sell records. Nah, every lyric, every fuckin' verse, was real life for me.

Search knew I was hood. He was always trying to rescue me from myself, like Puffy rescued Biggie from the street life and thrust him into a hit record. But I was a dangerous bitch on so many levels. I was one of the gang leaders and when shit popped off, they came to me for direction. I couldn't look soft or weak. I had a reputation to uphold and the million dollar checks weren't coming in yet, so I had to eat and survive somehow. But was I contradicting myself. Where I assumed Rico was a distraction for Mouse, the street life was my distraction from the music business. We both had our demons; for me, it was my temper and salacious behavior. It could also easily interfere with my dreams.

The black Acura I was in moved south down Soundview Avenue, toward Soundview projects. Winter was driving; Crystal and Meme were in the back seat. We continued to blaze and get hyped. Two blunts were being passed around, and each bitch had a weapon in their hands, either a pistol or a knife: something deadly, something to make a vicious statement tonight.

We were only a few miles from our destination: Soundview Housing. Denise and her crew had to get got tonight. They put one of our own in the hospital the other day. Dandy was only fifteen years old, and now she was lying in the hospital with twenty-five stitches across her face from a razor. She had been jumped by Denise and four other bitches. Four against one wasn't a fair fight and Dandy was a small girl. That bitch Denise took getting her ass beat down by Mouse personally and came after someone who she assumed was weaker than her. We couldn't let that slide so easily. It was a must that we retaliate. Now it was my turn to fuck that bitch up. I couldn't wait.

As I rode toward the beef, I could hear Search now talking to me. *Sammy, get out the car, this ain't worth it. You have a promising career ahead of you. Don't fuck it up!* He would have done anything and everything to stop me. That's why I didn't tell him everything. I wasn't going to be talked out of this shit. This life, it was still a part of me. It was still the woman I was: on some gangsta shit. I still had to live here daily.

Crystal interrupted my thoughts when she blurted out, "What's up wit' you and Mouse?"

"What you mean what's up wit' us? We still tight," I replied with a bit of an attitude.

"I'm just sayin', Sammy, I be seeing her and Rico kickin' it lately. He took her shoppin' and everything. You know she fuckin' that nigga," Crystal continued.

"Mouse is a grown woman, Crystal, why you talkin' 'bout her business for? She do her thang and I do mine."

"I'm just sayin', I haven't been seein' the two of y'all kick it like that lately. I just wanna make sure everything cool wit' y'all."

"Everything cool, so shut the fuck up about it!" I shouted.

Crystal knew not to fuck with me. I didn't want to hear Mouse being talked about, even if it came from a friend's lips. That's how much respect I had for her. I passed Crystal the blunt and she took a few pulls.

"You good?" I asked Crystal.

"Yeah, I'm good. I ain't mean no disrespect to you or Mouse," she apologized submissively.

"A'ight, its cool. We gonna find these fuckin' bitches tonight and put in that work. Okay?"

She nodded.

Winter navigated the Acura through the busy Bronx Streets. On a balmy spring night, it seemed that everyone was out and about. We tried to keep ourselves inconspicuous. The last thing we needed was NYPD lights blaring behind us when we were getting high and riding dirty. The closer we got to Soundview, the more hyped I was becoming. I was ready to kill this bitch. Denise usually stayed with her cousins out that way; it was known she had peoples in those housing projects. She was living in Edenwald, but the bitch felt more comfortable in Soundview. Now it was time to make her feel very uncomfortable. The South Bronx was another and entirely different location. It was a few miles from where we stayed at, and our beef with them went back since my mother was my age. Soundview was also notorious for violence, gangs, and drugs. It was once home to Pistol Pete and the Sex, Money, Murder gang, Fat Joe, and others.

Winter made a left on Story Avenue, and we slowly rode through enemy territory. We were never welcome around this area. Edenwald Blood Vixens and these bitches out in Soundview were like oil and water: we would never mix. We all were cautious, but we were on a mission. I knew that at any given moment, things could go terribly wrong for us, even deadly. But I didn't give a fuck; thinking about Dandy lying up in Jacoby Hospital with her face bandaged and fucked up, it put me over the edge. That might as well have been Mouse in the hospital. Denise fucked up, and she went running to enemy grounds because she had family out there. But they always say you can run but you can't hide, especially from me. I didn't give a fuck where that bitch was at; I was coming for her, even if she was in hell.

Soundview was lively tonight. It was a replica of where I came from, with the sprawling project buildings, dilapidated store fronts and bodegas, and busy streets, but positioned in the South Bronx. I stared out the window, crouching low in the passenger seat with the 9 mm on my lap. Winter steered the ride from block to block. The Acura turned some people's heads with it light tints and alloy rims. It was stolen. Winter had skills when it came to stealing cars. It was her forte.

We cruised through the area for fifteen minutes, still trying to be inconspicuous. I was getting impatient. "Damn, where the fuck is this bitch at?" I uttered.

"She's around here, Sammy. We gonna find that bitch," Winter assured me.

I didn't know if I wanted to put three holes in her or cut up her face like she did Dandy's the other day. Shit, just forty-eight hours ago, I was in a Manhattan studio recording a track with Macky, kicking it with Mouse and making something happen, and now I was riding dirty with the pistol on my lap and looking to hurt or kill someone. Strange how twisted shit could become so fast.

It was a quarter to ten at night. A few NYPD cruisers passed by us, but they didn't fuck with us, thank God. We continued our search and smoking on blunts. We drove down Randall Avenue, Roosevelt Avenue, Soundview Avenue, Lacombe Avenue, and the backstreets for almost an hour and we still couldn't find this bitch. But I wasn't giving up. I didn't come out here for nothing.

"Yo, this bitch is ghost, fo' real," Meme uttered.

"She know we comin' fo' her, that's why," Crystal added.

I remained silent. The only thing on my mind was revenge. I couldn't help but to become frustrated. I was itching to get at this bitch. Denise had it coming. She ran her mouth too many times, always spreading rumors and gossip, and she was a fuckin' bully. This time, I planned on shutting that bitch up permanently.

"There go that fuckin' bitch right there." Crystal pointed out.

I turned, and there was Denise walking out of the corner bodega on Roosevelt Avenue with one of her cousins. It took about an hour for us to find this bitch. I was determined and wasn't leaving the South Bronx until there was blood spilled. I glared at Denise; the bitch was smiling and looking too comfortable. I was ready to change that feeling and shake that bitch out of her fuckin' skin.

The pistol in my hand was ready to do some damage. Edenwald Blood Vixens was ready to put in that work. I eyed that bitch like a hawk, watching her smoke a Newport and chat with her older cousin, Angie. Angie had a bad and notorious reputation in the Bronx, too. We had a few violent run-ins with each other over the years, and tonight was about to be another one. I was glad to have the 9 mm on me though. Big, bad Angie was known to carry a knife or razor on her all the time and she wouldn't hesitate to cut a bitch. She had to be around when they cut up Dandy. It was perfect.

Winter parked across the street from the bodega Denise came out of. She waited for me to give the signal. We covered our faces with the red bandannas, representing our blood set, and were ready to cause trouble. And like lambs approaching the slaughter, these two bitches were coming in our direction.

I didn't take my eyes off of them for a second. I opened the passenger door, placing one foot on the pavement and leaving the other in the car. I was poised to strike. When they came near, I erupted from the car; my crew was behind me, the red bandannas covering our faces and the pistol in my hand looking menacing.

"Denise," I shouted.

She turned and was unaware of the threat looming her way. I hid the pistol from her view. She frowned, and her cousin did the growling.

"What the fuck you doin' on this side of the BX, bitch!" Angie shouted.

"Fuck you, bitch!" I shouted back.

Harsh words were exchanged. They came at me. Angie already had a box cutter in her fist. She was too predictable. But before they could come closer, Crystal and Meme lunged at these bitches with their fists swinging.

"Dumb bitch!" Meme shouted.

Meme caught Denise with a hard right to her face, and then Winter caught a few hits off that bitch too. These two moved like lightning and struck like thunder. Denise was caught in the storm. They attacked Angie next; she swung the box cutter at Crystal and tried to cut my friend in her face. But Crystal was fast on her feet. I wasn't about to have that happen to my friend. I showed my hand, the 9 mm, and screamed, "Y'all bitches better back the fuck down!"

Instantly, both of them became frozen with fear. I aimed the gun at Denise. It was too easy to take her life in the blink of an eye. I was always told you don't pull out a gun unless you were ready to use it.

"Bitch, what you gonna do wit' that?" Denise shouted.

Every breath in me was ready to kill this bitch. I hated this bitch with a passion, but I could hear Search shouting at me: *Please, don't do it, Sammy. I have so much invested into you. You have a lot to lose.*

Search was my conscience. I swear, this nigga had wings and was sitting on my shoulder. I was the devil on the next shoulder. Fuck it, then, I ran over and started pistol whipping this bitch across her skull with the butt of the gun. The steel against her flesh was messy. The bitch hollered and dropped to the concrete with a gaping gash across her head. I was all over her like stink on shit. I wanted to crush her fuckin' skull in. Crystal and Meme were beating the shit out of Angie in the middle of the street; without a razor or knife in her hand, she was fuckin' useless. Winter and I were stomping and beating Denise violently into the concrete. She was no match for us. Like always, the bitch was all bark but no bite.

"That's for Dandy, bitch!" I screamed madly.

My hands and the gun were bloody. Denise was sprawled out against the concrete in serious pain. Her whimpering echoed through the Bronx street. Angie was bloody and beaten badly just like her cousin. We left them bitches exposed and bleeding like squashed insects. The damage had been done, our statement told very loudly.

We retreated to the car and Winter sped off, tires screeching as she made a sharp U-turn in the middle of the block. We sent out a strong message to these bitches: don't fuck with EBV, Edenwald Blood Vixens. I felt vindicated, especially seeing Denise's face split open like a zipper. Not only was she pistol whipped by me, but Winter sliced that bitch's face open with a razor in her hand. I loved it. An eye for an eye.

We were gone before the first police car came rushing to the scene. Have EMS clean up our mess. We got back to Edenwald in no time. The first thing I had Winter do was dump the car somewhere far and set it on fire. We had no more use for it.

We all went back to Crystal's place and smoked a few blunts and sipped on some Cîroc peach. I wanted to get twisted tonight. With a lot on my mind, being with my ride or die bitches gave me some comfort. I only wished Mouse was with us. She would have loved to see Denise in that much pain. But I felt things were changing and I was powerless to stop it.

Smoking three blunts and finishing off a bottle of Cîroc Peach before dawn came, I ended up crashing on Crystal's couch for a few hours.

It'd been twenty-four hours since that brutal clash, and already word had been circulating through the streets about it. The confrontation in the South Bronx had been ringing out like Sunday bells and my name came along with it. Denise received thirty stitches in her face from the pistol whipping and the razor cutting. We had that bitch looking like Frankenstein. I felt no remorse at all. Angie was more fortunate; she only received a few bruises, a black eye, and a ripped-out weave, but her pride was crushed. She had put a green light on me in the streets. Supposedly, I was a marked woman for death. I wasn't going to lose any sleep over it. I'd been through it all and Angie and her threats didn't scare me. Warring and heartache was in my blood. I came from that lifestyle, and

I was part of a vicious blood set that would kill for me. Being a high-ranking member in my set had its advantages. Once a person has joined a blood set, it was for life; you couldn't leave the set or flip to another set. And this was my life, until music became big for me.

I'd been a female blood since I was thirteen. My status and reputation preceded me. I wasn't the oldest member, but I had a more extensive criminal background that gave me love and respect in my hood and on these streets. A set leader isn't elected but rather asserts themselves by developing and managing the gang's criminal enterprises through their reputation for violence and ruthlessness and through their personal charisma. I was that bitch that everyone looked up to.

We were over fifty deep in my set, from bitches to niggas, and we symbolized hard wherever we went, because bloods, especially EBV, have a strong sense of commitment to their set and are extremely dangerous because of our willingness to use violence both to obtain the respect of gang members and to respond to any person who disrespects the set. My crew, my bitches, was more to muthafuckas, like our male blood counterparts, than helping them carry weapons, hold drugs, or prostitute themselves to make money for their set. EBV, we had a fierce reputation and we did our own thing, made up our own rules.

We identified ourselves through various gang indicators such as colors, clothing, symbols, tattoos, jewelry, graffiti, language, and hand signs. Usually, we wore sports clothing, like team jackets that showed our colors, Chicago Bulls, San Francisco 49ers, and the Phillies.

The most commonly used Bloods symbols included the number five, the five-pointed star, and the five-pointed crown. These symbols were meant to show the Bloods' affiliation with the People Nation, a large coalition of affiliates created to protect alliance members within the federal and state prison systems.

I loved my peoples and I understood my history. The history of how something started always engrossed me, from the history of how the Bloods started to the history of our country, America, music, and much more. Society called me violent, but I was smart, intrusive, and inquisitive. I was beauty, attitude, and brains, a deadly combination not to fuck with.

But with me being Hispanic, and my family belonging to the Latin Kings, there was some conflict in the beginning. The history of the East Coast Bloods originated in Rikers Island. The United Blood Nation, simply called the Bloods, was formed in 1993, within the New York City jail system on Rikers Island's GMDC, C73. GMDC was used to segregate the problem inmates from the rest of the detention center. Prior, the Latin Kings were the most prevalent and organized gang in the NYC jail system. The Latin Kings were targeting the blacks with violence, and the black inmates, who were organized by some of the more violent and charismatic inmates, formed a protection group, which they called the United Blood Nation. By 1996, there were thousands of Bloods running the NYC streets and establishing ourselves as dominant, violent, and a ruthless organization. We were feared and we were respected. And there were the initiations into the Bloods, which meant robbing and slashing someone to join, maybe getting sexed in if you were a bitch, which meant fucking at least five niggas in one night, killing someone, or sometimes you were in because of your pedigree.

I was thirteen; Mouse and I were determined to join, and we weren't trying to get sexed in. Our pussies were still tight and pure at the time. With us being Hispanic and our fathers belonging to the Latin Kings, it was hell. But we weren't going to be rejected. Mouse and I had to rob and slash someone in the face to prove ourselves worthy and vicious enough to join. I was willing to do it. It was the fall, Mouse and I walked around the busy Fordham Road late in the evening when people were coming home from work, exiting from the subway and getting off the buses. Everyone seemed distracted by something else other than us; we were only two young and harmless teenagers wandering about, or so it appeared to be that way. But they had no idea the danger we was about to create for some poor individual.

I spotted my target. She was a black woman in her early twenties, nice looking, maybe a college student, maybe not. I didn't care about her occupation or her goals; she was only an agenda for me, my way inside the Bloods. I followed her around for a few blocks, the sharp razor concealed in my hand. Where she went, I went. She seemed happy and pleased about something, going from store to store, shopping for a child, maybe hers, or not. It wasn't any concern of mines.

As I neared her, my heart pounded like drums banging in my chest. This wasn't personal; it was just something I had to do to prove myself. Mouse flanked me. The others, the older Bloods, were watching us from a distance. Once this incident went down, it was recorded and we were in. When my target exited the children's clothing store with a few bags in her hand, I had to strike.

Mouse walked ahead of me and purposely bumped into the bitch, to create a distraction for me.

"Bitch, watch where the fuck ya goin'," Mouse had hollered at her.

"Excuse me," the woman had replied, looking confused.

"You heard what the fuck I said," Mouse hollered back.

When she wasn't looking, with her back turned to me, I rushed toward her and it happened so quickly. I didn't even know I was doing it, but I was. I quickly cut her face, feeling the razor open up the right side of face like a hot knife slicing through butter. Suddenly, there was blood everywhere. She screamed madly, dropping her shopping bags and clutching her wounded face tightly. I had blood on my hands, but the deed was done, mission accomplished. Mouse and I took off running. I didn't know this woman, but her pain and suffering was my way into a gang. As we ran, I could still hear her screaming in agony from a block away.

A week later, Mouse performed her initiation by cutting up some male in his early thirties. We caught him parking his expensive Benz on Jerome Avenue. He was in a suit and tie, looking like a banker or something. Mouse glared at him and without any hesitation, before he could press the alarm to his ride, she rushed him and slashed him across the face repeatedly. He screamed in pain, the blood gushing from his wounds. We took off running and made our way toward the nearest train station, jumping the turnstile and hopping on the train before the doors closed. Mission accomplished.

From there on, we were in and nothing nice to play with. We did whatever we had to do to get our respect. Mouse and I knew that as long as we had each other's back, we were impervious to anything. But sometimes, the enemy can come from within.

To see my mother just lying there in the bedroom after taking her medication was hurtful to me. Her HIV was crushing her. She was dying slow and I couldn't do anything about it. She had been sick for ten years now, afflicted with that nightmare that I dreaded. She had some good days and bad days. But there were more bad days than good this past year. I was the one taking care of her even though she rarely took care of me when I was growing up. It seemed like she didn't want to take care of herself; death was becoming more inviting with each unkind breath and aching bone inside of her. I could have been bitter toward my mother, but I still loved her despite her negativity toward me since the day I was born.

My mother was one fuckin' bitch. Her mouth was harsh and always slick like oil, and her ways were very wicked. My mother's past had finally caught up with her. From fighting, drug dealing, shootings, stealing, prostitution, and drug use, Dana Perez used to be one of the baddest bitches in the Bronx. From what I heard, none of these bitches could hold a candle to my moms back in the days; from her magnificent looks to her Coca-Cola shape, she had it going on.

Before I was born, my mother was running things in the Bronx, moving serious weight and selling drugs for my father and my uncle who were once kingpins in the late eighties and early nineties. But then things drastically changed after I was born. The feds came for my father, Ricky Perez, who was a prominent Latin Kings member, and they gave him a life sentence, and the streets murdered my uncle. He was shot fifteen times while seated in his Benz on Boston Road. The streets were saying that the hit came from his own peoples.

At five years old, I moved into the projects—Edenwald. And then when I was eight, my comfort in the hood was being with Mouse all the time. Coming from the same background, having a dysfunctional family, surviving the streets, we could relate to each other. And when my moms went crashing from the high life she used to live, to now turning tricks on the block back in the days for cash or drugs, and caught the monster from sucking and fucking niggas raw, things done changed.

I stared at my moms for a long moment. The bedroom was dark and it felt so still in her room. She was asleep and looking too frail in her dingy nightgown. Her immune system was shutting down rapidly. Her body was attacking her. She had morphed into a completely different woman. The drugs and HIV was destroying her. Her beautiful, long black hair was gone, now nothing but a knotty shag on top of her head. Her shapely figure was now a memory. She looked more like a broomstick. The only thing she had left from her past was me and her memories. It was a shame.

I didn't want to become her. I was better than her. I wanted to be a star, and when I reached the top, I was going to stay on top. This shit with the streets, the gangs, being poor, and my moms wasn't going to be forever with me. Fuck that! My moms once had the glamour and riches. I was determined to do big, big things by any means necessary.

I closed the door to my mom's bedroom and went into my own bedroom. My room's décor was so shabby, with peeling paint and cracked walls, black mold on the walls and scattered clothes everywhere. My room was sparse with furniture; I didn't have the luxuries of a radio or a TV to be entertained with, but only having a single mattress, no bed frame, and a beat-up dresser with missing drawers. It was like that everywhere in this apartment. The sink in the bathroom had partly fallen off the wall and was at a strange angle, having been clogged up with mastic, and the sink looked like it had been cleaned about once in the last ten years, and the kitchen was falling apart, with the only food in the fridge was week-old Chinese food and spoiled milk. And our carpet hadn't been vacuumed for a while, as cigarette stains and dust piled up.

How did I live like this? I spent most of my time spending the nights at friends' homes or on the streets. I always wanted to get away from this hell. It felt so much like a prison in here. Most times, I would just lie on my mattress either daydreaming or coming up with a few rhymes to spit. I thought about the recording session the other day with Macky, Search, and Mouse. Things went well after a rocky beginning. I was pleased. I stayed around to learn a few things about being an audio engineer and observed a few seasoned rappers do they thing in the studio.

Afterward, Mouse went her way with Rico and Search and I went to get a bite to eat at this twenty-four-hour diner on the east side. It was two in the morning with Search and me dining on pancakes, hash browns, and sausages.

I was a little tired but I wasn't rushing to go home. There wasn't anything for me at the apartment; it wasn't home for me. Search was devouring his meal, chewing with his mouth open and trying to talk to me all at once.

"Let me tell you something, Sammy. You are one of the most talented females I know, and you can take this music career so far. The world is gonna know your name soon, because you have what it takes. You can sing, rap, dance, and you write your own shit," he had proclaimed.

Where was he going with this? I had wondered. I done heard all of this before. It was nothing new to me. I took a sip of apple juice and was amazed at how much food Search was able to scarf down at one time, reminding me of *Hungry Hungry Hippos*.

He had continued with, "What I'm trying to tell you, Sammy, is sometimes people can hold you back. You understand what I'm saying to you?"

"Not really."

"I know you're close with Mouse and you probably feel you owe her something. But have you ever thought about becoming a solo artist and doing your own thing, in case the group thing doesn't work out for you?"

At first, it was unthinkable to separate myself from Mouse. You either took us as a team or you didn't take us at all. We had an unbreakable bond like that. However, if the situation escalated worse with her and Rico, then I reluctantly might have to take that route. But for now, we were still a team and I wasn't abandoning my friend so easily.

I had locked eyes with Search and said to him, "For now, we are still rocking as Vixen Chaos, Search. She's my friend and yours too."

"I really have nothing but respect for you, Sammy. Yes, she's a friend. But don't get pulled under and drown yourself too when you're trying to save another's person's life," he had warned me.

Those were real words spoken to me. I had nodded.

"I know Mouse though, Search. She's focused like me," I had said, trying to defend my friend's action.

"It sure didn't seem like it tonight. And if she continues with that kind of action, then I'm afraid gonna have to drop her, Sammy. It's nothing personal, but business. I mean, coming an hour late to a studio session, and then bringing Rico into our business, I can't tolerate that, Sammy. I just can't," he had proclaimed.

What could I say to the man? He was absolutely right. He lost out on money and time. "I'll talk to her, Search."

"Please do that."

We had finished our meal and left the diner. Search had driven me back home. It was three in the morning when I had walked into my apartment. I just wanted to sleep for hours without any interruptions. There was a lot to think about, me leaving Mouse and going solo. It was a crazy idea, almost unthinkable. So why was I entertaining it, or even thinking about it, since Search had brought it up? Perhaps I was starting to have some doubts.

Days after my talk with Search and that clash with Denise and Angie, I found myself on the rooftop of my building, smoking a cigarette and gazing down at Edenwald like I was a watchman or something. I loved chilling on the roof because I liked being on top. I had a lot to think about. The streets were heating up and police came to my door the other day. I wasn't around to know what for and I wasn't trying to be around. It wasn't the first time police came to my apartment looking for me, but I hoped it would be the last. They didn't have a warrant for my arrest or anything; I guessed they just wanted to question me. I didn't like questions from any type of law enforcement. I made sure to be ghost for a few days.

I took a few more pulls from my burning Newport. I exhaled and continued to fixate my eyes from the stars above to the dungeon below. There was such a great distance from up there to down there, like the poor and the rich. Up in the sky, everything was bright, peaceful and alluring. Looking below, it was the dungeon; everything was fucked up, trashy and grimy. Survival of the fittest, real talk. If you was weak in the dungeon, then you was a cow waiting to be slaughtered by the wolves, the predators that lurked everywhere.

However, tonight was a quiet night in my hood: no gunshots, not yet anyway, and no police or EMS sirens blaring. Everything felt like it was on pause or hiatus, even my recording sessions. I was ready to go back into the studio and start recording again. I felt like a greenhorn fiend; after that first hit, I was ready for more. Search was a busy man, but he always made time for me. So I was shocked when he wasn't returning any of my phone calls. Then it dawned on me: he had to be upset with me. I assumed that he heard about the incident in the South Bronx. It wasn't a shock that he would find out about it. People talk, and they always talked about me.

When Search finally did call me back, he barked, "Sammy, what the fuck is wrong with you?"

"Search, why you screaming on me?" I retorted.

"Are you crazy? You think I wouldn't find out about you fighting and pistol whipping Denise over by Soundview? Do you want to piss everything away, everything that you worked so hard for?" he exclaimed.

I was silent. Even though he was screaming at me and I had a low tolerance for muthafuckas yelling at me, I couldn't say anything.

"Sammy, listen to me, this gangster shit with you, it can't go on. You either want something better for your-self, or you don't. There's no in-between, no gray area. I'm willing to invest into you heavily, like I've been doing. But if you gonna continue to be a risk to yourself and me, then I can't do it. I can't afford it," he exclaimed.

I sighed.

He added, "You have too much damn talent to be fuckin' up like this, Sammy! You do! Don't fuck it up; don't throw away your future."

"I won't," I replied sheepishly.

I respected Search, because like me, he didn't sugarcoat shit. He was blunt and raw. I knew he cared for me. He liked me yes, but he was a great friend, too. What Search didn't know was that Macky had slipped me his number on the low before we left that night and he wanted me to call him. I wasn't naïve; he wanted to discuss something with me that was more than business.

After Search barked on me, I had Macky's number in my hand and was tempted to call him. But was it cool mixing business with pleasure, and to go behind Search's back when he was already upset with me and had a thing for me? I was attracted to Macky and it'd been a minute since I had some dick run up in me.

I stared at the number with the 347 area code and decided to call him. His phone rang a few times before his voice mail picked up. "Hey, this is Macky you reached. If this call is that important then leave a message and I'll get back to you. If not, then hang up and try your luck next time," his voice mail said.

It was cute. I thought about leaving a message, but decided not to. It would have been nice to hear his voice personally, but I wasn't the one to leave messages, especially if it wasn't that important.

I flicked my cigarette over the edge, sighed lightly, and went back inside my building. I did enough looking up at the stars and daydreaming. It was too beautiful a night to be cooped up in my crappy apartment. But with little cash and no car, my choices were limited.

Commonly on nights like tonight, I would spend time with Mouse and some other friends doing something fun. I needed to get high. I called my weed guy to make that special delivery. Some haze or kush going through my system was something I needed. After calling my weed guy, Cheo, I waited in front of my building. He came fifteen minute after my phone call in his black Chevy with chrome rims and dark tints. Cheo understood the routine. I met him in the building stairway for the transaction. With cops steady patrolling and cameras always watching, it was too risky to do anything out in the public, especially since I had five-o looking for me and my name was involved with a fight and assault.

Cheo entered the lobby with a smile, looking like Barney Rubble with his short ass. He always had a crush on me, but he wasn't my type at all. He was short, high yellow, and corny. Ugh! The one thing he had going for himself was driving a nice, tricked-out Chevy and having some of the best weed in the Bronx. Everybody called Cheo for that good, good smoke.

"You ain't wit' ya partner in crime tonight?" he asked, looking around for Mouse.

"Nigga, we ain't attached to the fuckin' hip. Why you lookin' around fo' her for? It ain't like she lookin' for you," I quipped back.

"Shit, you could have fooled me. Y'all always together, especially when y'all tryin' to get high and shit. What, y'all broke up or somethin'?" he replied with his wisecrack.

"You a fuckin' dumbass, Cheo, so fuckin' stupid!" I exclaimed. My harsh mouth was nothing new to Cheo. He'd been the subject of verbal abuse so many times from me; I was starting to think he liked upsetting me and hearing me go off. "Nigga, I called you for one thing, and why you in my fuckin' business for? Do I be in ya fuckin' business, Cheo?"

He shook his head and chuckled somewhat. "Damn, I was just askin' and tryin' to make conversation wit' you, Sammy."

"Well don't!" I spat.

"It must be that time of the month, then," he wise-cracked.

I was ready to smack him. It happened with him every time I got weed from him. The nigga didn't know how to sell his shit and leave. I was surprised police didn't bust his ass yet. He was so fuckin' sloppy, from his style to his wardrobe. And it wasn't a wonder why he was still single. Females found him repulsive and lame. He only sold weed to try to be somebody.

"Cheo, why you so fuckin' ignorant? That's why you ain't getting no pussy now."

His whole demeanor changed. "Why you gotta play me like that, Sammy? I get pussy."

I laughed. "From who?"

"Don't worry about it."

I continued to laugh, playing his heart, and said, "Just give me what I call you for. I don't have time to discuss ya pathetic love life."

"You's a cold bitch, Sammy."

"What you called me?"

"Nothin'," he replied sheepishly.

Cheo went into his pocket and pulled out a phat-looking dime bag for me. It was kush. My eyes lit up. I paid him his money and hurried out the stairway to walk to the twenty-four-hour bodega on 233rd Street. I needed to purchase a cigar and some snacks. I left Cheo standing in the stairway, drooling over something he wish he had—me.

The walk to the bodega was a peaceful one. The projects never slept, but tonight it seemed comatose. Thank God there wasn't a long line at the bodega, either. I could get what I wanted and leave. I got my White Owl and a few bags of potato chips. Before I took two steps away from the store, I saw the 650i coupe come rolling up with Jay-Z blaring. It was Rico. I wasn't in any mood to see him at all.

He stepped out of his flashy Beemer, clad in a wife beater and jeans along with his tattoos showing and jewelry gleaming in the night. He flexed his chest and muscles my way and smiled. I didn't smile back, cocky son of a bitch! I was ready to leave and didn't have shit to say to him. But he had something to say to me.

"What, Sammy, you can't say hi to me anymore?" he asked with a grin.

"Hey, Rico," I said dryly.

"What got you comin' out here so late?" he asked.

I showed him my White Owl blunt and chips. He nodded and continued to smile. For him to be such a hardcore gangster, I had to admit though, Rico did have a nice smile and a nice body.

"Yeah, it's gonna be that type of night for me too," he responded.

Rico came closer to me. I took a few steps back from him and frowned. I wanted nothing to do with him. He frowned too.

"Damn, you act like I got the plague or somethin'. I thought we were friends, or used to be, Sammy."

"I ain't got any beef wit' you, Rico."

"Then why every time I come around you always mean mugging me and giving me attitude?" he asked.

Because he was fuckin' with my best friend and I knew he was going to be a distraction for her, that's why. She was already screwing up because she was supposedly in love with him. I swear, this nigga must have had the super dick in his jeans. I didn't tell him that though. I continued scowling at him.

"Ya too beautiful to be always lookin' at me like that, screw face and shit. What, you mad 'cause I'm fuckin' wit' Mouse?"

"Nah, y'all two look cute together," I lied, being sarcastic.

He chuckled. "Yeah, whatever. I always feel that tension wit' you."

"What do you want from us, Rico?"

"I'm just tryin' to be a cool friend to y'all, and have a word wit' you when you give me the chance, too," he said coolly. "How far do we all go back, Sammy?"

"A long time," I replied feebly.

"Shit, ya pops and my pops both are locked up together, and they used to run heavy wit' the Latin Kings back in the days. But to let you know, I'm nothin' like my pops," he stated.

"So, what are you like then?" I asked.

"It's been a long time since we hung out. You remember when we were fourteen and fifteen?"

I did. But things were different now. Rico was a smooth talker. He was a man with the gift of gab. Yeah, we all had history, but not all history was good. And most of my history wasn't that good.

I didn't know why I was lingering in front of the bodega after I got what I needed. Maybe I was lonely, and we did have history together, and truthfully, there was nothing else to do. And he was an exciting guy, but I knew from experience that he was nothing but trouble.

Rico went to the small revolving window and picked up a few blunts, some beers, and some snacks. It was inevitable to have the munchies right after smoking. When Rico got the things he needed, he focused his attention back on me. I started to walk off, he called out to me. "Sammy, it's late, let me give you a ride back to ya building."

"Nah, I'm good," I replied.

"Sammy, c'mon, let me give you a ride. I ain't no threat, you know me," he said.

That was the problem, I did know him.

Rico stood by his car with his eyes fixated on me. I stopped and didn't keep it moving when I should have. I turned around and looked at him.

"It ain't like I'm driving you miles away. You just up the way. It ain't no thing to take you home," he added.

It was late, and I was tired. I released a frustrated sigh and walked his way. I looked around first, making sure everything was clear. The streets were still empty. The last thing I needed was for someone to see me get inside Rico's car and start having the wrong impression about things.

Before I climbed inside, I said to him sternly, "You better take me straight home."

"Where else I'm gonna take you, to the moon?" he joked.

"Ha-ha, ya so damn funny. Do I look like I'm playin' wit' you?" I quipped.

"You safe wit' me."

I climbed inside the luxurious car and remained cautious. It probably wasn't the smartest idea to get inside his car, but I did it anyway. I was impressed by the interior, comfortable leather seats. Rico got behind the wheel and started the car. He placed one hand on the steering wheel and the other out the window, away from my direction. Smart idea. He pulled away from the curb.

Jay-Z continued to play. "99 Problems" was blaring. I loved this track. I was getting into the lyrics until Rico decided to turn the song down. I looked at him and he looked at me. This nigga had something to say to me.

"You a wild girl, Sammy," he uttered, then smirked.

"What you mean by that?" I asked with attitude.

"I heard what went down in the South Bronx the other night. You and ya crew just didn't give a fuck," he said.

I was defiant. "I don't know what you talkin' about."

I wasn't trying to snitch on myself. Rule number one when it came to the streets and the game: shut the fuck up. There were always too many people fuckin' talking, and I hated when muthafuckas were in my damn business.

"I heard Denise is in really bad shape," Rico informed me.

"And you actually think I give a fuck about that bitch!" I shouted.

"Hey, don't get upset wit' me. I was just telling you somethin'."

"You know what, Rico, you can let me the fuck out right here," I exclaimed.

I was ready to reach for the door handle and step out the moving car. We were only a few blocks from my building. I didn't mind walking the rest of the way. I didn't ask for a fuckin' ride anyway. Now this nigga wanted to be in my business. Rico observed my sudden frustration and wisely changed the subject.

"Don't get agitated about it, Sammy. I apologize if I upset you."

"Just shut the fuck up about it!" I chided.

Rico glared at me. Yeah, niggas and bitches wouldn't get away with talking to Rico like that. He didn't tolerate disrespect from anyone either. But like he said, we had history. We went way back together.

"You like Teflon, Sammy. You know that?" he said.

I scowled harder. "What?"

"Never mind. But I wasn't tryin' to disrespect you. I was just talking," he said.

I wasn't listening to him anymore. I couldn't wait to get the fuck out his car. Already, he was pissing me the fuck off.

"But I need to talk to you about somethin' important when you cool down."

"I am cool!" I snapped.

"If that's cool, then I would hate to see you upset," he replied.

We were coming closer to my building, thank God. How could a man who was fucking irrelevant in my life upset me so quickly? Maybe because he was fucking Mouse had me wanting to hate him.

Rico stopped in front of my building, put the car in park, and left it idling, indicating that he wanted to talk some more. I really didn't. I opened the door. He reached forward and grabbed my arm, trying to prevent my quick exit. I looked at him like he was crazy.

"Sammy, don't leave yet. I wanna talk to you, pull ya coat to somethin'," he said hurriedly.

I blew air out of my mouth. I should have just gotten out his car and not given a fuck what he had to say. But once again, I did the opposite. I locked eyes with him and gave him his minute to talk.

"You always have been a smart and talented girl, Sammy."

"And what that's supposed to mean?" I asked with a raised brow.

"Look, you and I have somethin' in common and that's to get ours and make it to the top, by any means necessary."

"You already seem to be on top by the look of things," I quipped.

"I dream bigger. You doin' it ya way and I'm doin' it mines," he stated lightly.

"Your point is?"

"I ain't gonna beat around the bush. I'm sure Mouse told you that I'm ready to invest in y'all. I wash your back and you wash mine."

"Rico, why would I want to get in business wit' you?" I asked.

He reached under his seat and pulled out a wad of cash. The money was in hundred- and fifty-dollar bills.

"Because, this is what life is all about, making money, and I makes money. This is what I do out here," he said with conviction.

The giant wad was impressive. It was something that I truly needed in my life. So many things could change when you have money and success in your life. I gazed at Rico's wad of green; I estimated he had about ten stacks on him.

"Nice," I replied dryly.

He chuckled, like my comment was an insult. "Nice?"

What did he want from me, to sweat him or something?

"What I'm tryin' to tell you, Sammy, I think you and me would make a good team," he added.

"Team? A team doin' what? And what about my girl, Mouse? What the fuck you tryin' to say here, Rico? You playin' my friend? You tryin' to fuck wit' me?" I refuted.

"It ain't even like that, Sammy."

"Then what the fuck it's like? You know what, I shouldn't even be in this car wit' you. I know ya a fuckin' snake, Rico. Don't fuckin' talk to me," I shouted.

I jumped out his car and slammed the door so hard I almost thought I shattered his window. I didn't even give him time to explain himself. I rushed away, cursing at him. For some reason, I didn't trust him. I didn't want to hear anything else he had to say. Team? Rico saw a good thing and wanted in. I was about to blow up, and that's when the leeches come and wanna try to suck you dry. He had Mouse on his hook, but he wasn't going to have me. Fuck him!

Chapter Seven

Mouse

I was a woman in love, and a woman in love would do anything for her man, probably even die for him. Rico had my heart on lockdown, and I was his, signed, sealed, and delivered. There was no hesitation to it. The entire projects knew about our love, and Rico proclaiming me his, which was the best thing in my life. We'd been dating for several weeks now. Bitches hated on me from left to right. I moved in with him, a huge "fuck you" to my father. I was loved and protected, also well taken care of.

We were fucking and sucking each other off like rabbits. Nah, rabbits weren't getting freaky like us. We were just nasty with it. Rico was banging my pussy out like he created the punanny. And we fucked everywhere: indoors, outdoors, in the car, on the car. My pussy was his home, and he rested his big, long, and hard piece of flesh inside of me like daddy should do.

The drug game was becoming good to him, and it was being good to me. If Rico had it, I had it, and we had lots of it. I did whatever to please my man, and sucking his dick like a porn star in the front seat of his 650i coupe was nothing new to me. I loved doing it. I loved pleasing him, especially when he was so quick to please me with comfort and protection. Every day, I wanted him so badly. I wanted him to be my lover forever. I didn't want to share him with anyone or question his fidelity.

My lips were wrapped around his hard dick with him being reclined in the driver's seat. His moans were evident of me pleasing him satisfactorily with his hand entangled around my hair, my head bobbing up and down in his lap. I wanted to suck his dick like no other woman had ever done. I wanted to lick every inch of him. I wanted to enjoy him, swallow him whole, deep-throat that big dick with my spit running down his balls.

I pulled out my tits as I sucked his dick. I wanted Rico to play with my nipples while I was sucking his dick and tell me that he loved me and loved the way I gave him head. My tongue coiled around his mushroom tip. I could feel his dick throbbing inside my mouth. My sweet lips continued to glide around him like they were on ice, up and down on his nice-sized dick. I didn't even want to come up for air. I wanted to lick his nuts and feel them rolling around my tongue.

"Shit, baby, I'm about to cum," Rico grunted.

I sucked his dick harder and faster; the pressure from my lips was making him squirm in his seat. I heard a sharp intake of breath as I enveloped him with my mouth. Rico's knees started buckling, even though he was already seated; if not, he would have fallen over from the sweet intensity of my lips against his manhood.

I licked every inch of his hard dick as his breathing got louder and louder like always. My mouth enveloped him completely and he began moaning uncontrollably. I used my lips to pleasure and my tongue to torture, but the kind of torture that ushered in the most decadent release. Rico shut his eyes. He felt the warmth of my mouth and the softness of my lips slide sensually up and down his erection. Harder, faster, deeper, and wetter. There was only one goal: pleasing.

I wasn't worried about anyone witnessing my naughty act. The tinted windows on his car prevented anyone from having a clear view of us. I loved the way Rico's dick felt in my mouth, how when he was about to cum, he would thrust his dick into my mouth like it was my sweet pussy he was fucking.

I cupped and tickled his balls. He continued to grunt and have his eyes closed.

"Ooooh, baby, don't stop, that feels so fuckin' good right now. Oh shit! You about to make me cum. Ooooh, oh shit," he cooed.

"You like that? Huh, you about to cum?" I said teasingly, stopping my actions momentarily.

"Hells, yeah. Keep goin', shit keep going," he said feverishly.

I exposed a sinful smile. I wrapped my lips around his pulsating cock again and I violently gave him some head. I could feel him about to explode. He was becoming harder in my mouth, like concrete with my saliva saturating his bottom half.

"Shit, baby. Ooooh. I love you! I fuckin' love you!" he strongly proclaimed.

Oh my God, did he just say to me that he loves me? I was smiling heavily on the inside. Hearing that was precious. It seemed like the words flowed softly, sweetly from his lips like honey dripping. I wanted to kiss him. My heart had jumped. This was an emotional moment for me.

I sucked and jerked him off simultaneously. I definitely wanted to give him an explosive ending. The look on my man's face was priceless. I was ready to feel his release in my mouth. Yes, I was ready to swallow every last drop of him.

After a few harder sucking and licking on his erect cock, Rico exploded his semen into my mouth like a geyser going off, and I took it all in like a professional. I permitted for his babies to swim around in my mouth for a moment, savoring the taste of my man and then I swallowed. It all went down my throat like Kool-Aid. Rico looked spent and satisfied. As his woman, I did my job thoroughly. He pulled up his jeans and zipped them up. I wiped my mouth and fixed my clothing. I then looked at him and asked, "Do you really love me?"

I know it'd only been a few weeks, but you knew when you were loved and were in love with someone. I believed in love at first sight, and I was in love with Rico.

"You know I do," he replied.

I wanted to hear him say it again. I'd never heard a man tell me that he loved me. Not even my own father would utter those three special words to me. It was so nice to hear them. I wanted to hear him say it to me over and over again. I wanted to drown in his love and escape in passion. I couldn't help but become emotional and wanted to tear up. I wanted to be told that he loved me over and over, and over, until the end of time. But he didn't. His reply to my question was, "You know I do." I didn't get too downhearted about him not saying them again. Yes, I yearned to hear "I love you" said to me once more. But we were having a very pleasant evening and I didn't want to ruin it with desperation about hearing him tell me that he loved me again. I was afraid that if I pressed him about it, then it would run him off. At least he said it to me. I found great satisfaction in that.

Rico started the car and drove away. We were going to Edenwald. He needed to take care of business out there with his crew. I wasn't in my man's business like that. I was playing my position, like a good woman should do. I was staying at his place for the moment and living comfortable for once in my life. I didn't have to worry about my abusive father, or bitches coming at me over some bullshit. But I did miss home and Sammy.

I was quiet in the car, nodding my head to Alicia Keys song that he had playing for me. "Unthinkable" had me in the zone. Her lyrics were so tantalizing and so true, especially for me.

It's becoming something that's impossible to ignore,
And I can't take it.

The only thing I wanted to do was love my man, write lyrics and rap, and get rich and well known with Sammy. That's all. It wasn't that hard. I deserved it. I deserved Rico and happiness.

We arrived at Edenwald in no time: 233rd and Baychester Avenue. It seemed like everybody living in the projects was outside getting into something, mingling, laughing, and gossiping. There was different type of music blaring from every direction, and the men and hustlers were loitering on the corners and playing dice in front of the bodegas, and the residents were taking advantage of a beautiful spring day. I noticed a couple of my girls walking about. I wanted to say hi, but Rico had important affairs to take care of.

I felt like that bitch riding around in the passenger seat of my man's 650i. The windows were rolled down with a breeze gently blowing against me. I was getting so much attention from everyone. It was a beloved moment.

We pulled up to the towering buildings on East 229 Drive North. The parking lot filled with cars. He parked and asked if I wanted to wait in the car. I didn't. I wanted to stretch my legs and walk with my man. I stepped out the car with my red bottoms hitting the pavement and a new attitude. I was looking fabulous in my denim Guess jeans that accentuated my young, thick curves, and my white ruffle-front cami top that made niggas scream out, "Whoa!"

Rico concealed in my purse the 9 mm he always carried. I didn't mind carrying it for him. He was my boo and females rarely were harassed by police like that, especially one looking like me, too fine. And I was used to packing guns, even shooting them at muthafuckas who tried me or my crew. Rico understood that I could hold my own. I could be his gangsta bitch and his classy bitch all in one.

We strutted toward the building in front of us. I had to shake my head. Out of all buildings, why did he have to come to this one? It sat on the corner of East 229th Drive North and East 229th Street. It was Denise's building. I had too many enemies inside and clashes with a lot of bitches in that building. It was a place I wanted to stay far away from, but I didn't run from anybody, especially when I was with Rico. I knew he had my back.

I was already getting the stares from people we passed who recognized me. Some were deadpan and some were screw faces aimed at me. *Yeah, it's Mouse, bitches, and look at me now*. People looked displeased that I was walking with Rico and had the audacity to walk into Denise's building after what Sammy and my gang did to them in the South Bronx. Yeah, I heard about it, and it was music to my ears. Sammy was my bitch, and my only regret was that I wasn't with them when it happened. The streets were saying that Angie was hunting for my friend and Denise was finally home from the hospital and her face was fucked up. She was going to be scarred for life. And she was cooped up somewhere recovering; and nobody hadn't seen the bitch since she was discharged from Lincoln Hospital. But hearing what they did to Dandy, those bitches came off lucky, because they were still alive.

Dandy was my bitch; she was only fifteen and she was a sweetheart. Yeah, she was EBV, but she was still in school and always a pleasure to be around. We all looked out for her. She had no parents, they both were dead, so she lived with her elderly grandmother, and she didn't have any brothers or sisters. We were her sisters. Dandy was also a beautiful girl. The projects were saying she reminded them of Lauren London, Lil Wayne's baby mama, and when they cut up her face, it was only hate. I was disgusted when I heard the news. But the tension was escalating. When you been in the streets as long as I have, you know this was only the beginning of something bigger.

Angie was YGB, Yung Gangsta Bitches, Crips Alliance, running the South Bronx. She did have a fierce reputation and a swarm of people that were loyal to her. But we didn't give a fuck. Our beef went back since we were young and our set was ready to ride out and bang hard with anybody at any time. But real talk, Rico was a blessing in my life; his name rang out too. He was practically running shit from East 233rd down to East Gun Hill Road. And he had our back, increased firepower, and muscle.

I stepped into the building with Rico. We walked toward the elevators and waited. The lobby was quiet; the spring heat had drawn everybody outside for some fresh air, even though the air in the Bronx wasn't that fresh. But waiting in the sweltering lobby was a bitch. It was too hot.

We stepped into the smelly and pissy elevator. Rico pushed for the ninth floor. It quickly ascended. I was quiet. I wasn't nervous; it just felt awkward being behind enemy lines, especially after all the shit that done went down in the past month. We stepped onto the ninth floor and I followed Rico to apartment 9F. Already, I could hear music blaring from the apartment. Rico knocked. We waited. Someone came to the door and looked through the peephole.

"It's Rico, open up," he said with authority.

There was no hesitation. The apartment door came open and Rico walked inside. I was right behind him. Once inside, it was obvious that this was a trap house, or trap apartment. There were about six goons present and the living room was prevalent with drugs, mostly keys of cocaine being broken down for street distribution, pills and guns displayed everywhere. The weed smoke was heavy. Two young boys were heavily engaged playing *Madden NFL* on the giant flat screen.

The eyes fixated on me meant I looked really good, like Beyoncé herself was in the room. I was eye candy in the place. I stood behind Rico silently. Being in a room filled with hardcore thugs and killers wasn't anything new to me. I was EBV and well known out here. I had respect like Rico, but my man was notorious and no one dared wanted to disrespect me. I was Rico's girl and that meant a lot to everyone in the room.

I noticed a few familiar faces in the room too, even a nigga I fucked a few months ago, Feach. He only looked at me. He had no words and I had nothing to say to him. His crazy killer ass gave Rico dap, said a few words to my man, and he went back to work, breaking bricks down at the table and weighing shit on the scales accurately. Every piece of drug paraphernalia and automatic weapon was in the apartment. The DEA and ATF would have a field day if this place ever got raided.

"What y'all niggas got for me?" Rico asked.

One of his goons stood up and went into one of the bedrooms. He shortly came back out with a black book bag and handed it to Rico. It was obvious the bag contained cash, probably lots of it, in the tens of thousands. It's the only thing that would bring Rico into the projects: money. Rico was moving shit wholesale, maybe three or four keys a week in these projects and others. And those he knew well, they got their shit on consignment.

"We gonna need that re-up real soon, Rico. Shit is moving really good out here," the man said.

"I'll holla at my connect first thing tomorrow morning," Rico replied.

The man nodded and smiled.

I looked around the apartment more. It was definitely far from being someone's home. The front door was steel plated and painted black. The apartment windows were blacked out. The rap music was still playing but it had been turned down so Rico could hear himself talking, and the goons inside either were busy with the bricks on the table they were cutting up and breaking down and smoking, cigarette or weed, or playing *Madden* or *NBA Live* on the Xbox.

Rico didn't socialize much with anyone in the projects. He didn't get his hands dirty unless he had to. He had been there and done that: shot niggas, murdered niggas, got locked up, and been in the trenches of warfare. Usually, he had his right-hand man, Nine, with him and handling his street affairs. But from my understanding, Nine had received a year sentence a few months back, and was on Rikers Island for violating his parole and assault.

Rico walked up to this man who seemed to be in his late twenties. "Jo-Jo, you making sure security is tight around here, right?" Rico asked. He stared powerfully at the man, who was lean with dark skin with long dreads.

Jo-Jo nodded. "Yeah, I'm on point wit' it, Rico."

"You making sure the young ones are going up and down these stairways, perpetually making sure there ain't no trouble brewing, and you got lookouts on the rooftop?"

"Rico, we tight wit' our shit. I know it's hot out here."

"A'ight." Rico was always on point. He still clutched the book bag in his hand. He decided to call over one of the young kids playing *Madden*.

"Mike, c'mere," Rico called out.

Mike hurried over to Rico like he was being called by a strict parent. He looked fourteen, but his eyes and demeanor showed that he was very mature in these streets and probably been through and seen more than the average man in his short lifetime.

"Hold on to this fo' me," Rico said to him. Rico handed him the book bag. Mike took it without any problems. It appeared Rico had some trust for him because that bag was precious. I fixated my eyes on Mike. He was a little cutie and in a few years, I knew he was going to be a terror.

While Rico was talking to Mike, I had to use the bathroom. I took it upon myself to find the bathroom without asking.

"I gotta use the bathroom, Rico," I said to him.

"First door, to your right," he said.

I made my way toward the bathroom, but I soon noticed someone coming out of one of the bedrooms. I stopped in my tracks and gazed at this person. It was a female. She made her way toward me, to the living room, and when I saw her identity, I scowled heavily. She was a foe of mines. It was one of Denise's peoples, Keysha. She saw me and glared at me. The bitch was one of the girls Sammy and I fought a few weeks back. Me and my bitches had that bitch on the floor and we went ham across her head and tried to beat her into a coma. The bitch had the audacity to be in the same room as me. I was ready to pop off. But it was clear that she was there only because she probably was fuckin' one of the niggas in the apartment.

Rico noticed the sudden tension between her and me. He quickly stepped in between us, knowing I was ready to charge, and said to us, "Okay, y'all two ladies play nice now. I can't be having that bullshit up in here. You know this, Mouse."

"Fuck that bitch!" I exclaimed.

"Fuck you too, bitch!" Keysha retorted.

I took a few steps toward her and was ready to lunge at this bitch and cause havoc on her. Rico held me back. I was so heated that I almost forgot where I was at and was ready to cause mayhem in his spot. That would have been disrespecting my man and his business. And Rico showed me nothing but respect since we'd been together.

Rico continued to hold me back though. We exchanged harsh words, giving the men in the place a little show. I was ready to tear that fuckin' bitch apart with my bare fuckin' hands.

"Mouse, you need to calm the fuck down," Rico shouted at me.

"I am calm. But I'll be even calmer when I fuck this bitch up," I exclaimed.

"Bring it then, stupid bitch!" Keysha shouted.

I wanted to, but I wasn't going to touch that bitch right now and piss Rico off even more. I had the gun on me, too; there was no telling what I could have done to Keysha in the heat of the moment. Rico was already upset that we were bringing unnecessary drama in his place. He glared at Keysha and then asked harshly, "Who this bitch belongs to?"

"She's wit' me, Rico," someone answered submissively.

He was a beefy and shirtless goon, with his upper torso swathed with intimidating tattoos. He looked like trouble, but he didn't bring any while standing in front of Rico.

Rico was blunt with his response. "Get this fuckin' bitch out of here right now and don't bring her back to this place. Fuck she hangin' around here for!"

"I'm sorry, Rico. I didn't mean any harm," the beefy thug replied sheepishly.

I smirked at Keysha while Rico was humiliating her in front of everyone. She didn't say a word. It was a golden moment. I still wanted to beat her ass and was tempted to follow her outside into the hallway and get it popping. I kept my cool though. She was quickly escorted out of the apartment, but before her exit, Keysha locked eyes with me and said, "This ain't over, bitch!"

"I'll see you around, bitch," I spat.

Fuck her!

I loved Rico so much more for doing that for me. He showed and proved I came first. I was important to him. After Keysha left, we left. Rico didn't like hanging around the projects for too long. He kept it moving like the wind blowing. We left the building with Mike carrying the book bag filled with cash to his car.

With it being a warm and balmy night, I wanted to go for a nice drive somewhere with my man, maybe the beach. I loved the beach, and the ocean. Since growing up, the ocean had been a place that was so picturesque and tranquil for me.

I'd learned to swim at the YMCA when I was eight years old. There was something about water that was so soothing and relaxing. It was a place where I could clear my head and get away. I used to get on the F train from Manhattan after transferring from the 5 train coming from the Bronx, and ride it to the last stop in Coney Island, Brooklyn. I would sit on the beach and stare at the ocean for hours. I would be alone. But there were a few times when I would bring Sammy with me. We would marvel at the atmosphere and just talk for hours. Being in Brooklyn, we weren't bad girls or some gangster bitches. In a different borough, far away from the Bronx, we were or seemed to be two regular teenagers just chilling on a spring or summer day.

It'd been almost a year since I'd been to the beach. I wanted to go tonight. I wanted to spend a nice time with Rico on the boardwalk, perhaps walk barefoot through the sand, maybe hold hands and talk while we gazed at the ocean. Yeah, it was probably farfetched thinking with a man like Rico, but a bitch could dream. However, since I'd been kicking it with Rico, my life had become a bit calmer. I would mostly stay at his place writing lyrics, watching TV, relaxing and fucking and sucking my man.

I climbed into the passenger seat of his car. Mike placed the book bag in the trunk and Rico got behind the wheel. We were leaving Edenwald. The night was peaceful so far. I turned on the radio and listened to HOT 97. Rico pulled out the parking lot and turned right onto 229th Street. When he came to a stop at a red light on the corner of 229th Street and Laconia Avenue, I turned my head and saw Sammy, Tina, Chyna, and La-La walking toward the corner. It was good to see my bitches again, even if it was from the car. My clique was looking fierce and strong.

Sammy noticed me in the car with Rico and looked at me. We had spoken via phone a few days ago, and everything was still cool between us. She told me that Search had another show lined up for us; this one was in the city, Midtown Manhattan, at the Manhattan Center Grand Ballroom. And then she was trying to get us more time to record in the studio. I was ready. I really wanted to get out the car and chill with my clique for a moment, but Rico was in a rush to get somewhere else.

"Sammy, Chyna, La-La, Tina, what's up y'all?" I hollered.

"Hey, Mouse!" my clique shouted back at me in unison.

They were excited to see me. They rushed toward the car before the light could change green. I could barely hug everyone from where I sat. But we still greeted each other with friendship. There wasn't any hate, but all love for me. They were all glad to see me happy and doing well.

"Hey, Rico," Chyna, Tina, and La-La said.

Rico greeted them halfheartedly. He was ready to drive off.

"Damn, look at you, Mouse, styling and looking all nice and shit. I love what you got on," said Tina, admiring my outfit for the evening.

"It's nice, right." I smiled.

"Bitch, you got on red bottoms?" La-La asked incredulously.

"Yup!"

"Ooooh, I need me a pair of those," La-La said.

I chuckled and smiled.

"When you gonna come chill wit' ya bitches again, Mouse?" Chyna asked.

"I'll be back around," I told her.

"Don't be forgetting about us," said Tina.

"Oh, guess who I just ran into," I blurted out.

My clique was ready to hear who.

"Keysha's trifling ass," I let be known.

"Where you saw that bitch at? We been lookin' fo' her," said Sammy with a grimace.

"She was at Rico's . . ." I started, but I had to stop myself from saying too much. I already knew I said too much when Rico cut his eyes at me, giving me a stern warning that I had a big mouth. "I saw her over by Denise's old building, walking," I informed them faintly.

"We 'bout to fuck that bitch up then," Chyna hollered.

I saw the fire building in their eyes. They were ready for some action. I so badly wanted to jump out the car and go with them, but I couldn't. The light changed green and before Rico pulled off, I locked eyes with Sammy. We were still kicking it, but not like before. She didn't have much to say to me at the corner, and I wondered why.

"Mouse, get wit' us, okay?" Chyna screamed out.

I waved good-bye to them. Damn, I missed hanging out with them. But my life was with Rico now; and the only disadvantage about that was I wasn't able to kick it with my clique like that anymore. He had a new life planned for us, and I didn't mind; it was perfect. He didn't want to see me in the streets anymore and risking death or incarceration. He loved me, and I loved him.

Chapter Eight

Sammy

I took a cab to the train station at Eastchester, and got on the number 5 train that was heading to the city. The only reason I didn't take the cab into the city was because it would have been too expensive and I didn't have that kind of money. I also couldn't be seen on the city bus with the outfit I had on and the way I was looking—stunning.

It was early in the evening. I had a date with Macky. We finally talked and he wanted to take me out somewhere nice in the city. He volunteered to pick me up from my building, but I turned down the offer. The last thing I needed was muthafuckas being in my business, and I didn't want Search to know about my date.

I wanted to show off my body and well-toned legs, so I decided to wear this sexy and sensational sexy mini dress that featured a halter-style silhouette with the plunging cowl neckline, along with flattering side-ruched skirted bottom and embellished bodice, and an open back with jewel accents that added a little something extra to my style. It only cost me forty dollars off the Internet. I sported a pair of high heels that made my defined legs stretch to the heavens. I definitely didn't look eighteen.

I got on the 5 train and I was already turning heads. I wasn't worried about any trouble coming my way; I held my clutch tightly and inside was a .22 pistol. It was easy to conceal and lethal. I had enemies out there and couldn't be caught slipping. The train wasn't crowded for a Friday evening. I took a seat near the door, crossed my legs, and minded my business. This creepy old guy who was sitting opposite of me kept giving me these chilling looks. I guess he liked what he saw, but I was way out of his league. The way he looked at me I felt was impolite. *I mean, you can glance, nigga, but don't stare and drool too hard.*

I rolled my eyes and smirked. He kept staring at me. I was starting to become uncomfortable.

"You have a problem wit' ya fuckin' eyes?" I asked the old man with contempt.

"No. I just think you are a really beautiful woman. It's like heaven came down to earth to bless up with a moment of bliss," he returned with his toothless smile.

He made me smile after hearing that. "Thank you."

"No, thank you. I'm having a wonderful night just by looking at you."

I chuckled. His appearance was shabby and dirty, but his mannerism was priceless. I gave him a quick show by slowly uncrossing and crossing my legs, giving him a glimpse of the pink G-string I had on. It was for charity. He smiled even harder and his eyes bulged out from his head.

He got off at the next stop. The old man's eyes weren't the only set of eyes watching me. I guess they couldn't help themselves. It was true beauty in front of them. I huffed, though, because not all attention was good attention. It was going to be a long train ride to the Midtown area. I was supposed to meet Macky at Penn Station. Before I left, I called and told him that I was on my way. He still insisted that he'd drive to the Bronx to come get me; it wasn't out of his way. I declined.

It was after seven p.m. when I exited the train station on Thirty-fourth Street, Penn Station. It was exhausting coming from the BX and transferring trains to get to my destination, but I was finally here. I moved behind the crowd in the major intercity train station and a major commuter rail hub in the city and emerged into the bustling, concrete jungle. Thirty-fourth Street, like always, was noisy and busy. The towering buildings seemed to reach the clouds and the people were always so busy coming and going that they wouldn't know if the world was ending.

I immediately got on my cell phone, dialed Macky's number, and began looking around for him. I was lost in the crowd, but I stood out in my sexy attire. I became a distraction for the men, and a few ladies who passed by me. Their eyes without delay shifted either from their girlfriends or Smart phones on to me. I heard someone utter out, "Damn!"

Sorry fellows, I was someone else's date for the evening. And if I told them that I was only eighteen, they probably wouldn't even believe me. From the sexy attire to the makeup I wore, I looked to be in my mid-twenties.

"Hello," Macky answered.

"Yeah, I'm here, I just walked out of Penn Station. Where are you?" I asked him.

"I'm double-parked across the street. I'm in a silver white Jaguar XF," he said.

He was driving around in a Jaguar. It had to be a nice car. I moved through the crowd toward Eighth Avenue and looked deeply for the car he had described. I spotted Macky in seconds. He was standing outside his car looking around for me. We saw each other. He waved me over. I smiled and said to myself, "Damn!" He was looking fine and his vehicle was nice! The car was a four-door sedan with a permanent sunroof and had the best aerodynamically designed body.

I waited for the heavy traffic to pass. The yellow cabs ruled the Manhattan streets. They were some crazy-ass drivers who always seemed to try to hit you purposely. When the light was red and traffic stopped, I strutted Macky's way. It seemed like he couldn't wait to wrap his arms around me. He was smiling greatly and looking good in a white V-neck T-shirt, a pair of boot-cut denim jeans and white Nikes. His dreads were flowing, his dark skin gleaming like the moon, and the only jewelry he wore was a white gold Rolex and diamond-studded earrings.

He threw his arms around me and hugged me tightly when I approached him. "It's good to see you again, Sammy. Damn, you look so beautiful," he said in delight.

"Hey, and thanks," was my sparse reply. I was still skeptical but I was also curious about him. I wanted to see what he was really about. It just felt awkward going behind Search's back to a man he introduced me to, and was a good friend of his.

I climbed into the passenger seat of his Jaguar XF. The interior was impressive and had a trendy appearance with its expensive cream-colored leather seats and gleaming wooden veneer. The instrument panel used pale blue backlighting, and he had a one-touch glove compartment. I felt like a queen in his car.

Macky got behind the wheel and navigated his way through the thick evening Midtown traffic. "Why didn't you want me to pick you up from the Bronx? It wasn't a problem for me," he said.

"I just didn't," I dryly replied.

He didn't push it. Cool.

We were headed to downtown Manhattan. The sun was slowly fading behind the towering city buildings and night was forming, which was creating the city into a multitude of hues from block to block. Macky placed a CD in the CD drive and R&B started to blare through a ten-speaker 400w audio system with an MP3. I didn't recognize the song or the artist singing.

"Who is this singing?" I asked.

Macky nodded his head and replied, "She's gonna be the next big thing in R&B. Her name is Tina Green, and she's from Newark."

She had a beautiful voice. But why did he have me listening to her?

"I'm managing and producing her," he added.

It was nice to hear. Her voice was golden. Her vocals pulled you in and hypnotized you. The song she was singing was a genuine love song. I could tell she had her heart broken, maybe one too many times by a trifling-ass nigga. I nodded to the song. Macky said he did the beat. It was catchy, and so was the hook:

I'm steadily feeling so small, so unseen
I survived; 'cause I tried
But how long will I stride?

"She's about to blow up soon. She just signed to RCA records a month ago, and received a half-million dollar advance. And she might go on tour and open up for Jill Scott," he proclaimed.

"Wow, that's nice," I said, wishing it were me who had the record deal and was going on tour.

Having half a million dollars and a record deal with a major record company would change my world. I would definitely move out the projects and buy me a nice car. Me and Mouse would go on an extravagant vacation somewhere far, maybe to the West Coast or to one of the West Indies islands. I always heard it was paradise out there. I really never had been out of New York; the farthest was maybe New Jersey with a friend. But I could definitely see us sitting on the beach, feeling that tropical breeze and warmth, looking fabulous in our bikinis, and sipping on drinks with our underage asses.

Damn, why did some people have it so good and I didn't? I wondered why Macky was telling me about this woman's career. I didn't know the woman. It wasn't me. I was happy for her. Now it was time to be happy for me.

"You can become her," Macky said to me.

"Her? I need to be me," I replied.

"I mean, you got it, Sammy. She only sings, you can do both, exceptionally, too," he praised.

I smiled.

He turned onto the West Side Highway and drove south. The traffic was thick like a fat bitch's thighs. He was taking me to this downtown restaurant called Delmonico's Steakhouse. It was expensive and classy place on the west side, near the Hudson River.

"So, when you think it's gonna be my time to shine?" I asked him.

Macky smiled, like he knew something I didn't.

"What?"

"I have a surprise for you," he said.

"Well, tell me."

"I'll tell you during dinner."

I hated surprises and I hated waiting. I wanted to hear what he had to say now. This anticipation of hearing what he had to say to me was building up inside of me. But I didn't want to ruin the moment, so I went along and had to wait until we arrived at the restaurant.

Twenty minutes later, after fighting heavy traffic and careless drivers, Macky pulled up to a nice-looking restaurant that was nestled on a cobblestone street in the heart of the Meatpacking District of the city. There was valet parking. Macky and I stepped out, he handed the valet the keys, and we walked inside. I never had been to anything so elegant before. There was fine dining inside and outside. It was such a beautiful night that many patrons decided to dine outside. There was causal chitchat and laughter, the mood so polite I felt awkward and nervous.

Macky took my hand and smiled. "You'll be okay," he said.

I smiled.

We walked hand in hand into the restaurant. Inside there was gilded ceilings, oversized oil paintings, ornate chandeliers, and rich mahogany paneling: the scene for America's first fine-dining restaurant.

The maître d' seated us at a lovely decorated table in the upstairs dining room to experience the restaurant's full grandeur, overseeing the street below and the highway. Macky was a gentleman and pulled out my chair for me to sit.

"Thank you," I said.

"You're welcome."

It was something I had to get used to. We sat opposite of each other and talked. Macky talked a little about his music career. He was twenty-nine and been producing, managing, and making magic happen since he was seventeen. I was reluctant to talk about myself. He didn't believe me when I said I was only eighteen. He respected my honesty though. But I gave him a quick rundown of my background. We talked a little about Search. I told him how long we'd been friends and how good of a man Search was. He agreed. I also told him that I didn't want Search in my business. He agreed again.

The waiter came to us; he was well dressed in black and white, distinguished with his foreign accent and the gray streak in his hair. He was courteous to us and ready to take our orders.

"Ladies first," said Macky.

I stared at the menu; everything seemed so new and pricey. I gawked at food that you only saw and heard about on TV. I didn't know what to order. The two men were waiting patiently for me to say something, but for once, I was stuck on stupid.

Macky noticed the confusion on my face and he intervened. "We'll both have the boneless rib eye steak, and on the side some king crab macaroni and cheese and Delmonico potatoes. Also, a bottle of white wine. The good stuff."

The waiter wrote everything down and responded, "Right away, sir." He walked away.

"Thank you," I said.

"It's not a problem."

Our conversation continued. He was so easy to talk to and so fun to look at. I mean, from his genuine smile and dark skin, to his neatly styled dreads that extended to his shoulders, I could chew him up and taste him slowly.

"You are so beautiful, Sammy," he kept repeating throughout the night.

I kept blushing and thanking him.

Strange though, here I was dressed up and looking marvelous with my legs and curves showing, and forgot that I had a .22 concealed in my clutch. I wondered what Macky would have thought if I told him about the gun on me. But I wasn't stupid; it was for my protection, and even though I was far away from the Bronx, there was no telling where my enemies could be.

My lifestyle was crazy, and I kind of understood where Search was coming from.

Our food came and everything looked delicious. The boneless rib eye steak looked like it was ready to melt in my mouth and slide down my throat. We started to eat and continued our talk. Macky brought up his artist Tina Green again.

"I do magic in this business, Sammy. Tina Green, she's only twenty-one years old, and had nothing going for her. She came from the slums of Newark, like a rose buried under concrete. I dug into that concrete and pulled her out. With my help and my beats, within a year she was signed to RCA records," he proclaimed.

"I need that in my life right now, Macky," I said.

"What's that?"

"A change," I told him.

"And it will come. When you have talent and know the right people, make the right connections, anything's possible." He reached across the table and gently took my hand in his. He massaged them and grinned.

"Sammy, I can make it happen for you," he continued. "I've been in this game a long time. I know the workings of this music business like the back of my own hand. Two years ago, I took the R&B group Ready & Trend, who I saw weren't being paid right with the label they were with, and I did the unthinkable. I went to their label and renegotiated their contract on a record that was already out. Their label gave the group a two million dollar advance, and double their point spread."

I was impressed.

"I can pull you out of the concrete too, Sammy. In fact, the surprise I have for you is, how you would like to do a track with Tina Green and be on her record, maybe even write some songs for her?" he mentioned.

Oh my God. Was he serious? "Are you serious?" I asked, taken aback.

"I'm so serious. I don't bullshit when it comes to making money and producing good music."

I was ready to lunge across the table and hug Macky dearly. Shit, I wanted to give him a firm kiss on the lips. But I contained myself. I smiled profoundly, like this was a big step into achieving my dream. Macky smiled also. He was heaven sent, fo' real. I couldn't wait to tell Mouse about this. *Hold up, he didn't mention Mouse at all. And what about Search?*

I looked at Macky and asked, "What about Mouse? She's gonna be on the track too, right?"

"Mouse is talented, but I only need one of you on the track, and you're the chosen one. But I didn't forget about your friend," he said.

I couldn't do this without Mouse. I was thinking heavily. Macky noticed the sudden dubious look on my face and said, "Listen, Sammy, I know you care for your friend a great deal, and you don't want to be selfish. But think about it, you doing this track is a step up for the both of y'all. You understand me? It puts both of you in a better position. And if Mouse is the great friend you always say she is, then she would want you to do it."

He did made sense. "And Search?"

"Search is a friend of mine, you know this. He's your manager, too, and they always come out right."

"I wanna tell him. I don't want it to seem like I'm goin' behind his back being sneaky and setting up deals on my own. Search's been riding with us for a year now. I can't do that to him."

Macky smiled. "I understand. Shit, how old are you again?" he joked.

I chuckled.

"But you are good peoples, Sammy. I want to see all of y'all come up and make it big. And with my help, it's going to happen."

I had butterflies in my stomach. This was for real. Finally, we had the right connections to go somewhere and it was a step out of the projects and poverty for us. We were definitely expected to get paid for a track with Tina Green. I didn't know how much, but it was something.

We finished our meal and had a wonderful talk. Macky escorted me out the door and the valet brought his car back around. Being the gentleman he was, the chivalry continued for the night. He opened the passenger door for me and I climbed inside his Jaguar XF. I was on cloud nine and still couldn't wait to call Mouse and tell her the good news.

We drove around the city for a while. I was listening to a few more of Tina Green's songs and I liked her style. She reminded me of a young Mary J. Blige. She was raw and her voice distinctive. I was so wrapped up in a track she made called "Black Butterfly" that I didn't realize we were crossing over the George Washington Bridge, and heading into New Jersey.

"Where are we goin'?" I asked.

"It's another surprise," he said.

I didn't sweat it. It had been a wonderful night so far.

"'Black Butterfly' is the track I want you on," he said.

"Fo' real?"

"Yes. It's missing something, and I finally know what it is. I think the two of y'all will kill that track and when it blows up, everyone's gonna be asking, 'Who's that girl rhyming?' It's Sammy," he said convincingly.

I was like a wide-eyed schoolgirl in a whole new world. I was already thinking about lyrics to go with the beat. It was going to be a hard rhyme. My debut had to be on point. I had to show out, like Snoop did on the *Deep Cover* soundtrack or DMX's first appearance in the video for LL Cool J's single "4, 3, 2, 1." I had to stand out, maybe more than the primary artist.

Macky continued to drive. We were in New Jersey, moving north on Henry Hudson Drive. It was a remote location near the waters and swathed with trees. We parked in this empty parking lot near the shoreline. It had a spectacular view of the GW Bridge, which was so colorful at night, and the New York City skyline, which gleamed on the other side of the river like the Emerald City in Oz. It was dark and quiet. Macky killed the ignition and sat back in his seat. He looked at me and smiled.

"You comfortable?" he asked.

"I'm good," I replied.

The last track had played on the CD and it reverted to playing the first track. I looked around: no cars, it was only us. The time on the dashboard read eleven-fifteen p.m. Macky leaned in closer to me and showed off a glib smile. His eyes were fixated on my meaty thighs and chest. Okay, this was getting too creepy for me.

"You know I'm gonna look out for you, Sammy," he said.

"I know."

"I'm doing a lot for you, because I believe in you," he continued.

I was listening.

"So, with that said, what are you gonna start doing for me?" he asked coolly.

"What?"

"Look, I do you a favor and you start doing me a few favors," he had the nerve to say.

I wasn't a fool. I understood what fucking favors he was talking about. Out of nowhere, he quickly undid his jeans and pulled out his dick. *What the fuck?* I thought. But I had to admit, it was long, black, and thick—about nine inches.

"You suck my dick tonight, and I'll definitely get you on this track with Tina Green and put you out there within six months. I can make you a star, Sammy," he said, sounding so fuckin' greasy all of a sudden.

I scowled. "Nigga, are you fuckin' serious?"

"Just suck my fuckin' dick, bitch, and you gonna get put on," he barked.

This muthafucka just morphed into some demon spawn instantly; his chivalry left so fast. I wasn't sucking his dick, I didn't give a fuck who he was. The moment was gone, ruined, and I saw my chance at success flying out the door.

"Fuck you, muthafucka!" I cursed. "I ain't suckin' shit!"

"Bitch, I spent money on you tonight, took your ghetto ass out to a nice restaurant, showed you a good fucking time and you wanna act the fuck up! And I'm ready to put you on. Bitch, you fuckin' owe me something," he shouted.

I was resistant and ready to hurt him. Out of the blue, he lunged for me and punched the shit out of me. I was stunned for a moment. He hit me like I was some man. He then gripped my hair violently and pushed my face into the glass so hard, I thought it shattered. I then felt him forcing my head into his lap.

"You gonna suck my dick tonight, bitch!" he exclaimed. "And if you fuckin' bite me, I'll fuckin' kill you, bitch!"

Where did this demon come from? He had me fooled completely.

"Get off me! Get the fuck off me!" I screamed.

The tip of his dick was rubbed against my face. I felt his pre-cum smearing across my cheek. He was strong and tried to get me to open up my mouth, but I continued to fight.

"Suck my fuckin' dick, you ghetto-ass bitch!" he screamed madly.

He was attacking me. I was hit again, this time on my side; it felt like he cracked my ribs. But he took the breath out of me with the blow. I reached up and clawed the right side of his face. My nails dug into his skin roughly and he hollered. But he was still forcing me to please him, either from doing oral or pussy. Now he was trying to rape me in the front seat of his car. He was forcing my legs open and pulling up my dress simultaneously, exposing my pink G-string underneath. He ripped my underwear from me like it was a rubber band popping. His hand grabbed around my neck and he squeezed.

"Get off me! Stop it!" I screamed from the top of my lungs.

I kicked and punched him, but he was a monster. My clutch bag was on the floor. I scrambled with my right hand to find it, while I fought him with my left. I had the .22 inside, but never thought I would need it to prevent from being beaten and raped. I continued to fight. I punched, scratched, and kicked this muthafucka repeatedly until I finally hit a nerve on him that made him jolt and hurt. I caught him in his balls; my knee went thrusting upward and connected with his family jewels. He fell back, howling from the pain. Now was my chance.

I quickly removed the small pistol from my clutch, and while Macky was holding his balls in pain while he was against the driver's seat, I struck him with the butt of the gun repeatedly.

"Muthafucka!" I screamed.

I was all over him, pistol whipping this nigga until his face was red. Now I was the monster on top of him.

"You know who the fuck I am?" I shouted. "I'm EBV, nigga. Fuck you! Fuck you! Fuck you!"

I felt his nose breaking and his teeth shattering. I was going to kill him. I had never been disrespected like this in my life. I aimed the pistol at his face. My eyes were bloodshot from crying and anger, but before I could shoot this asshole in his fuckin' face, he pushed me off of him. I went flying into the other seat. He went for the gun and there was loud pop that exploded inside the car.

I scrambled to get outside. I didn't know who was shot, me or him. The passenger door flew open and I crashed in a thud to the ground on my side. I crawled on my hands and knees against the rocks and dirt and then spun over on my back and glared at the car. The gun was on the ground also, away from me. Macky stumbled from the car, screaming, "Fuckin' bitch, you shot me!"

He was bleeding more. He had been shot, but it wasn't life threatening. The bullet had zinged by his ear and he was still a threat.

Macky looked dazed and confused. I continued to watch him stumble from the car and stagger my way. I was scared. There was lots of blood, more on him than me. I jumped to my feet, when he snatched up the gun and I ran away. I popped off my heels and took off sprinting. I had to get away. I didn't even turn around to see if he was chasing me. I soon found myself lost amid the thick shrubbery and trees that seemed to go on for miles. I didn't have a clue where I was. I only knew that I was somewhere in New Jersey.

I ran for what seemed like forever. I didn't cry out for help. I was scared to, thinking my cries for help would lead him to me. I was tired and breathless. I propped against a large tree and unruffled myself. There was no one around me, only darkness and a peculiar surrounding. I pulled out my cell phone and wanted to dial Mouse's number. I had to get home. I had to leave here. I started to dial my friend's number, but abruptly, this wave of grief overcame me and I found myself crying hysterically. I dropped to my knees with my face in anguish and my heart pounding immensely. It felt like I almost couldn't breathe. Once again, my future was nothing. It was all a lie. I wasn't sucking or fuckin' anyone to get a record deal. I was a gangsta bitch, but I wasn't a slut or that desperate to sleep with a nigga to sign a contract.

My life was still in danger, though. That maniac was still out there with my gun in his hand, and the only thing I could think about was making it home. I felt weak, hurt, and alone. I dried my tears, touched my bruises, and stood up. I thought about Search. I felt I betrayed him. I shouldn't have gone behind his back and got with Macky. It turned out to be a serious mistake.

I had to find my way home and be careful. I looked at my cell phone; there was barely a signal to make a call. I had to roam around and find a signal. It took me twenty minutes to find a decent signal where I was able to make a phone call. I hurriedly dialed Mouse's number. It rang.

"Please, pick up. Please, pick up," I prayed.

"Sammy?" I heard Mouse answered.

She sounded like an angel on the other end of the phone.

"Mouse, I need your help. Help me," I cried out.

Chapter Nine

Mouse

Every day is a beautiful day when you have peace of mind. I was intoxicated with love and lust. For me, being with Rico and in love, the sun shined brighter, the birds sang louder, and every step was more assured. And my moans bounced off from wall to wall with ecstasy. His touch sent a warm tingle throughout my body. Rico was hitting this pussy from the back. Our intimacy was so strong, our connection with each other unbreakable. I was curved over, knees spread against the carpet, feeling his masculine penis part my moistened lips, exposing my hardened clit; and my breasts flapped away from his hard thrust inside of me.

"Ooooh, fuck me, Rico. Ooooh, shit, baby, love me right," I cooed.

We both were buck naked in the living room. The sixty-inch plasma flat screen was playing a muted *Friday After Next*. We had stopped watching it a long time ago and began entertaining each other passionately. I loved the way my boo was all over me, sliding his hard cock in and out of me effortlessly. He gripped my hips and I felt his hard dick pounding me, making me scream, tears in my eyes and ready to receive his precious gift while I was getting thoroughly fucked.

The dick pounding inside me made me bite my lips as I tried to hold back the moans and sounds of pleasure. I always longed to feel his erection invade and manipulate me. I gave him all access to every part of me; if he wanted to fuck me in the ass, I wasn't going to stop him. We just needed some Vaseline and patience. I felt every inch of him inside me; my womanly juices was all over him.

I thought he wanted to cum inside me from the back, but he turned me over and I spread my legs for him. There was something comfortable about lying back and feeling your lover pleasing you from head to toe. I wasn't being selfish, just completely satisfied. I wrapped my legs around him with him on top of me, blanketing me with heated passion. We kissed fervently and he fucked me profoundly while pulling my legs back to my chest, exposing me completely and giving him all access.

We switched positions again; I climbed on top of him with my nipples crushed against his chest and my breath panting against his. He slipped his arms around me and filled his hands with my ass, his dick piston inside of me. He was all I could think about. He was filling every gap inside of me with his powerful and thick machine.

"I'm cumming," Rico cried out.

"Cum for me, daddy," I said loudly, feeling my entire body dancing with excitement.

He felt so good inside of me with me being on top of him, straddling his fine physique. He cupped my breast and gripped my ass, grunting like an animal. My pussy had him speaking in tongues and his face twisted with ample pleasure.

"I'm coming, baby, shit!" he groaned and squirmed underneath me.

I worked my thick and shapely hips against him like a race jockey pushing his horse for the win. He squeezed my ass with both hands and grunted with a lasting passion. I felt his penis growing and throbbing harder inside of me. A few more thrusts into my pink luscious lips that engulfed his dick and I felt his strong release within me, his semen swimming around in me, with the sexual rawness turning us into an entwined bliss.

I lay against my man's chest and exhaled. He wrapped his arms around me and held me like a blanket of comfort. I closed my eyes and rested for a minute. I needed that dick. It was only round one with Rico with more sexual pleasures to come. The man had stamina. His energy level was high and he could go for another two rounds at least until he was finally done sexing.

It was a quiet night in our home. With my eyes closed and Rico's breath nestling my ear, I was about to be in slumber land. But my cell phone ringing and vibrating on the table disrupted the peaceful and calm moment. I wasn't going to answer it, thought to just let the voice mail pick up, but something inside me told me to answer it.

I pulled myself away from Rico's pleasing grasp, hearing him say, "You really gonna answer that?"

"I think it's important," I replied.

It was almost midnight. He sat up and watched me rush for the cell phone buck naked. The caller ID showed that it was Sammy calling. It had to be important. I started to think something terrible had happened: who got beat down, who got shot, or who was locked up?

I snatched the phone from the table before the last ring and answered, "Sammy?"

I couldn't even speak a sentence when I heard Sammy frantically shout into the phone, "Mouse, I need ya help! Help me."

"Sammy, what happened? Sammy, where are you?" I shouted with worry.

"He tried to rape and kill me," she exclaimed. It sounded like she had been crying.

I couldn't believe what I was hearing. "What? Who tried to fuckin' kill and rape you?" I screamed out. "Sammy, fuckin' talk to me, what is goin' on?"

By now, Rico was off his ass and came toward me with a concerned stare. "What's goin' on wit' Sammy?" he asked.

With tears streaming down my face, I replied, "I don't fuckin' know!"

Rico took the phone from my hands and said, "Sammy, talk to us. Where the fuck are you?"

I was going crazy. Someone tried to rape and kill my best friend. I was ready to go ham, call up our crew, bring out the pistols, and look for this muthafucka who was living on borrowed time. I just needed a name from Sammy, that's it.

"A'ight, just stay there. We on our way there now; just keep ya phone on," I heard Rico say to her.

"Where is she?" I asked Rico frantically.

"She's in New Jersey, by the GW Bridge, near some park or shore," he told me.

New Jersey? The GW Bridge? I was confused.

I hurried to get dressed, putting on anything within my reach. Now wasn't the time to be looking cute. We didn't have any time to waste. Rico pulled out a few pistols from the bedroom and stuffed the 9 mm into his waistband and handed me the .45. I concealed it on my person and we rushed out the door.

Under the cover of night, we hurried to his ride. I jumped into the passenger seat with my mind racing with so much shit. Who the fuck did Sammy go to New Jersey with? And why?

We rushed toward Jersey, getting on the Cross Bronx Expressway and racing to the bridge. Traffic was sparse, and while on the way there, I kept calling Sammy's phone. We knew she was near the GW Bridge, but we needed a specific location.

We got to Sammy an hour later. It was hard trying to find her, her calls kept dropping, but we finally did. She was near a dark road by some rocky shore and looking a fuckin' mess. I didn't even give Rico a chance to stop the car and park; I hurried toward her and ran to aid my friend.

"Sammy," I called out.

She looked at me with these hurt and angry eyes. Her tearstained face was dirty and bruised, her dress was torn, and she had blood on her. I automatically started to think the worse. When I reached her, I hugged my best friend tightly. *Oh my God, what happened to her?*

"Talk to me, Sammy. Where is he at? Is that muthafucka still around here?" I shouted at the same time looking around the area to see if there was anyone else, but nothing. No one else was around.

I got nothing but silence back from Sammy, though.

Sammy was strong. This incident didn't break her. I knew it didn't break her. She was shaken up, but Sammy was going to bounce back from this and someone out there was a dead man walking, he just didn't know it yet. We only needed a name and the pistol would do the screaming.

I locked eyes with Sammy and asked her, "Sammy, who the fuck did this shit to you? Just give me a fuckin' name and they are dead."

She didn't answer me. Rico finally made his way over with the screw face and pistol in his hand. He was ready for some conflict, but it was only us in the mix. The perpetrator was probably long gone from here.

"Who the fuck did this to you, Sammy?" he also asked.

There was still silence and anger with Sammy. I understood the anger, but why was she so fuckin' silent?

"Fuck that, we taking you to the hospital," I said, grabbing her arm.

"I'm not goin' to no fuckin' hospital, Mouse," she finally spoke, pulling away from me. "I'm okay!"

"Well, damn, at least we know you can still speak," I replied dryly.

"Give us a name, Sammy, and I promise you by week's end, he's dead," Rico said with conviction.

"I just wanna go home and get some rest," she replied coyly.

"You not gonna tell us who the fuck did this to you?" I asked angrily.

"I just wanna go home and chill, Mouse, that's all. Forget about it," she returned with a slight attitude.

"What?"

"Fuck it, let's just go," Rico chimed.

I was becoming upset with her for not telling me who it was who tried to rape and kill her. This shit was serious and she was taking it lightly. Whoever it was, he wasn't going to get away with it. I promised her that.

We walked back to the car in silence. Sammy crawled into the back seat and I climbed inside behind her. The stillness was troubling me, but Rico and I didn't continue to press the issue. I wanted to, though.

Why wasn't she saying who the nigga was? Was it someone close to us, in our circle or clique? Was she in shock? Was it Search? Nah, he wouldn't have done the unthinkable to Sammy. We were all friends and Search wasn't that kind of dude. And Sammy wasn't the type to trust anyone, and why the fuck was she in New Jersey? So many questions I wanted to ask her, but why ask when this bitch wasn't trying to answer anything?

Shit, we were Edenwald Blood Vixens, we always looked out for each other, thick and thin, blood in, blood out, and nothing had changed since I got with Rico. I was still Mouse, that bitch ready to pop the fuck off at the drop of a hat.

Rico pulled off and started heading back to the bridge. Sammy seemed to be lost in her thoughts. I gazed out the window, staring at the water below and the city skyline from afar. It was a beautiful night, but the mood in the car was so sour. I was still itching to find out who the nigga was. I glanced back at Sammy; she carried a stone-cold expression. She had some minor bruises and cuts; in spite of that, she was fine in my eyes. Maybe she needed to rest and clean up, collect herself and get her mind right, and then she would tell us what went down.

How did my night begin so perfect and end up so fucked up? But this been our life for so long. It was like you expected shit to happen when things been cool for too long. I started the spring being in a new and loving relationship and we were grinding in this music business. And then just like that, shit can go so wrong within the blink of an eye.

We arrived at Edenwald and pulled up to Sammy's building. I wasn't leaving her alone for the night. I planned on being by her side until everything was cool with her and she told me what happened. Rico was cool with it. He dropped us off and went about his business. I walked with Sammy into the building lobby and then into her apartment. Our turbulent homes were similar, her with her sick mother and me with my abusive father. The apartment was dark and reeked of a foul odor. There wasn't anything nice in Sammy's apartment; everything from the little furniture they had to the pots and pans in the kitchen looked run-down and hand-me-down. And the foul smell came from the bathroom; there was a backed-up toilet.

In her bedroom, Sammy stripped down to her underwear and just climbed into her bed, which was only a shabby mattress against a dirty floor. She threw the sheets over her head and closed her eyes.

"Just lock the door when you leave, Mouse," she said to me in a nonchalant manner.

"So, that's it?" I spat. "You not gonna tell me what happened to you? You just gonna go to sleep like everything is good?"

"I just wanna sleep, Mouse, that's all."

I sucked my teeth with aggravation. I couldn't believe this shit. What was she trying hide from me? Was she scared about something or someone? I wasn't leaving though. I was going to sleep on the couch and talk to her in the morning. I closed her bedroom door and let her be.

The next morning, I woke up to find Sammy smoking a cigarette in the building hallway. She was seated with her back against the wall, knees up and puffing in silence. I walked up to her and asked, "Everything okay with you?"

"Yeah, I'm good," she replied coolly.

"So, you gonna tell me what happened last night?" I asked.

She took another pull from her cigarette and looked up at me with this deadpan gaze. "I'm not tryin' to talk about it right now, Mouse," she replied.

"You know what, Sammy? I'm ya best friend, and I always gonna have ya back. But right now, real talk and shit, I'm startin' to feel some type of way. Some nigga out there disrespected you to the third degree, and you tryin' to take this shit lightly. The muthafucka shouldn't even be breathing right now," I exclaimed heatedly. "You can't even give me his fuckin' name."

She took another pull from the Newport and continued to remain nonchalant about the situation. It was pissing me off.

"Just leave me alone, Mouse. I'm good," she replied softly.

"What?"

Sammy stood up, took one final pull from her cigarette and flicked it down the hallway. She looked at me, deadpan. I didn't know what was on her mind.

"We still gotta do this show at the Manhattan Center next week," she had the audacity to bring up.

I didn't give a fuck about doing a show right now at some Manhattan Center. I cared about my friend. "Are you serious, Sammy?" I exclaimed.

"The show don't stop, it goes on, right? I'm good, Mouse. Don't worry about me, I can handle myself. It was nothing. I just blown it out of proportion."

I glared at my best friend. I seriously wanted to smack some sense into her head. "So you calling me up after midnight, with you crying, and pleading for me to come pick you up from New Jersey is blowing shit out of proportion. Wow. Really? Sammy, what the fuck is wrong wit' you? This ain't you!"

"Mouse, just fuckin' drop it, a'ight? I'm okay and let's just do this show next week. That's all that matters," she proclaimed.

I heard enough. She was talking crazy. I retorted, "Fuck you, Sammy! I'm here for you always, and it seems like you don't trust me or somethin' to tell me what happened. So fuck you!"

I stormed off, marching down the stairway. When she didn't try to call me back, it angered me so much more. I was ready to put my fist through one of these brick walls. I continued to march outside the building. I was so upset that I was feeling sick to my stomach. Suddenly, this nauseated feeling came over me and I hurried to the nearest trashcan and threw up chunks. I started to feel lightheaded and weak. I needed to eat something. Thinking and worrying about this bitch had me ready to pass out.

I walked farther from Sammy's building, and being back in my old hood always felt great. I wasn't rushing to go back to where I rested my head; sometimes, it was just too quiet on Rico's block, and when he wasn't around, I would be bored to death. It felt like I was becoming his housewife or somebody. I was cooking for my man, cleaning, and he was always in the pussy or I was sucking his dick like a porn star. I'd been out of the loop for almost two months and I just needed to chill for a moment.

I figured since I was around the way, I might as well go by my old apartment and pick up the rest of my things. Hopefully, my father wasn't home or didn't change the locks. When I got to my building, it was still the same. It hadn't been that long since I moved out, but this nostalgic feeling came over me. I walked inside and took the elevator to my floor. I had my keys already in my hand and slowly approached my apartment. I put my ear to the door and listened: silence. No music was playing and there was no loud talking. It meant nobody was probably home. I twisted the key and pushed open the door. The shades were drawn and it was dark inside. It smelled, too. The kitchen was a mess, dirty dishes piling up in the sink, trash overflowing in the trashcan, molded food displayed on the messy table with roaches crawling everywhere; it was horrendous. The rest of the apartment wasn't any better, clothes and trash was everywhere, and remnants of what looked like a large get-together showed.

I walked toward my bedroom, but then this sick feeling came over me again. I hurried to the bathroom and dropped to my knees in front of the porcelain toilet, which was already disgusting with shit floating inside the bowl. I cringed at the sight of it and threw up anyway. *Yuck!* I continued to float my head over the toilet. It smelled so badly. I couldn't take it anymore and continued to throw up in the sink. When I was done spilling shit from my stomach, I wiped my mouth and went into my old bedroom.

Everything was gone. My bed, my posters, my stereo, CD collection, clothes, shoes. The room was barren, like looters rushed in and picked me clean. *What the fuck!* I wasn't worried about the clothes or shoes, Rico bought me tons of stuff, but the sentimental things I had in that room was gone, like the stuff Sammy bought for me over the years, and the locket pendant necklace in sterling silver that I kept in my top drawer; it was gone. It was a gift from my mother before she died. Pictures that I had under my bed of me having good times with Sammy, Tina, La-La, Chyna, and ex-boyfriends were gone; and ones that were plastered on my wall were all torn down. There was nothing left, the memories taken. I wanted to cry. How could my father just come into my room and have so much lack of respect for my things, stuff that I held dear to my heart?

The closet was emptied out and there was even urine in the corner. *Oh my God.* I hadn't been gone that long, and it seemed like my bedroom was treated like some crack house or flea market.

I all of a sudden heard someone entering the apartment. My heart skipped a beat and nervousness came over me. It had to be my father. Maybe it wasn't such a good idea to come back here. I left for a reason. I slowly walked into the hallway. I heard him in the living room, and he wasn't alone. I wanted to leave. The radio came on and Spanish music started blaring.

"*Ve que,*" I heard my father say.

"*Me gusta que,*" the next voice said.

I didn't know what they were doing, but I could tell it wasn't anything nice at all. I looked into the living room and saw my father seated on the couch with a bottle in his hand. It was early in the morning and he was already drinking. He had another man with him who was unfamiliar to my eyes. The nigga was young and lanky. I never saw him around the hood before. I huffed. I had to pass him to make my exit, and it was clear that he was twisted.

But what I saw next clearly disturbed me. My father took a swig from the bottle in his hand and leaned back in the couch with his legs spread. He unzipped his pants and pulled out his dick. *What the fuck!* The dude with him leaned over in his lap and took my father's dick into his mouth.

Oh my God! I was shocked.

I witnessed the unthinkable, my father receiving a blow job from another man. I was disgusted. He was a fuckin' faggot. My father moaned with his hand gripped around the back of the man's head, shoving this nigga's face farther into his lap. I wanted to cry. He was a high-ranking member of the Latin Kings. He was a killer and had bitches going crazy for him back in the days. This was impossible to see. This faggot's lips were wrapped around my father's thick dick and I wanted to throw up again right there.

"Ooooh, yeah. Suck that dick. Yes. Yes. *Se siente tan bien,*" my father said.

"You like, *papi,*" his gay lover replied.

"*Me encanta.* You my bitch," said my father.

I gasped from hearing and witnessing this appalling act. They heard me. The man stopped sucking dick and jumped up, and my father rose up from the couch, pulling up his pants, and came charging my way. I had nowhere to run.

"Who the fuck is in my house?" he shouted.

I tried to run for the door, but he caught up with me and grabbed me from behind and pulled me back aggressively into the room. I fell backward, landing on my side. He stood over me, scowling, and shouted, "Mouse, what the fuck are you doin' here? What the fuck did you just see?"

"I didn't see anything," I hollered.

"You lying!" he screamed.

I could smell the liquor on his breath from there. He kicked me in my stomach so hard and the wind was knocked out of me. I doubled over, and screamed loudly from the pain.

"What did you fuckin' see, you little bitch?" he screamed.

"I didn't see anything," I shouted.

"Stop lying to me!"

He kicked me again, striking me in my side with his boot and the pain shot through me like I was being dipped in ice-cold, arctic waters. I screamed out from the pain and begged my father to stop. He never stopped. The beating continued. This time his fists landing on me next, like I was a gym punching bag, and I folded up into the fetal position. Why had I come back?

"I'm no faggot, Mouse!" he screamed. "I'm no fuckin' faggot!"

I didn't respond. I was too busy trying not to black out from his savage beating. I was paralyzed on the floor, feeling wetness on my face. I was bleeding. My body ached and my mind was spinning.

"Hector, stop it! Stop it!" I heard his faggot boyfriend scream out.

"Shut the fuck up!" Hector retorted.

"I can't be a part of this, Hector. Isn't she your daughter?"

Hector went over to him and punched the man in the face so hard, his face seemed to explode. "Shut the fuck up, you fuckin' faggot!" my father screamed madly. "You fuckin' faggot! You violate me!"

The beating shifted from me to him. The man was trying to defend himself on the couch, while my father's hard blows rained down on him. He screamed out. Hector was going crazy. I knew he had to have stopped taking his medication. His outbursts were becoming more violent. I feared he was going to finally kill me or his lover. But I had a moment of freedom from the abuse. It hurt, but I stood up and while my father was distracted with his gay lover, I bolted from the apartment.

I heard him chasing me. "You little fuckin' bitch! C'mere!" he screamed out.

I ran. He continued to chase. I didn't have time for the elevator; I crashed through the stairway and scrambled down the stairs with my eyes flooded with tears.

"You better not tell anyone about this, Mouse! Or I'll fuckin' kill you. You shut up, Mouse! You shut the fuck up and better not tell anyone." His voice echoed in the stairway.

I went rushing out my building like a bat out of hell and toppled over someone who was entering, making them spill the groceries they were carrying. We both went crashing against the pavement. I received a few scrapes and cuts, but I was far from okay. I started to feel lightheaded again. It was hell again for me. I took a few steps toward the street and passed out.

Chapter Ten

Mouse

I was pregnant! I was five weeks pregnant. Wow! But it wasn't hard to believe. The way we were fucking and the way Rico was coming inside me, raw, too. It was inevitable. It was late May with Memorial Day right around the corner, and I was in the hospital. I was admitted into Monteriore Hospital by Gun Hill Road after the incident with my father. I was lucky to be alive. He could have killed me. When I passed out, so many people came to my aid and rushed me to the hospital. The doctors treated me and took a blood and urine test and found out I was having Rico's baby. Besides that, I was fine. I only spent two days in the hospital and was being discharged.

The beating from my father wasn't too severe like the others I had received before. I was a strong bitch. Police had come to my room to question me about it, and asked if I wanted to press charges against him. I wasn't snitching on my father. I was that type of bitch to keep her mouth shut. No matter what, he was still my father and I wasn't telling. It was the primary rule of the hood, the ghetto: if you ain't gettin' bag stay the fuck from police, if niggas think you snitchin they ain't tryin' to listen.

But the police informed me that they were looking for my father. There was already a warrant out for his arrest. When he couldn't catch me, he went back to the apartment and nearly beat that other faggot to death. The man suffered a broken nose and ribs, shattered jaw, and he was violently sodomized with a broom stick to his anus and he suffered internal bleeding and tearing. My father was sick. He had finally lost it and went over the edge. I was just glad that I didn't have to deal with him anymore.

I was excited and scared at the same time about being pregnant. I was going to become a mother. Damn, finally, somebody knocked this pussy up and I was going to be a baby mama. I was just glad it was Rico's baby. I was a 110 percent sure it was his, no doubts about it. Me and my child were going to be taken care of. I loved Rico and he loved me, and now we were about to become a family. It was going to be his first child as well.

There was so much to think about. My father was fuckin' gay, or bisexual. How did he hide it from me for so long? Did it happen in prison? It had to. His rage almost tore me apart. He was so strong and violent. I thought about his lover; what had happened to him? When Rico found out about the abuse, he was furious. The minute he heard the news, he rushed to come see me at the hospital. I was in the emergency room being treated and he charged in like he owned the place.

"Mouse," he had hollered with trepidation. "You okay?"

I had smiled when I saw my man coming for me. It was great to be loved by someone like him. I had nodded, and replied, "I'm okay, baby."

He had seen the minor bruises and cuts on me and he went berserk. "Did ya father do this shit? I'ma kill that muthafucka!"

He had said it in front of the doctors and nurses. I wanted him to calm down. He had already expressed that he was about to commit premeditated murder. The last thing I wanted was for him to get locked up, and then where would I be?

"Rico, just calm down."

"Nah, fuck that, I told you what I was gonna do if he ever put his fuckin' hands on you again," Rico had exclaimed.

He was scowling heavily and was making a scene. His temper was flaring. It was a side of Rico that was so scary. I noticed the bulge underneath his shirt. He was concealing his pistol and didn't do too good of a job. If I saw it, then who else could see it? Police and security were already outside the room, and with Rico not thinking straight, he was jeopardizing his freedom.

"Rico, I need a hug, come hug me," I had said to him, extending my arms.

He walked over, and when I pulled him into my arms, I quickly whispered in his ear, "Baby, ya gun is almost showing underneath ya shirt, please fix it."

"Oh, shit," he had whispered back.

We both subtly tried to conceal his pistol better while anyone wasn't really paying us any attention. Rico zipped up his light jacket and became calmer. He lost the temper and we just talked. It was a good thing I was the only one on point and no one else was.

The next day was when they told me I was pregnant. Rico was by my side and I told him the news. He was nonchalant for a moment. It was scaring me.

"You pregnant," he said, looking stoic.

I smiled and nodded. "They tell me that I'm six weeks."

I'd been fucking with Rico for almost two months now, and before him, I hadn't had sex in maybe five or six months.

"Wow, we gonna have a baby," he said.

I beamed profoundly. He said "we." He didn't try to deny his child or my fidelity, because he knew I was a faithful bitch. I couldn't help but release a few tears of happiness and hug my man strongly. I didn't want to let him go. My world was changing and things seemed to becoming sweeter. But then I started to think about Sammy and wondered about her. It was obvious she was going to be my baby's godmother, there wasn't any doubt to that. I couldn't wait to tell her the news. But where was she? I figured she had to hear that I was in the hospital and would be the first to come see me. But also, she just went through that incident of almost being raped and killed, and she wasn't saying shit. We both had a terrible incident happen to us within forty-eight hours of each other.

When Rico left the room to make an important phone call, I huffed a great deal. Rico was the first person I told about my pregnancy and Sammy needed to be the second. Was I still upset with her for not telling me what had happened and leaving me in the dark? Yes, a little. But this news of me having a baby had triumphed over everything and made me get rid of any ill feelings I had that morning.

I tried to call Sammy numerous times from my phone, but she wasn't picking up and then her phone started going straight to voice mail. I was worried about her. It felt like things were changing between us.

I was dressed and ready to leave the hospital room. I was waiting for Rico to get back. He was my ride home. I walked toward the window in the room and gazed out. I was on the eighth floor and had a marvelous view of the Bronx. I could see the Bronx River Parkway and gazed at Woodlawn Cemetery from afar. It was ironic, a hospital located not too far from the cemetery. With my eyes fixated on the cemetery, I thought about so many of our friends who were buried there, from homies we knew and bitches from our clique who had fallen because of gang violence. I always thought about death; the way we lived it was just a touch away. I was only eighteen, but it felt like I lived two lifetimes of shit and going through hell.

I gazed outside thinking about death while rubbing my stomach that now carried life inside it. Was the baby going to be a boy or girl? I was wishing for a boy, a little Rico running around and being so handsome and charming just like his father. I stood by the window thinking until Rico came back and we were ready to leave.

"You okay?" I asked him.

"Yeah, but I should be askin' you that," he said to me.

"I'm okay, baby."

He picked up my things and we left the room. The next time I wanted to see a hospital was when I was giving birth to a beautiful baby boy or girl.

We exited from the front entrance of the hospital and Rico escorted me to the car. He was so helpful every step of the way. I got inside and felt at ease. My face was healing, but my spirit was still heavy. Where was Sammy? Why hadn't she called and why wasn't she picking up her phone?

Rico took me to a nearby IHOP and I dined on pancakes and bacon. We had a great conversation and already I was thinking about baby names. I was going to make a great mother; I knew I would. I lost my mother to the streets and drugs when I was ten years old. This baby wasn't going to lose me. I was going to be around forever to take care of my seed, to nourish and protect him or her. I already started to feel motherly. I was already changing.

After IHOP, we went back to the house. Rico made sure everything was okay for me. He didn't stay long; he was back out the door fifteen minutes later. He claimed it was more business he had to take care of. He was a hustler, always on the go, the streets were calling and there was money that needed to be made. I understood. It wasn't like he never made time for me. He did. But now that I was pregnant with his baby, I didn't know what to think. I really wanted this family. I wanted us to work and live him harmony and comfort, like the families I grew up watching on TV: *The Cosby Show, Family Matters, The Fresh Prince of Bel-Air, My Wife and Kids, The Parent 'Hood,* and others.

I used to envy how other black families lived. They had it so easy and always seemed so happy. A mother and father living in the same household, and making money, with more than two bedrooms, was incredible to me. Because where I came from, having both parents living with you in the projects was, if not impossible, then rare.

But life for me and Sammy wasn't a TV show, it was a horror movie, real talk. However, we survived many horrors shows and kept it moving. With this baby growing inside of me, I had enough of the horror and wanted to star in my own *7th Heaven.* This baby wasn't going to go through the hell that I'd been through. They were going to have so much better. It was a promise.

I went into the bathroom and lifted up my shirt to see my stomach. I started to rub my belly again. I gazed at my reflection and imagined what it was going to feel like to be pregnant. I was definitely going to lose my curvy shape and probably get fat. I didn't want to get too fat. Maybe I would still be able to fit my clothing or shoes for a while. If not, then Rico was going to have to take me shopping for a whole new wardrobe. I heard about the morning sickness; it was a fucking pain. But the feeling I wanted to experience the most was having this baby move around inside of me and feel it kicking against me. That is true indication of life.

It was late May and the heat was blazing like the sun was personally giving the Bronx a bear hug. I was already sweating. I was gonna be pregnant during the summer, fall, and wintertime and it was cool with me. I planned on being comfortable in my nice home and lying up with my man as my belly grew bigger.

Memorial Day was a big thing in our hood. There were barbeques, block parties, cookouts, and house parties. Sammy and I used to attend everything popping in the hood, from sun up to sun down, and until the wee hours in the morning we showed our asses and had a good time. We used to wear the skimpiest shit and caught all the niggas' attention. It was fun having the boys hollering at us; even grown men tried to talk to us. Sammy and I was always the hottest thing moving in the projects, probably in the Bronx, too. For years, we always partied hard and did what the fuck we wanted to do. And now with a baby growing inside of me, it was going to slow me down. I didn't care though.

Being in the house alone, I needed to talk to someone. I was dying to share the news with Sammy. She had to be the second person I told about my pregnancy. It wouldn't be right to tell anyone else about it before her.

I dialed Sammy's number for the umpteenth time today. I desperately wanted her to pick up and talk to me, not just to tell her about me being pregnant, but to find out what was going on with her among other things. We really needed to talk.

I sat near the window with the phone to my ear and was steady hearing it ring and ring. She didn't pick up. It went straight to her voice mail. Damn, was this bitch avoiding me? I asked myself. What did I do to her? I hung up with frustration. It was a sunny and beautiful day with a breathtaking life growing inside of me and my best friend was nowhere to be found or reached.

Exhaling heavily, I wanted to get high, but I was pregnant now, feeling different, and I didn't want to become that type of mother who was drinking and smoking while carrying her baby. I always found that to be disgusting and selfish. I always wanted to smack a bitch when she risked her baby's health by doing that type of shit. But I couldn't be the one to throw the first stone at someone when my house wasn't even that clean.

My scars from my father, both physically and mentally, were healing. I didn't want to think about my father; that muthafucka could burn in hell for I cared. I was gonna be nineteen soon, and surely fading from being that scared ten-year-old little girl after my mother died. I was a woman, the type of woman my mother intended me to be. And even though she was on drugs and in the streets, my mother always loved and cared for me.

With my father in and out of jail all the time, it was mostly us growing up. She lived a hard life, and I was right behind her living a harder life. But with my moms, I felt protected around her all the time and truly loved. She was a junky, smoking crack and turning tricks in the hood for drugs, but best believe no one ever disrespected her daughter, who was me. She would always fight hard for me, like a lioness protecting her babies.

The thing I respected most about my mother was that she never got high in front of me or Sammy. She didn't want us to see her demons because we were her angels. And she always tried to turn shit into sugar. No matter how bad a situation we were in, from poverty to violence, she would always try to see the bright side of things and wanted to make her baby girl smile.

The one thing my mother used to tell me was, "Mouse, sometimes the bitter truth is better than a sweeter lie."

And we were living in the bitter truth.

I always said that my mother wasn't the average woman, or junkie. She fell in love with the wrong man at a young age, who also mistreated and beat her, and the only good thing that came out of her turbulent relationship was me.

My father was hell on earth. I tried to love him so many times, but I hated him. The best thing for me was to stay away from him. He would never get to see his grandchild, ever. He wasn't going to corrupt such an innocent life that would come from my womb. He would not lay hands on my blessing. My baby was going to be an angel, and the devil couldn't have them.

The next few hours I spent in the house bored. At first I started to write lyrics and rhyming to myself. I had a few new joints that I wanted to write down and spit, especially one for my unborn child. I walked around in my underwear with a pen and pad in my hand and started to recite, "When ya born, the world is yours, but no one ever tells you the world is a fraud, they say we all are born into sin, so how can we ever win, no silver spoon, in this home utensils was a luxury, eatin' wit' my hands was the come up fo' me, poverty takin' shots at me, prosperity was lookin' small to me, cry for the light, willin' to die for the light, but darkness was a right, lights out, bills blowin' up like C4."

This was going to be a hot rhyme. I was always hyped to talk about the way I lived and where I came from. By early evening, I had about three pages of rhymes written. I was ready to get back into the studio and start recording. Just getting out of the hospital after being beaten by my mentally disturbed father and being pregnant had inspired me even more.

When seven p.m. came around, I had nothing else to do but start to worry about Rico. He hadn't called me all day, and I tried to hit up Rico's phone a few times, but he wasn't answering. Becoming a little worried about him, I tried to call a few of his friends, but they hadn't heard or seen Rico all day. Now my worrying was starting to transform into panic. I was ready to get on the bus or catch a cab and take my ass to Edenwald.

I stepped out of the gypsy cab on Laconia Avenue to see blaring police lights in front of me. Something major had happened. There had to be at least a dozen cop cars in the street stopping vehicle traffic and pedestrians from entering what looked like a crime scene. There were so many people outside looking behind the yellow crime scene tape that looped around the block.

I paid the driver, handing him a ten dollar bill, and rushed toward the scene.

"What happened?" I asked someone.

"Somebody just got shot and killed," they said fervently.

Panic started to overcome me. I started to think that something had happened to Rico; maybe it was the reason why he wasn't picking up his phone or calling me back. I hurried to see what went down, praying it wasn't my man dead. It would be so fucked up for Rico to be murdered on the day he found out that I was pregnant. I had this sick feeling in my stomach that I was going to know the person murdered. This hunch was eating me alive. I practically ran toward the crime scene with tears streaming down my face and anguish tearing my heart apart. I pushed my way through the thick crowd surrounding the incident and gazed at the center of attention.

It wasn't Rico dead, thank God. The body hadn't been covered yet; the murder had just happened and the man dead was contorted in death. The crimson blood was pooling underneath his wretched, torn frame and staining the concrete. He had been shot four times, twice in the head and twice in the chest. He was sprawled on his back, clothes looking dingy, and eyes cold and closed to death. I fixated my eyes on his gruesome demise; there was no remorse in my soul for him. No tears falling for him. I would never have to worry about him hurting me again. He was no more. My father was gone. He had found himself on the other side of the barrel, and brutally lost. He was a bad man and his time finally came.

I saw people starting to look at me, making the connection, whispering to each other, probably making assumptions. Police and detectives were walking around, inspecting the body, being nonchalant toward death and investigating a homicide. I didn't want to be a part of it. I already understood what came next, questions and interrogations. I probably was going to be the first person they came to, and I wasn't going to make it easy for them.

Then a sudden thought popped into me: *Rico! Did he kill my father? He did.* If not himself, then he probably hired a shooter to do the deed. It was ironic how my father was brutally shot down days after he put his hands on me. Rico had promised me that he would kill Hector if he ever touched me again. *Oh my God, he actually did this, for me.* Was it the reason he left the house so early, and didn't pick up his phone when I called? My heart started to beat so fast. I quickly walked away from the area, hoping that I didn't create too much attention by being there and leaving. I wasn't going to cry for my father and I didn't want to be bothered with it.

I decided to head back to Sammy's place and see what she was doing; the projects' attention was grasped with the murder of a notorious gangster named Ozone, my father. It was going to be a big thing and I was nervous for Rico. My pops was old school, still dangerous, and he did have people who loved him and would be looking to avenge his death.

Where was Rico?

I called him numerous times as I walked toward Sammy's building, but he still wasn't picking up. I needed someplace to chill for a moment. The daughter of a slain gangster walking around alone wasn't too cool. I didn't want people coming up to me and giving me their condolences and asking what happened. I didn't give a fuck.

When I reached Sammy's building, my clique was chilling outside, smoking a cigarette. I saw Tina, Chyna, and La-La gossiping about something. They stopped when they saw me. Immediately, they came up to me, hollering, "Mouse," and hugged me strongly.

"Oh my God, Mouse. I know you heard already," Chyna said sadly, giving me a hug.

"Yeah, I already know."

"I'm so sorry about ya father," Tina said.

I was nonchalant. I didn't want to hear about him, but they were going to tell me anyway. "It is what it is," I replied coolly, being stoic.

Here it was, the day I had some exciting news to tell everyone, and my father's murder trumped everything. I was so upset. The only thing I could say to them was, "Y'all see Sammy?"

"Nah, she ain't been around all day," said Chyna.

It figured.

I didn't want to be outside, and the girls thought the same thing, because police was everywhere, swarming the projects like bees. They were harassing everyone and we didn't want to be bothered with it. We all decided to go back to Tina's place, since her mother was at work and it was the most comfortable.

An hour later, the girls were passing around a phat joint and talking about my father's homicide, almost forgetting that I was in the same room with them. It didn't bother me though. I was thinking about Rico. I asked if they'd seen him around lately, and they answered no.

I watched them smoke and was tempted to take a few pulls too. When they passed me the joint for my turn, I turned them down.

"Mouse, you ain't smokin'?" Chyna asked.

"Nah, I'm good," I replied.

"Damn, Mouse, why you ain't smoking?"

They thought I was sad about my father's death; it was far from the reason. With it being a gloomy night, hearing police sirens blaring outside, I was itching to tell them about my condition and lighten things in the room. I gazed at my friends and said to myself, *fuck it!* I wanted Sammy to be the second to know, but since she wasn't picking up her fuckin' phone and was nowhere to be found, I decided that Chyna, Tina, and La-La were friends too, and they could be the second to know.

"I'm pregnant, y'all," I blurted out.

"What, bitch!" they all hollered.

"Oh my God, congratulations, Mouse. You about to be a mommy," La-La said excitedly.

"Yup!" I smiled.

"It's Rico's right?" Tina asked.

"Bitch, hells yeah! I ain't been fuckin' anybody else."

They all hugged me dearly, and were genuinely happy for me. But in the pit of my stomach, I felt sick and guilty. Sammy, why couldn't she just have picked up her phone?

Chapter Eleven

Sammy

The show must go on; it was something that I kept telling myself. After Mouse had left, ranting and cursing at me, I went back into my apartment, locked myself in my bedroom and began writing. I pretty much stayed there the next couple days. The words poured on to the paper like rainfall. My mind was going crazy with so many things. I was upset, angry with myself for being so naïve and being so fuckin' weak and got caught slipping. Macky had caught me off-guard. I really thought he was a nice guy, and had my best interest at heart. I was so wrong. I wanted him dead. He had violated me on a level that there was no coming back from. But I was also upset and crying because I came so close, I thought he was for real, but he was an asshole, and it seemed like I had to start all over again.

I was excited about being on Tina Green's track and networking with the music moguls. I wanted to take that step to success. And within the blink of an eye, it was all gone, never mine to have in the first place. But why? That muthafucka had played with my emotions and career, and he tried to rape me in the middle of nowhere. I didn't know what to say or do. Mouse was pressing for me to give her a name, but I refused. She was ready to kill him too. I think I wanted to do it myself. But it was a sticky situation. He was a friend of Search's and well known in the business. And what if word got out? I felt I would have been blacklisted, criticized, laughed at, and my music career would be finished before it even got started, because who was I to accuse this top-notch producer of rape and assault? I had a long criminal record. He probably didn't. I was in a gang, well known in the streets, and probably on the verge of gang warfare with Angie and the YGB Crips. The conflict with Angie was growing. So, I had a lot to think about. Macky wasn't going to get away with what he tried to do to me, but now wasn't the time for more conflict in my life, especially after I went behind Search's back to meet and network with him in the city. And when I also was on the verge of recording something with a known artist without Mouse being involved. I felt guilty about it. Things were already hell enough for me, and I didn't need Mouse mad at me with her feeling betrayed. I was already mad at myself.

And if I told Mouse, and Rico, they would have gone after him without any hesitation. Rico would have killed him. I wanted him dead, but he had to suffer. Fuck that. They say revenge is best when it's served cold.

I sat by my window writing: "So she's forever hoping and lovin, but her future ain't so cunning, holdin' on to you know what's wrong for you, lovin' Mr. Wrong after all the shit he's done to you."

It was late in the evening and Mouse had been calling me all day. I ignored her calls. I wasn't in the mood to talk to anyone. I wanted to be alone. I wanted to write. I wanted to think. I wanted to perform at the Manhattan Center next week. It was a big show for us, and I didn't want anything to interfere with us performing.

As I was writing, feeling the sun setting and the night rising, I heard the far-too-familiar sound of gunshots ringing out, cutting through the air like a cold chill.

Bak! Bak! Bak! Bak!

The shots echoed throughout the projects common like kids playing. I didn't flinch. I didn't care. They were frequent like poverty in this place. Things don't change. I heard someone screaming, another life gone, snatched away, heaven or hell now their permanent home.

I sat by my window and continued to write: "Shit is real, who the fuck cares, death is near, now who's sincere, spread ya last tears, wipe ya fear, 'cause no one really the fuck cares, this asshole of a place home to me for so many years, mind trapped in the dungeon, chained down like a POW, lookin' up hoping for at least one star to fall, shoot up like a rocket."

I wrote and wrote until I couldn't write anymore and my fingers started to cramp up. My room was silent; the shabby display indicated true poverty. I heard police sirens blaring outside; another crime scene was to begin. I needed to get away. Mouse was able to escape, so why couldn't I? I tried to call Search, but his phone was going straight to voice mail. We needed to talk. I started to think that maybe he had heard what happened and was purposely ignoring my calls. Maybe Macky went to him and twisted the truth about everything, badmouthing me and making me out to be the villain.

Suddenly, I found myself crying again, and the more I wiped the tears away, the heavier they became. I removed myself from the window and sat on the floor. I felt alone. I felt like a failure. I had my crew and my clique, but I wanted so much more, from success to wealth, and even love. I knew I was contradicting myself about love. I wanted to run from it, but who could I run to, besides Mouse, for a shoulder to cry onto. For someone to wipe away my tears as they fell and talk comfort and certainty into my ear, and listen to grief with care. Someone to cheer me up when they saw me frown. In a way, I was hoping to find some intimacy with Macky, and the stupid muthafucka would have gotten my goodies if he would have been patient and hadn't turned into a fuckin' monster. He fucked it up. He fucked me up, emotionally. I wanted some dick, because it'd been a minute since I had sex, but you didn't take from me, and didn't extort me.

Subconsciously, I thought, I was jealous of my best friend. Did she find something with Rico that I truly wanted for myself? When she and Rico came to my aid, and seeing the two of them together, it stirred something odd inside of me, and I couldn't pinpoint it. I just escaped a monster and here was Mouse, arriving with her Prince Charming.

I cried some more. I never cried in front of anyone. Outside the apartment, I was that bitch. I never looked weak or scared, never ran from a fight or any conflict. I took beef head-on and always won. But in my bedroom, with these four threadbare walls swallowing me up, I felt so weak and scared. I felt alone. Where was my direction going?

I tried calling Search again. We needed to talk. But his phone went straight to voice mail. I hadn't seen Search in almost two weeks, and it wasn't like him to just disappear on me. He would always let me know what was going on. But after the studio and the talk at the diner, he seemed aloof around me.

I needed to escape. Being cooped up in my room and drowning in my tears wasn't doing me any good. My sorrow was becoming crippling, and it wasn't like me to hide from anything or anyone. I got dressed. I threw on a pair of jeans, a T-shirt, and my sneakers. I put my hair into a long ponytail and left the room. I checked my mother's bedroom, but she was gone. I couldn't be concerned with her; she was sick, but she was still a grown woman who did whatever she wanted to do.

I walked out my building and saw the blaring police lights a few blocks down with a large crowd gathered around the crime scene. I didn't have time to be nosey. It was a shooting, probably a body or two. After years of enduring the violence and bloodshed, you start to become numb to it all.

I headed to Search's apartment. Was he ignoring my phone calls? I wanted to speak to him personally. He lived a few buildings from me, near the school playground of Cardinal Spellman High School on Schieffelin Avenue. Search's building was always quiet, unlike mine. It was a good distance, but a nice walk. During the duration, I ran into a few friends who were rushing to see who got shot on Laconia Avenue.

"Sammy, you ain't comin' to see what happened?" Kenny asked.

"I don't give a fuck about that," I spat.

He shrugged and he and few others kept it moving. I didn't want to see death. I'd been seeing death since I was a kid. I'd been seeing a lot of things since I was a kid. It was time to see other things. It was time to really do me and shine.

When I arrived at Search's apartment, I knocked on his door a few times, but there wasn't anyone answering. He lived alone. I didn't see his green Durango parked on the street either. I was about to leave, but a neighbor of his opened up her door and said, "Hey, Sammy, you lookin' fo' Search, right?"

"Yeah, where is he?" I asked.

"I'm surprised he didn't tell you, he left a few days ago, went down to ATL to do some show with some group of his and see some agent," she told me.

I was dumbfounded and hurt. "What? Are you serious?" I asked, being dubious.

"Yeah, that's what he said to me when he asked me to watch out for his place."

"You know when he'll be back?"

"I think next week," she said.

"Thank you," I said.

I just wanted to disappear. How could Search leave for Atlanta and not take me with him? He always knew that I wanted to travel, especially get out of Edenwald for a few days. I was so crushed that when I took the concrete stairway down to the lobby, I didn't exit the stairway right away, but sat against the concrete and the tears leaked from my eyes again. I was pissed, angry, and bitter, and felt betrayed all in one.

Why would Search do me like this?

The hurt was eating away at me. I wanted to become violent. I wanted to really hurt somebody, because it seemed like someone was always hurting me. I dried my tears; I didn't want anyone to see me crying. I walked out of Search's building with my head up and a hard look.

Fuck Search, I cursed to myself.

I could do this without him. If he was still upset about that incident at the studio and in the South Bronx, then he could kiss my black ass. He always wanted to fuck me, but we were only friends, and if he felt some kind of way about Rico talking to me about business, because I always kept it real with him, then fuck it. I had gone to Search and told him what Rico had said to me that night he gave me a ride home. And I told Search that I wasn't Mouse, I wasn't interested in having any dealings with Rico, but if he took it the wrong way, then Search was an asshole too.

It was dark out. I didn't want to go back to my apartment. I wanted to leave the projects, but once again, with no car and no funds, I was trapped like a stag. I wasn't thinking straight. It felt like I was walking into darkness and couldn't see. I wandered to the playground and sat on the bench alone. I lit a cigarette and tried not to think about Search being in ATL without me. But the harder I tried to forget about him, the more bitter I became. We were supposed to do this together and now I was by myself. And this muthafucka didn't have the audacity to tell me anything.

Hours passed with me sitting in the dark, and on the bench thinking. I rhymed to myself as I sat by myself. The night was my audience, my pain a motivation. I freestyled while puffing on my fourth cigarette and tried to ease this grief. The solitude was somewhat a comfort, but not much comfort. I could still hear the drama going on in the projects, another wild spring where police were everywhere and I just wanted to be somewhere else for a long moment.

After four hours, smoking five cigarettes, spitting about fifteen rhymes to entertain myself and trying to clear my head, the drama in the projects seemed to be settling down. The sun was long gone, but the spring heat at the end of May remained. I felt like a statue sitting on that park bench. The streets seemed to be quiet and my tears were drying. I took a deep breath, flicked away the final cigarette in my hand and reluctantly started my walk back to my building. I crossed the street, gazing at Edenwald, the dungeon I felt trapped in, like a prisoner of war.

The moment I crossed the street, I heard rap music blaring from an oncoming car and noticed the 650i coupe drive by me. It made a sudden U-turn in the middle of the street, coming back my way. It was no mistake that it was Rico. He was the last person I wanted to see.

The car pulled to the curb and Rico hopped out with his wild smile. "Sammy," he called out.

"What, Rico?" I shouted. "Now is not the time to fuck wit' me."

I wasn't in the mood to deal with his silly antics tonight. But Rico still came my way, not caring what I just said to him.

"I just wanna holla at you about somethin'," he said.

"About what?" I said with attitude.

He had one of his goons seated in the passenger seat toking on a blunt and looking at me like I was a sandwich to him. I screwed up my face and sucked my teeth at Rico's clown-ass nigga.

"What's up wit' you? Why you out here in the dark, alone? You know somebody just got bodied on the other side, cops are everywhere in this bitch," he said to me.

"I'm a big girl, Rico. You ain't gotta worry about me."

"Somebody gotta worry about you, Sammy," he returned. "You holdin' out okay from that incident the other day?" he asked with concern.

"I'm good. I don't need you or Mouse holding my hand."

"Sammy, I ain't tryin' to hold ya hand. I'm not in that kind of business. I know you that woman to hold ya own and handle yours. I always respected you fo' that. You is one down-ass chica. And if you ain't tryin' to talk about it, then I understand. I'm not gonna press you about it like Mouse did. But let know, if you need a nigga, I got ya fuckin' back, real talk. It can be about anything. And whoever was the *puta* that put hands on you, when the time comes, you just point and I'll do the rest," he proclaimed genuinely.

Rico's eyes were fixated on me with this thoughtful passion. For once, he wasn't saying any bullshit from his mouth. He was being a friend who was truly concerned about me. I came back with a simple, "Thank you, Rico."

"I'll do anything for you, Sammy. You and Mouse, I love y'all. And despite what happened between us back in the days, I'm not that man you think I am. I wanna see you and her get on top. You are so fuckin' talented, Sammy. Don't ever let this place bring you down. You hear me?" He sounded like the father I rarely knew.

"I hear you," I replied.

"I shoulda seen the type of woman you was back in the days, but you know we both were so young and naïve," he said.

"Yeah, we were and you shoulda."

There was this nostalgic moment between us. We locked eyes. Our history started when I was thirteen and he was seventeen. Rico had me selling drugs for him. For months, maybe a year, I hustled crack, weed, and pills for him in the building stairway twenty-four-seven. I pushed pills and crack like I was the neighborhood ice cream man. I was on the verge of becoming a school dropout anyway. I rarely went to school, had thirteen absences in one month. I was too busy getting money and didn't have any parents to punish me. My father was locked up and my mother was a drug addict. I was left on my own so many times and knew how to survive.

I had a crush on Rico when I was younger, I admit, but he always said I was too young and I was just business to him, meaning I was only good to him if I was making him some money. He was always fine, but he always ignored me when it came to anything sexual. But working for Rico always came with risks. I had gotten beaten up and robbed for $500 one day, and it was a loss I had to pay back on my own.

Rico, however, found out who had robbed me. Two towering thugs from a different project took it upon themselves to violently rob a fourteen-year-old girl. When Rico was done with them, one was almost brain dead and the other was blinded in one eye with two broken legs. I was shocked that he didn't kill them, but he'd sent out a vicious message to his rivals.

The second incident happened when I was fifteen. I was shot at by a rival crew that was trying to muscle in on Rico's territory. A drug war had ensued and that was one of the most violent and bloodiest summers Edenwald endured. Nine people were killed in a span of two months, from June to August. Rico came out to be the victor, holding down the fort, but it came with a heavy cost. He had lost two first cousins that summer. He was close to both of them.

The third incident with Rico was when I had gotten arrested. I had sold drugs to an undercover cop and the jump out boys swarmed in on me like I was a terrorist. I was caught holding some serious weight, ten vials of crack, and some pills, along with a .380. I was taken into holding at the forty-seventh precinct and then down to central booking. But because I was a minor at the time, my bail was low and the judge hit me with two years' probation, a hundred hours of community service, and youth counseling when I was going back and forth to court. Rico didn't even pay my bail to get me out at the time, which was only $2,500. Mouse and my crew had helped me get out of jail. And I still held my own, didn't snitch or cry.

Six months after my arrest, Rico caught an assault and attempted murder charge. He had shot this kid five times and pistol whipped the nigga's bitch right after that. And this all happened because the nigga had the audacity to call Rico a bitch-ass nigga. Rico was fortunate to beat the serious charges against him, because the man and his bitch refused to press charges and cooperate with the police investigation, and didn't want to testify in court. However, Rico still had to do some time for the gun possession. He wasn't gone from the streets for too long, though.

He was back home a year and a half later, and got right back into hustling and controlling his block like he never had left. But by then, my feelings for him had changed. I was older, more mature, and he wasn't interested in me like that, so why continue to bother?

But yes, Rico was a very serious, coldhearted, and violent dude. He wasn't to be fucked with, especially when it came to his money. He and his crew were notorious in the Bronx: crack dealers and killers. Edenwald was his to run and control. He also was a mini celebrity in my hood. From the time he was twelve years old, his name had been in the papers.

Before he got into the street life, Rico used to play basketball. He was a point guard for many teams, including his junior high and high school team. He was nice on the court, skilled with a basketball like I never seen. At thirteen, he was playing better basketball than most men twice his age and dunking on rivals like he was Michael Jordan. They nicknamed him "The Puerto Rican Dream," because he was the only Puerto Rican on the courts doing his thing.

He had his picture in the news papers several times, been on TV, and in high school he was one of the most prominent players who had the chance to attain a full athletic scholarship and leave the hood to play Division I basketball at any college. Two things fucked him up: he always carried that stigma of his father being the ruthless drug dealer who shot two cops back in the days, and his lure for the street life.

It didn't take long for Rico to get into the drug game and make a hardcore name for himself in the streets like he had done on the basketball courts. This time, there weren't any referees to blow whistles at his fouls.

Deep inside, I always liked Rico. I had a crush on him from the time I was thirteen. And the only reason

I started selling drugs for him was to get close to him and have him notice me more. And then when he finally noticed me, I had a whole different attitude and I didn't want anything to do with him anymore. He could have had this pussy back then, when I was really young and falling in love with him, but things done changed. He had put me through a lot, and we weren't even dating each other.

I never told Mouse about my crush on Rico. We talked about everything and we never kept any secrets from each other, but for some reason, this was the only thing I kept from her, and I never knew why.

Rico looked at me like he didn't want to leave me alone in the streets. He acted like I was brand new in these projects. His goon was waiting quietly in the car, still puffing on his blunt and nodding to the rap music playing.

"Just be careful out here, Sammy," he said. "I know you a tough girl, but if somethin' was to happen to you, I wouldn't be able to live wit' myself."

I didn't respond to his statement.

"But you look really good tonight," he added. "You were always able to take a nigga's breath away."

"Seriously?" I replied dryly. But truthfully, I wanted to smile after hearing his comment. But I remained deadpan. "Thanks, Rico."

I was playing hardcore with Rico, but honestly I needed a friend right now, someone to talk to and help me out with my situation. I didn't want Rico to walk away from me. It seemed like I yearned for his company, somewhat.

"I heard Search is in ATL. Why didn't he take you wit' him?" Rico asked.

"He had his reasons. Why do you care for?" I replied matter-of-factly.

"His reasons. Yeah, okay."

"You tryin' to tell me somethin', Rico?"

"I ain't tryin' to start anything wit' you, Sammy. It's always love wit' me. But I've been wanting to pull ya coat to sometin' in a minute, but here's not the time."

"Then when?"

"Yo, I'm having somethin' next weekend at Cream. Come through, chill and have a drink wit' a nigga. We really need to talk about a few things, Sammy," he said.

I looked reluctant.

"I'm serious. Just come through as a friend, a'ight?" Rico pushed.

I thought about it. I thought about what he was saying to me. Did Rico know something about Search that I didn't know? I respected him for not telling any of my business in front of his friend. Rico was many things, and not always nice things, but the one thing about Rico, he was always real and was smart. He was the devil I did know.

"I'll think about it," I said.

"Just come through, Sammy. I don't want to have to drag you by the hand to have a good time," he joked slightly.

"You won't."

He started to walk back to his car. He stared at me before he climbed inside.

"Definitely holla at me, Sammy. I know we got a lot of things to talk about," he said lively. "And holla at Mouse. I think she has some important news to tell you."

He winked at me and got inside his car. I gazed at him for a moment, and for once in a long time, I didn't feel so hostile toward him. We actually had a decent talk. He drove away, leaving me with something to think about. I hurriedly walked back to my building, cutting through the projects quickly because I didn't want to get swept up in the shit storm after a homicide. I also had enemies of my own lurking about, and I wasn't going to get caught slipping again.

I was still unaware of the person murdered. I really didn't care. I just wanted to go back home and write some more. I wanted to release this raw storm onto the world, and show off my talents, because my fans were going to relate to me and understand my music. I couldn't be anything but real and raw on my tracks. I wanted to be heard with a craze. I was always working hard and so motivated. Living in squabbles, poverty, and horror for so long, I felt I had nothing left but to be completely motivated and make it happen.

The apartment was quiet; my moms was probably in the streets somewhere getting high again. Her past and her pain was another focal point when it came to my music. If she couldn't tell her story, then I would, along with mine. I knew I was a multiplatinum-selling artist ready to shock the world.

With it about to be dawn soon, I wanted to see the sun rise this morning. It was one of the few good things to look for in the projects. The sun rising was something that always came, even with rainy and cloudy days. The sun never disappointed, unlike so many things in life. I enjoyed the sun. The sun was a beautiful thing. It showed its presence everywhere, it didn't discriminate. Whether you were rich or poor, bad or good, black or white, you always got the joy and benefit of seeing the sun and experiencing its radiant warmth. Too bad success and prosperity wasn't the same way.

I sat by the window and continued to write again. As I wrote, for some strange reason, Rico came to my mind. I remembered him saying that Mouse had something important to tell me. I wondered what it was. Was is good or bad news? I had dissed her the other day, but I knew with Mouse all was forgiven. I also felt this slight shift involving us. A transition was happening between us that was making me feel uncomfortable. Something was changing, and I couldn't pinpoint what.

Several days had passed since I spoken to Mouse and Rico had invited me to his party. I became reclusive, staying in my apartment for hours writing and gazing out the window. I shut everyone out for a moment, even my best friend. Phone calls went to voice mail, and when people came knocking at my door I didn't answer it. Like Search did me, I disappeared for a moment, only walking to the store late at nights for food and snacks.

It was the weekend and a beautiful evening outside. But everything felt like hell to me. I was in a very foul mood. I had enemies everywhere, Vixen Chaos was in limbo, our music wasn't taking off like I hoped, and I felt abandoned by everyone. And when I heard about Mouse's father being killed, I should have called, said something to her, maybe gone to check on her, but I didn't. She never cared about her father anyway, so I knew she didn't need any condolences. She had Rico. I had nobody.

I continued to gaze out my window and noticed Rico pulling up on the block in his BMW. He looked handsome in a wife beater showing off his physique and jeans and Timberlands. He was alone, and perched from my window I watched Rico socialize with his cronies on the block. He was all smiles and Mouse wasn't anywhere around. I missed my friend, but I was going through a moment when I needed to be alone.

I thought about Rico's party tonight. I wasn't going to go at first, but watching Rico on the block, taking care of his business and looking happy, I changed my mind suddenly. I hadn't been anywhere in almost two weeks. I was becoming a hermit and it wasn't a cool thing to become. I was always the live one, being out in the streets and in the clubs, making a name for myself. I wasn't hiding from my troubles or anyone, but I just felt so overwhelmed by everything that I kind of shut down.

Fuck it; I was definitely going out tonight. I needed something to do, and I figured at Rico's party I could have a heart-to-heart talk with Mouse and also hear what important news Rico had to share with me. I was ready to listen. I was ready to advance, somehow and someway.

I walked into club Cream alone. I was dressed to impress in a pair of tight denim jeans that highlighted my thick curves, and long legs, and a tight stylish shirt that showed off my breasts. The heels I wore were sexy and cheap. I also sported cubic zirconia jewelry to look a little extra. I was dressed like a diva on a shoestring budget. I looked the part, but in truth, when it came to my wardrobe, I was faking it until I made it. Mouse was wearing the real stuff though: red bottoms, Chanel, Fendi. Rico had her looking phenomenal and I was wearing knockoffs and clearance stuff.

We hadn't signed a record contract yet, or had a hit song out, and she was already wearing designer clothing and living a somewhat rock-star lifestyle, thanks to Rico. I wasn't jealous of my friend; I was always happy for her. But I was just tired of being poor, and struggling to become successful, and trying to make it in America. Sometimes it seemed like it wasn't going to ever happen.

The DJ had Rick Ross's "Maybach Music" blaring and the place was live like a wire, and swelling with a crowd of about a hundred revelers or more. Instantly I caught attention from the men when I came alone. Their eyes shifted my way with transfixed stares from my top to bottom. I was always eye candy for so many people even with my fake and knockoff clothing.

I didn't come here to socialize with anyone. I only came to talk to Rico. I was ready to hear what he had to say, especially after Search left without me. I wanted to get out, chill for a minute, and have a few drinks.

Cream was a twenty-one-and-older club near the Major Deegan Expressway. My fake ID looked authentic and I knew the bouncer at the door. I told him that I was there for Rico's party and he let me slide through easily like ice going down a slippery slope.

The dance floor was packed, people grinding, sweating, and partying hard to the DJ's lively tunes like there wasn't going to be any tomorrow. I looked around for Rico and figured he could only be in one place, and that was the VIP section up top, overlooking the congestion of people below. I looked up and saw Rico's crew above. Everyone was partying hard, popping bottles, and wilding out. I headed their way, with niggas on me like white on rice as I moved through the crowd. They were pulling and grabbing at me, either wanting a dance or a minute of my time.

Muthafuckas were thirsty for a piece of me. I had to be harsh to some of these muthafuckas. Some assholes just couldn't accept an easy no or a polite, "I'm good," when I turned them down. But a harsh, "Fuck you!" or a nasty, "Get the fuck out my face!" was the language they understood quite clearly.

I pushed my way through the tight crowd and made it to the foot of the stairs that led up to the VIP area. One husky security guard was watching vigilantly for any unwanted company or trouble. Rico had enemies too, quite more than me on the streets. When the man saw me approaching, his look remained expressionless with his huge arms folded across his chest.

"I'm here for Rico's party," I told him.

His hard scowl didn't intimidate me. He didn't know who the fuck I was, and he looked like he was about to be trouble. But before he came with any callous refusal my way, I heard someone say, "Yo, she's wit' us, let her up."

The man nodded, moved to the side, and let me go up. Rico made sure to have security tight, sparing no expense with bouncers strategically placed around the club and having VIP locked down like it was Fort Knox. He was surrounded by his thugs and having the time of his life, but that didn't stop him from being on point. I saw him seated on the red velvet lounge chair with a bottle of Cîroc in his hand and some dumb-looking bird bitch sitting on his lap. I admit, he was looking good with his strapping physique in a black V-neck and his cornrows freshly done. He sported a Cuban-link fourteen-karat white gold chain around his neck and a Rolex around his wrist.

I looked around for Mouse, expecting that she would be in attendance too, but there wasn't any sign of her. I did want to talk to her.

Rico smiled heavily when he saw me approaching him. Out of respect for me, he quickly pushed the dumb bitch he had on his lap off of him and stood up. It looked like she was ready to curse him out and make a scene, but she was no fool. The bitch knew her position. She didn't want to fuck with me or Rico.

"Sammy, what's good. I see you made it to my party." Rico greeted me with a huge smile and hug.

I had everyone's attention in his circle. I was the best looking bitch in the room. And I was the only bitch in the room who had Rico's undivided attention like that. I always held his attention, whether I wanted to or not.

"Where's Mouse?" I asked him.

"She's home," he responded nonchalantly.

"So why isn't she out partying wit' you?" I asked with a raised brow.

He chuckled like a young boy. "She wasn't feeling too well, so she decided to stay home."

I didn't believe him.

"And you out here partying wit' the next bitch on ya lap. You better not hurt my girl, Rico," I warned him.

"Relax, Sammy, Mouse is in good hands. I take care of her," he replied coolly.

I looked at him like whatever. He offered me a drink and I accepted. Taking a seat next to Rico with the music blaring, he was already in my ear talking, trying to discuss business. The crowd around him cleared out, giving us some privacy, with it looking like Rico and I was a couple in the club. It wasn't a good look, and to be honest, I felt guilty sitting next to Rico in VIP with Mouse not around. We'd known each other for years, but it just didn't feel right. But Rico didn't seem to have a problem with it. He continued to drink and talk to me.

"You know ya too good to be fuckin' around wit' Search," he said in my ear.

"You tryin' to talk about a man who's not here to defend himself," I said in Search's defense.

"Is he tryin' to defend you? Do that *puta* got ya best interest at heart?" he replied gruffly.

"What you mean by that, Rico?" I asked.

"We gotta talk later, when there are less people around and it's quieter," he said, then took a sip of Patrón. He then continued with, "But for now, ya out the house, so have a good time, don't think about the hard ones, and let's have some fun . . . like we used to do back in the days."

I didn't want to be reminded of the old days with him. I was thirteen years old when we first met, and was so much a naïve little bitch back then. Sometimes history or the past should be left alone.

Rico poured me a drink, and then raised his cup filled with liquor and I lifted mines in the air. We toasted— about what, I had no idea. But the vibes were cheerful and relaxed; even some of Rico's hardest thugs and contract killers had smiles on their faces.

The night went on with me actually having a good time with Rico and his peoples. I danced and I laughed. For a moment, I felt like a completely different person: no beef, no drama, and I forgot about my nightmare with Macky. I was a strong woman and wasn't going to break so easily, but I wasn't going to forget about it. The club music was good and, in spite of being in a room with thugs and killers, there wasn't any drama or tension.

Rico and I started to dance. We moved in union with him grinding behind me in a slow wind, our hips gyrating to Ciara's "Promise":

> *And I've been kind of lonely*
> *But I'm looking for somebody to talk to*

It felt like those words were talking directly about me. And with Rico pressed tightly behind me, I quickly came to my senses and pulled away from him. It wasn't happening, and what the fuck was I thinking when I allowed him to grind behind me like that? It had to be the alcohol talking.

With the party winding down and the crowd thinning out, I was a little tipsy, and hated that I had to travel back home alone. It was quite a distance either by cab or public transportation. I made my way toward the exit. The Cîroc Peach and Grey Goose had me feeling nice. It was almost four in the morning and I didn't want to go straight home, but there was nothing else to do. I only had enough cash for the twenty dollar cab ride to my hood.

"You don't even have to worry about catching a cab, Sammy. I got you. I'll take you home," Rico offered. "We need to continue to chat it up anyway."

I looked at him, feeling this could turn into a huge mistake. I already felt some type of way that Mouse wasn't at his party, and I was. And then with us having a moment on the dance floor, it wasn't right. However, it was really late, I was tired and somewhat tipsy, and a ride home would save me twenty dollars and some time.

"Just take me straight home, Rico," I said.

"I got you, Sammy. Ya my homegirl, and I'm gonna always make sure you end up okay," he said.

I walked with him to his car with the spring night becoming a little brisk. We were alone approaching his parked 650i that seemed to glisten on the corner of the block. He opened the door for me and I slid inside like I was his girl. He was being a gentleman. I tried to be aloof. I just wanted to go home. He got behind the wheel and started the ignition. He lit a cigarette, took a few pulls, and then shared it with me. I needed a smoke.

Rico exhaled and looked at me. He then asked, "What you gonna do wit' yourself, Sammy?"

Why did he ask me that? I was ready to bark on him and hop out his car, but he continued with, "I know ya better than this. You ain't like these other bitches scavenging around, ain't got shit goin' fo' themselves, wit' four kids and countless baby daddies and whatnot. You sassy wit' it and you don't whore yourself out. You probably can count on one hand the niggas you been wit'. I always had respect fo' you. And you got talent, Sammy, real fuckin' talent, and ya fuckin' smart."

It was a raw compliment. I was listening. He got onto the Cross Bronx Expressway.

"Where you goin' wit' this?" I asked bluntly.

"How long you gonna let Search run you into the ground?" he asked me.

"What?" I asked with bewilderment.

"Sammy, there's more to that dude than you think. He ain't the man you think he is."

"And you are, Rico?" I replied sharply.

"Hey, my true colors show early. I'm still that nigga you know from back then. But Search, he can be a grimy nigga, and you shouldn't trust him."

"But I should trust you, Rico? You were the same man who couldn't pay my $2,500 bail when I was fifteen. That same nigga who involved me in drug dealing and a drug war. The same man who I was only business to, and sometimes treated me like shit when I had a deep crush on him."

"That was awhile ago, Sammy, and I truly apologize for the past and my actions. You are a good woman, real talk, and I love you. But Search, that chubby bastard, is only out for himself. Man, check out some of the company he keeps around him. I'm in the business of knowing things and finding out about people. And he went to ATL without taking you, or even having the respect to tell you that he was leaving. You think that was right?" he strongly proclaimed.

Rico had me thinking, and he was right about a few things. I hadn't spoken to Search in weeks. We were supposed to do that show at the Manhattan Center, but we never got the phone call confirming it. I didn't know what the fuck was going on. Also, the confrontation with Macky had me thinking extra hard. Macky was a good friend of Search and the nigga had me fooled. Macky was a monster, but Search had vouched for him, and if Search could be friends with a man like that, then there was no telling what other monsters Search associated himself with.

Rico continued with, "You and Mouse been fuckin' wit' the nigga for over a year, and what you got to show for it? No disrespect to you, Sammy, you still a broke bitch out here. And you can have all the talent in the world, but if you ain't benefiting from it and gettin' paid, what good is having it? At least when you were fuckin with me, I had you paid. You was making money. You was able to take better care of ya mother. You was able to live. Yeah, doing shows in the city is cool, but y'all gettin' paid for them shows?"

Rico looked at me and, for once, I kept quiet. The cat had my tongue. I could only shake my head no.

"So let me guess, Search is sayin' it's all about promotion right?"

"Yeah, he did."

Rico chuckled. "You see how Search is living. Nice green Durango he's pushing, the way his crib is laced out, the nigga can travel when he wants, and the connects he got in the business, and you mean to tell me you still out here trying to get a record deal, just now getting into the studio and fighting for scraps? What kind of manager is that?"

I didn't know if he was trying to brainwash me. What was Rico's motive? But I was becoming more aware about a few things.

"It takes money to make money out here. C'mon, Sammy, you know the game. You a hustler," he added. "You can get out here, grind, make ya own ends, and invest into ya own damn self."

I was. I traded in the crack vials for a pen and a pad, along with a hope and a dream. I didn't want to give up and wasn't going to give up. But I needed to make that paper again. I needed to breathe and exhale like Whitney Houston. I wanted to be different. I wanted to be brand new somewhere else.

Rico exited off the expressway. We were coming closer to home. Home was becoming a disaster to me. Rico was talking and I was listening. When we finally made to Edenwald, I had the urge to slap the shit out of Search. But there were always two sides to a story, and I wasn't just going to listen to Rico. He was a snake too.

Rico sat idling in front of my building and placed another cigarette into his mouth. I stared at my building. I hesitated getting out his car. I didn't want to go inside yet. I wanted to escape, even if it was for the night. I wanted to go somewhere far and chill.

Rico puffed and exhaled. He leaned back in his seat and said with a rakish smile, "You gettin' out, Sammy, or you gonna spend the night in the front seat?"

I didn't know what I wanted to do.

"A lot to think about, huh?" he added.

I turned to look at Rico, and I felt I was going to regret saying it, but I blurted, "Take me away from here, Rico."

He looked confused.

"I just wanna go somewhere for the night. I need to get away, Rico. I'm tired."

"Where you wanna go?"

"Anywhere but here," I told him.

"You sure?"

I nodded.

He put the car back in drive and spun it into a U-turn and we drove away. I closed my eyes, sat back in the seat, and imagined I was on an airplane somewhere leaving Edenwald behind me in the distance.

"You gonna be okay, Sammy, I got you," said Rico.

I was committing the ultimate sin in paradise. And this was a moment I wanted to take back, but I couldn't. I closed my eyes and gasped, having beads of perspiration formed on my forehead. The feeling between my thighs felt so good and intense with his body pressed into mines, my nipples crushed against his naked chest, my legs wrapped around him, and we moved together in unity, our two bodies becoming one.

I moaned as I grabbed Rico tightly, my nails scrapping down his back. He had taken his dick and slammed it into me in one thrust, breaking my months-long drought of not having any dick inside of me. His dick felt delicious, sliding in and out of me, hitting my spot like crazy, twisting inside of me, pounding me and stroking me.

I looked deeply into his eyes and it let me know that everything was going to be fine, saying he was going to take care of me. I didn't need to be afraid. And Rico, with the hunger of a starving man and the thrill of the first time, had penetrated me heatedly. I didn't plan this. The sex was spontaneous.

The hotel suite we were in for the night was a palace in my eyes. It was a place of grand luxury. It had all the amenities for a good time. The rooms were exquisitely designed to present a classic regal feel and you could live it up with the wet bar and plasma TV. The bedroom boasted a king-sized bed, and the granite bathroom displayed a deep, sunken oval tub and custom shower. The atrium-view rooms at the Marriot in the city offered a full-sized balcony or bay windows overlooking the impressive eighteen-story glass atrium. The Marriot was my temporary escape from the dungeon and fucking Rico was my eternal sin.

My mind wanted Rico to stop thrusting between my thighs, but my body ached for him to continue. I couldn't even think straight. I was so close to cumming and I just wanted to feel that explosion. His rhythm between my legs went from slow, to steady, and to hard and deep. He drove his dick up inside me over and over again. My breath panted against his ear. He was making me moan and almost scream with pleasure and ecstasy divine. I could feel my pussy grabbing his so hard manhood and pulling him deeper inside me.

It almost felt like I was a virgin all over again. My pussy was so wet and tight for him. When he pushed the mushroom tip through my tingling and pulsating pussy lips, I cringed underneath him, my face twisted in heated passion. I kept my eyes closed when he fucked me and passionately kissed me because I didn't want to see him. I only wanted to feel him. I closed my eyes and tried to shut out my wrong against my best friend.

"Damn, you feel so good. Ooooh, work that pussy, Sammy. Ooooh, fuck me," he cooed in my ear.

My hips gyrated against him. My moans seemed endless. His tongue explored the inside of my mouth as we started kissing excitedly. Our touch against each other felt so radiant. With him inside of me, I completely blocked the guilt I was committing from my mind, faded Mouse from my thoughts, and enjoyed the night with Rico. He was pulling my nipples, twisting them, and humping inside of me.

I felt the sensation. I felt the heat and the tingling between my legs at the same time. My breathing started getting more labored. I shut my eyes strongly, felt my body releasing and I was lost to the pleasure of the dick thrusting inside me.

"I'm gonna cum," I cried out.

"Cum on this dick, do that shit," Rico responded in a lustful craze.

I was bucking my hips in the air with Rico's arms around me, holding me closely, our bodily fluids were about to be entwined. My pussy was still grabbing his dick as he pounded into me relentlessly, grabbing my ass, and it was so good to him that his eyes started to roll to the back of his head with my slippery sensation pleasing him nonstop.

He kept chanting to me how tight and wet my pussy was. Faster. Deeper. He grunted louder and I moaned wildly. I could feel his dick swelling more inside of me, it was about to fill me with his seed. I didn't want to move. He uttered repeatedly, "I'm gonna cum. I'm gonna cum. Oh shit, I'm gonna cum."

It became a tune in my ear.

"I always wanted you, Sammy. Oh, god, I always wanted you. Oh, shit. *Tan bueno. Que cono es tan bueno*," his Spanish rolled off his tongue.

A few more hard thrust in me and I felt his hot cum splash inside of me. Rico shivered from the sensation. He pulled out and fell against me, exhausted and drained. I came too. My knees were shaking and all I could feel was pleasure. I drifted in and out of consciousness. Rico gazed at me. My heart started to beat rapidly. We couldn't turn back the hands of time. The dirty deed had already been done and the only thing on my mind was betraying Mouse.

What the fuck did I just do?

Chapter Twelve

Mouse

Rico not coming home was becoming a common thing, and I didn't like it at all. He didn't come home last night again for the umpteenth time and I was becoming worried about him. And I hadn't spoken to or seen Sammy in almost two weeks, still not telling her that I was pregnant and wanted her to be my baby's godmother. I didn't know if Sammy knew about my pregnancy. If so, why wasn't she calling me? What was going on? The night I was hanging out with our old crew, with us reminiscing about good and old times, I kept thinking Sammy was going to show up, but she never did. I was somewhat disappointed that she didn't. We hadn't hung out together and smoked blunts with our clique in a while. But without her, I still had a good time with Tina, Chyna, and La-La. Hanging out with them took my mind away from my worries. We had celebrated that I was pregnant. I wanted a night like that again, this time with Sammy there. But things were becoming different. I was spending too many days alone in this house and it was driving me crazy.

Also, the death of my father didn't have me tripping. I knew it was inevitable. He was a bad man trying to change, but change wasn't happening fast enough for him or me. I was so tired of the abuse, and then he being a fuckin' faggot was a shock to me. Death was more of an honor than disgrace. And even though I hated my father

I wasn't going to shame his name. And he wasn't going to be missed. But let him burn slowly in hell. Fuck him!

I looked at the time and it was almost noon. Rico didn't call and when I called him, he wasn't answering. This thing with him coming and going constantly, not answering my calls, being out in the streets doing God knows what, was becoming too frequent for my taste. I didn't want to accept it, but he was changing on me.

I sat in the lap of luxury, with all the amenities I needed for my comfort, but without my man around to enjoy it with I was becoming bored. I imagined myself a few months from now, with my belly protruding and the baby nearing, how life was going to be for me, especially after my baby was born. I thought about Rico killing my father. I didn't have any proof that he did it, but deep down inside, I knew he was responsible. What if they locked him up, gave my man a life sentence for murder? Would I be able to cope with it? It was a heavy and frightening thought.

I sat on the steps in the backyard listening to Keysha Cole's *Woman to Woman* album and nodding to the track, "Enough Of No Love."

> *What we had is now hers*
> *Let her know she can have it*

I thought about it and I would be damned if I let any woman have my man. I loved Rico dearly, and would fight for him. Was he perfect? He wasn't, but he was mine. He took me from poverty and placed me in luxury. I was having his baby. His seed was inside of me and I felt proud, because I was the first and wanted to be his only child's mother. And I wasn't going to become second to no bitch.

I sat under the hot spring sun writing my next rhyme and rubbing my belly. I guess I was getting practice in. Thinking about this baby growing inside of me made me think about Sammy and call her. It'd been too long since we'd spoken. I pulled out my cell phone and dialed her number. Her phone rang a few times and she finally picked up.

"Damn, bitch, it's about time you picked up. You tryin' to avoid me?" I said with some attitude. I was trying not to be mad at her, but I truly felt something was wrong with her, or between us.

"Hey, Mouse," she replied dryly.

"Damn, you act like you ain't happy to hear from me. What's up wit' you?"

"Nothin'. Another day, another hustle. What's up wit' you?"

"Sittin' around here waiting for Rico to bring his ass home. Have you seen him around the way?" I asked.

"Nah, I ain't seen Rico in a minute."

"If you do, tell him to call me. I know you don't fuck wit' him like that, but he startin' to get on my nerves," I said.

"Rico gonna be Rico, Mouse. You already know that."

"Yeah, yeah. Don't be trying to lecture me, Sammy."

"I got too much shit going on of my own to lecture anyone," she replied.

"I see. 'Cause you've been out of the loop for some time now. What, you was livin' on the moon or somethin'? I got shit to tell you, and I wanted you to be the second to know."

"Know what?"

"I'm pregnant!" I said excitedly.

"Pregnant?"

"Yup, doctors say I'm almost two months now. Shit, that means Rico knocked me up the minute he got wit' me in April. That nigga got some potent sperm." I laughed.

She didn't find it so funny.

I continued with, "And you know I want you to be my baby's godmother. There's no one else but you I want in my baby's life."

"Damn, Mouse, you really fuckin' pregnant by this nigga?" she replied gruffly.

"Yes, and it sounds like you ain't tryin' to be happy fo' me, Sammy."

"I am, but our music . . . us doing shows . . ."

"It ain't gotta stop. Shit, it ain't like I'm handicap, Sammy. I've been writing every day, comin' up wit' some new hot rhymes to spit. I'm just as motivated like you."

"This changes everything, Mouse."

"How it changes everything?"

"It does, Mouse. You gonna be a mother," she exclaimed.

"I know, right."

"How you gonna do this to me, to us?"

"What? *¿Perra eres celosa?*" I said, meaning, "Bitch, you jealous or somethin'?"

"I just care for you, Mouse, and I don't want to see you get hurt."

"I'm not hurt, Sammy, I'm happy. So be happy for me," I said.

I heard her snicker through the phone, like my happiness to her was a joke or something. I couldn't believe this was coming from Sammy.

"I'm sayin', Mouse, you ain't been wit' Rico no less than two months and you already pregnant by this nigga," she exclaimed.

"'Cause I'm in love, Sammy. That's what people in love do, they fuck and make babies, start a damn family, like I'm tryin' to do wit' Rico," I hollered back.

"And you really think Rico is a damn family man, Mouse. Like he gonna settle down wit' you and live happily ever after," she spat mockingly. "You is stupid if you truly believe that."

I scowled at her comment. It was very hurtful. I was ready to go off on my best friend. Words could hurt so much. I went from a smile to a frown the minute Sammy started coming out of her damn mouth about my business with Rico.

"It sounds like you really fuckin' hatin' on a bitch, Sammy. Why's that, huh?"

"I'm not hating, Mouse, I'm just tryin' to keep it real wit' ya ass. You ready to play Susie homemaker to a womanizing drug dealer. It's like if you was a nigga, I would be sayin' to you that you tryin' to turn a whore into a housewife. It just ain't gonna work," she said.

"You know what, Sammy, fuck you! Why you so fuckin' negative? I thought you would have been the first person to be happy for me, but it's clearly showin' that you ain't," I refuted.

"Mouse, all I'm saying to you is, open ya damn eyes and see for once. You always get blind by this nigga or the next."

"I am seeing, Sammy, and what the fuck you know about love? When was the last time you was in love and had a man in ya life? Maybe if you stopped being so fuckin' picky and get some dick in ya life, then you wouldn't be all up in my fuckin' business. *Pinche puta*," I shouted heatedly. "You a lonely-ass bitch, Sammy. *Puta, perra tonta.*"

It was a shot below the belt, but she came at me harsh, fuck it, I came at her even harsher. I didn't give a fuck anymore. It seemed our friendship was being tested, but it was on the verge of collapsing over some bullshit.

Sammy sucked her teeth and came back at me with, "You know what, Mouse? I'm tired of always carrying ya ass."

"You carrying me," I rebuked.

"*Sí*," she spat. "I'm the one always networking and pulling you in. I had so many chances to go solo, but I would turn it down because we a team. And now you get pregnant and fuck everything up. I was workin' hard for us."

"Bitch, go solo then. You think I give a fuck? I always been better than you anyway," I shouted. "*Besa mi culo, puto.*"

"*Pudrete en el infierno.*"

"*Pudrete, pinche cerda asquerosa,*" I shouted.

Our argument was getting heated. I wanted to reach through the phone and slap the shit out of her. Sammy kept on cursing and shouting at me. It was getting to the point where our words were stinging harshly and we might end up saying something that we might regret.

"Bitch, you ain't shit without me!" she blasted.

"Fuck you, Sammy. You ain't gotta worry about being my baby's godmother. They don't need a bitch like you in their life anyway. Do me a fuckin' favor, lose my fuckin' number! *Pinche puta,*" I screamed madly. "*Que te den por el culo.*"

She replied with a few vulgar curse words before I hung up on her. Suddenly I became emotional. My eyes were in full-blown tears and I burst out crying like a baby. How did it get to this point with her? What the fuck happened? It felt like I couldn't breathe at all. Everything was feeling restricted around me.

I thought I lost my one and only true friend in this world and it stung like a muthafucka. It felt like she was dead to me. The news of my pregnancy turned into this nasty and violent horror show between us.

I went back outside to get some needed air and feel the sun in my face. The neighborhood Rico had me in was so quiet and out the way from Edenwald. It would have been a headache to constantly travel back and forth to go hang out with friends. And I didn't have a car or license. So I was pretty much alone from day to day. The only comfort I had was Sammy and Rico. Now Sammy was acting like a bitch, so there was Rico, and I was getting tired of his coming and going. I wanted to smoke but I had to think about my baby.

I heard the front door open. It had to be Rico finally coming home. I went to greet him. I was sad and upset. I frowned at him when he walked inside. Rico looked at me; he seemed tired, like it had been a really busy day and night for him.

"Hey, Mouse," he greeted me lightly. I didn't get a kiss or hug from him. Just a simple "Hey, Mouse" like I was someone he was passing on the street.

"'Hey, Mouse.' That's the only greeting I get from you after you have been gone for so long, Rico? Seriously!" I spat.

"I'm tired," he returned.

"You tired of doing what?"

"I'm just tired, Mouse, just let it be," he said with a slight harshness in his tone.

"Rico, do you love me? I mean, do you really love me?" I asked with sadness and a dubious gaze.

"Yeah, I love you, Mouse. You about to have my first child. I took you out of the projects and moved you here. I provide you with everything you need. I protect you and I want you," he proclaimed.

It was good to hear. I needed some assurance. Sammy had put all this nonsense in my head about him. I wasn't stupid or naive; Rico was a good man. I had picked myself a winner. And he picked himself a good woman. I was ready to do everything for him, for our family and happiness.

Rico came closer to me. His eyes became softer toward me. He towered over me. He asked, "What's wrong wit' you, Mouse? Why you questioning my love for you all of a sudden? You don't trust me? You the only woman I want to be with. If I didn't, then you wouldn't be living like this."

"It just things did kinda happen so quickly and I was talking to Sammy—"

"What the fuck she had to say?" Rico interrupted me with a hard look.

"We had a fight over the phone."

"A fight about what?"

"I think she's jealous of me, Rico. I don't know why, but it feels like she's changing. I asked her to be our baby's godmother, and then we started arguing, and I can't even remember how the argument started."

I was in tears again. Rico placed his arms around me and comforted me. I placed my head against his chest and sobbed a little. I felt that stinging pain again. It was so hurtful. I thought about Sammy. I was tempted to call her back and apologize. Maybe I'd overreacted.

"Mouse, I'ma be honest, sometimes people closest to you can be the ones who hate the most. Sammy's a lonely bitch who don't have shit in her life. What music? She ain't poppin' off like that, especially fuckin' wit' Search. And she's showing you her true colors. You should just stay away from her, 'cause you goin' one way, the right way, and she goin' her way. I got ya back, Mouse. I already told you that I'm gonna invest into ya career. You better than her anyway," he said to me with conviction.

Usually, I would defend Sammy and curse Rico or any-body else out if they spoke one bad word about my friend, but I didn't. I thought maybe Rico was right. Sammy was starting to hate on me and show her true colors. When you finally have something special in life and you're doing good then people say you've changed, when it's really that they are the ones who changed against you.

"Don't worry about Sammy, she's the past and we are the future. We gonna be a family," he said.

I smiled heavily hearing him say that. I wanted nothing more in the world but to have a family of my own. I never had a true family of my own, except for Sammy. But that ship done probably sailed and drowned. Growing up in the streets, trying to survive, was a harsh, scary, and lonely feeling. And the baby I was carrying inside of me was going to be truly loved. I wasn't going to abandon them, abuse them, or hate them. I was going to really love my baby and become a better mother, a better parent to my unborn than my mother and father ever was to me.

I blew air out of my mouth. Rico continued to hold me in his arms, squeezing me gently. I exhaled. His masculine grip around me made me want to fuck him. But I had one more question to ask him. It wasn't that important of a question, but I just needed to know. I wanted him to be honest with me and confirm my suspicion.

Before I could ask Rico my question, he suddenly kissed me. It was a heated kiss that made me forget what I was going to ask him. His tongue swam around in my mouth and he gently began caressing my body, with his hands sliding down my back and cupping my ass. He was ready to take me somewhere that I always longed to go.

I felt my body weakening with his sensitive touch. He picked me up in his arms and carried me upstairs into the bedroom. He peeled my clothing away from me and had me exposed to him like the stars in the night. He looked at me pleasantly for a moment. His eyes danced across my naked skin. His hunger for me was growing inside of him.

"Damn, ya so fuckin' beautiful, Mouse. I love every inch of you," he said.

I beamed.

He came to me and dropped to his knees. He pulled me into his grasp, wrapped his arms around my thick thighs with my belly against his lips. He started to caress and rub my belly. He then kissed my stomach and said, "This is us, our baby. My baby is having a baby."

I smiled profoundly and exhaled. Rico was taking my breath away. He kissed my stomach again, so gently and lovingly. Then he rose up a little and placed one of my nipples into his mouth and began sucking it. I panted from the pleasure of his lips on my flesh. I touched the top of his head, played with his cornrows. My eyes closed, he danced his lips across my skin. He craved my body and it was my hot, wet core that was calling out to him.

"I love you so much, baby," I said faintly, feeling his lips press against my womanhood.

He parted my lips with his tongue. Oh, God, he was about to do me the honors, which was something he never done to me before: eat my pussy. He lifted me up and I floated in the air as he carried me to the bed. I was placed on my back. I spread my legs for him and awaited my moment of reckoning. My pussy was fresh and ready for him to eat. I noticed the swell of my brown breasts as Rico lowered his mouth to my sweet center. My slippery and sweet juices started to flow freely. He kissed between my thighs and then my pussy lips were parted slightly, exposing my sleek and pink center.

"I love you for this, baby," I said pleasantly.

"I know you will," he responded with a cocksure smile.

His tongue tenderly flicked at my clit, and it sent waves of pleasure all through my full body.

"Oh, God," I moaned.

He gripped my thighs firmly and centered his head into my middle. My body jerked and shook every time his lips sucked my delicate spot. The more Rico licked my pussy the wetter I became. I moaned louder and louder, squirming from the euphoric feeling that stirred up inside of me.

"Baby, I love you. I love you. Oh shit, I love the way you lick my fuckin' pussy. Oh, *se siente tan bien. Comer ese cono,* oh shit!"

The Spanish poured out of me. And I made it pour out of him.

"*¿Te gusta eso, no?*" Rico replied with a lustful smile.

It was intense.

"I love the way you lick my pussy. Oh, shit. Fuck. Fuck. Yesss, oh do that shit, baby! Do that shit! It feels so fuckin' good. *Eres el major, nena,*" I cried out.

Rico cupped my ass in his hands and pulled my pussy deeper into his mouth and drove his tongue deeper inside me. I was ready to fuck. I wanted to feel him inside of me now. My pussy was so wet it was leaving a wet spot on the sheets. I squirmed and wiggled. I was becoming frantic with my plea. I wanted to feel his hard, throbbing dick inside my pussy. He was making me cum from this tongue action. The way his tongue boxed and licked on my sensitive clit caused my legs to quiver and my clit to swell even more. I was lost in so much pleasure that tears began to flow from my eyes and then it happened. I came in his face. There was my loving, so thick and smooth, coating Rico's face. He didn't mind. My nigga was a fuckin' beast; he went on to doing me nice and I wanted that dick inside of me.

He climbed on top of me. I wanted to be fucked. I wanted to be penetrated by his beautiful, long, thick dick. I wanted that sensation of having Rico's dick rub my pussy lips, teasing me, sliding up and down my slit. I wanted to feel that hard dick thrusting into me. With Rico's full weight on top of me, he plunged that well-working machine inside of me and I gasped. He fucked me the way I loved to be fucked. He started slow and then gradually sped up with his rhythm between my legs, causing my face to twist into overzealous pleasure.

"Fuck me, Rico! Take this pussy! Fuck me!" I cried out.

I wanted him deeper and harder inside of me. My nails scraped down his back and dug into his ass, pulling him deeper and deeper inside me. He put that thick dick into me like he was a well-oiled machine. I didn't want my baby to stop.

From behind, he grabbed my hips and took me to a higher level of sexual pleasure. My tits swung while he thrust with all his might and then he put his finger in my ass. I cringed a little from the double penetration, but it was such an exhilarating feeling that I buried my face into the pillow with my ass arched for him and howled; my pussy was ready to explode for him again.

I climbed on top of him and rode that dick, rubbing my clit up and down his long shaft while he squeezed and fed on my tits. Our final position was him climbing back on top of me and with my legs pressed back and him fucking me like the king he was.

"I'm gonna cum!" he howled.

"Cum inside me, baby," I howled back. Shit, I was already pregnant.

I could feel his dick pounding in me; it was making me scream and making tears come into my eyes. Our bodies were glistening in sweat and I longed for that explosive finale with my man. I could feel it coming and then he did, he shook against me and grunted, discharging all of his seed into me and filling me completely. I held him closely and breathed out. The sensation had enveloped me entirely.

For a moment, we cradled together in silence. I was savoring having Rico lie against me. I was stroking his braids gently and was snuggled in the place between his chest and neck.

"I love you so much," I whispered in his ear.

His orgasm and my orgasm had hit us hard. He had left his mark inside me; I could feel his seed growing in my stomach. I really wanted to give him a son. But if he happened to be a girl, then she was going to be the most precious baby girl on earth. He continued to cradle me and I did the same.

"I love you, baby," I whispered again in his ear, and then I drifted off into a peaceful sleep.

Good dick would do that to you.

I woke up a few hours later. Rico wasn't by my side. I was shocked to see him gone. I didn't know what time it was or how long I'd been sleeping. But once again, I found myself alone. I jumped out of bed. I was still naked. It was dark out; the place was quiet like a cemetery. I glanced at the time on the dresser and it was after nine p.m. I didn't realize I was so tired.

I donned a robe and left the bedroom looking for Rico. I knew he didn't leave. I went through the whole house calling out to him, longing to feel his touch again.

"Where are you, Rico?" I called out.

But he wasn't answering.

The house was dark. I turned on the lights in the kitchen and saw the note he had left for me on the fridge. I removed it and quickly read it:

> *Babe, had to leave to take care of urgent business, be back in a few hours. I had fun with you and you're the best, love you!*

I puffed with irritation and crumbled the note in my hand and tossed it into the trashcan. I wanted him here with me, but like always, he would come home, fuck me, and then leave like he didn't live here too. What good was it to have a home when your man constantly left you in it alone? If I had my own car, then it would probably be different for me. I quickly got on my cell phone and called him. His phone didn't even ring; it went straight to voice mail.

I was angry. "Muthafucka!" I cursed.

When I heard the beep, I left a message. "Rico, so you just gonna fuck me, put me to sleep and then leave? Where are you? Call me back, baby, when you get this message. I'm missing you already."

I pressed 2 to make the message urgent. I tossed my phone and felt some kind of way. What the hell he doing out there? The streets couldn't possibly be keeping that man busy. I went back into the bedroom and plopped down on our king-sized bed and rested against the green silk sheets. I gazed out the window while lying on my back. The quietness was somewhat becoming annoying for me. I missed the sounds of the projects, the loudness that boomed into my bedroom window when I stayed with my father. Mount Vernon was just too still and quiet some days for me.

I turned on my stereo system and popped in a Mary J. Blige CD and listened to my girl Mary tear it up about love, drama, and heartbreak. Damn, I could relate to so many of her songs. My own life was love, drama, and heartbreak.

Chapter Thirteen

Sammy

"Fuck that bitch," I shouted.

"What you about to do?" La-La asked.

It shouldn't have even been a question about what I was gonna do. I felt disrespected. My name rang out and I was a fire that couldn't be put out. I was always a bitch about action and I was fuming. My mind was set on one thing: violence. It was the core of my existence.

I snatched the snub-nosed revolver from Chyna and was ready to march out her apartment. I was scowling and cursing. I was ready to hurt and destroy this bitch. And I wasn't the only one who was ready to do some damage. Our teeth were showing and we were going to be more than just bark.

It had gotten back to me that Angie was in my hood looking for me. They said she was armed and she was in a black Chevy with three other bitches searching for revenge. YGB had the audacity to come to Edenwald and come with guns. I wasn't scared; I was ready to go head to head with all those bitches. I was already angry and hyped after my fallout with Mouse; now this drama with Angie was adding more fuel to my raging fire.

Sporting some coochie-cutting shorts and a sexy tank top, I had nowhere to conceal the snub-nosed revolver. It was a small handgun, but I had nowhere to place it on my person. But I wasn't leaving the house without it.

Tina had come bursting into the apartment and shouted, "Yo, Sammy, these bitches are still driving around lookin' fo' you!" She then screamed excitedly. "What you wanna do?"

"You already know what the fuck I wanna do!" I shouted.

"That's what I'm fuckin' talkin' about!" Chyna hollered.

We wrapped our hair up in red doo-rags, put Vaseline on our faces, removed earrings, and armed ourselves with a few weapons. It was on. La-La, Chyna, and Tina were all behind me. These bitches wanted to go to war and I was the general leading the charge. Angie and her dirty bitches were about to feel so much wrath that hell was gonna feel like paradise to them after we were done with them.

I couldn't believe this dumb bitch had the audacity to come to my hood and start some shit with me. It was on. I was ready to tear this bitch apart like a lion does to meat.

We stormed out of the apartment and out of the lobby like some vicious bitches, which we were. I gripped the snub-nosed in my hand, keeping it to my side. Already, we gripped people's attention. By the way we were moving residents already knew there was some shit brewing. They seen the gang colors and our angry attitudes, and a few people followed us like we were leading a civil rights movement. Everybody wanted to see a fight. The projects wanted to be entertained by violence; they didn't care at whose cost.

We all marched toward 233rd Street where I heard Angie and her crew were parked and waiting. I wanted to open fire on her ass and leave her dead where she stood. I was tired of whooping bitches' asses; let my gun do the talking.

Being a few blocks from where these bitches were at, the intensity was growing and the drama unfolding. The outcome was unpredictable, but I was ready to make it predictable. They were strapped and we were strapped.

EVB against YGB; it was always violence and bloodshed between both gangs. There was dangerous history between us.

I was marching with a storm of bitches behind me, scowling, and anxious, and determined to hurt and damage any bitch who was trying to form a weapon against me.

"Where the fuck they at?" Chyna shouted.

We continued to march toward 233rd and before I could cross the street, Rico's 650i came to a screeching stop in front of me and my clique. Rico jumped out from the passenger seat, scowling. I was surprised he wasn't driving. It was one of his goons behind the wheel. He came at me and shouted, "Sammy, get in the fuckin' car!"

"What!" I was dumbfounded by his harsh action and words.

"I said get in the fuckin' car, Sammy!" He roughly snatched me by my arm and yanked me toward his ride like I was his personal bitch.

I yanked my arm free from his grip, glared at him, and shouted, "Rico, get the fuck off me! Who you think I am?"

He glared back. He looked down and noticed the snub-nosed in my hand.

"I ain't playin' wit' you Sammy! Let me talk to you," he said sharply.

"About what?" I exclaimed. I didn't have time to deal with Rico's shit. I was focused on one thing: going at Angie and causing her some serious bodily damage.

My crew was also dumbfounded with the way Rico came at me. He may have had Mouse brainwashed and thought he owned her, but I wasn't that bitch. Shit, give a nigga some pussy a few times and muthafuckas don't know how to act. Yeah, we fucked again and again, behind my friend's back. The dick was good and he had me hooked. We had some kind of spark between us. I didn't see it coming, shit just happened. But I wasn't his bitch for him to control and embarrass in the street.

Chyna, La-La, and Tina were all looking at me crazily. And I knew they were all thinking, *why is Rico tripping with Sammy? Isn't that Mouse's nigga?* He was creating the unwanted attention that I did not need.

"Sammy, get the fuck in the car!" he protested with a hard stare.

I didn't want to continue to challenge Rico. We were all ready to fight, but he was adamant in pulling me into his car.

"Rico, what's ya problem?" Tina spoke up.

"Shut the fuck up, Tina. This ain't ya fuckin' business," Rico rebuked.

"What, Rico?" Tina spat back.

"You fuckin' heard me."

Tina didn't care. She was ready to smack Rico. She stepped forward to confront him, but Chyna pulled her back. Things were starting to get out of control. We didn't need any beef with Rico. I saw the driver step out from behind the wheel and he was six feet tall, full of nothing but muscle and ugliness. He looked like a human pit bull. He looked fiercely at us and seemed that he was ready to growl about something. It was getting scary.

"Fuck it, Rico, I'll go wit' you," I shouted.

"Just get in the damn car, Sammy. Stop makin' shit so fuckin' difficult," he barked at me.

Reluctantly, I climbed into the back seat and Rico got into the passenger seat. The door slammed like I was being locked into a jail cell. Chyna, Tina, and La-La all looked lost. They were helpless to do anything. Rico didn't even acknowledge them. He frowned harder at my girls and turned his back on them, like they were all trash. I didn't even get to explain anything to my peoples or tell them bye. The car sped away and Rico turned around glaring at me and shouted, "What the fuck is wrong wit' you, Sammy?"

I was lost. "Huh?"

"You ready to fuck everything up. You think I didn't know what was about to go down? It's a good fuckin' thing I was around the way to stop you from doin' some dumb shit," he screamed.

"So, I'm supposed to let this bitch come into my hood and threaten me. You fuckin' serious, Rico?" I screamed back.

"You about to get this money. Fuck that bitch!"

"No, fuck you!" I shouted heatedly.

"Bitch, what?" He leaned over his seat in a threatening manner and I thought he was about to lunge at me and attack. "Sammy, don't fuckin' play games wit' me. Fuck that bitch Angie and YGB. I got things planned for us."

"What, Rico? You think just 'cause I'm fuckin' you that you can treat me like any other bitches?" I hollered.

"I want you to get this money."

"And I wanna get this money, Rico. I need to get paid. But damn, let me just go and fuck this bitch up. And you don't fuckin' control me."

"I'll handle that, you better than that gang shit, Sammy." Here was a drug dealer trying to judge me. Ironic.

"Where we goin', then?" I asked.

"Away from here for a moment," he said to me.

I sat back in the back seat and pouted. I still had the snub-nosed on me. It was fully loaded, but I had no use for it now. Rico sat back in his seat and talked to his thug driving. I gazed out the window, zoning these muthafuckas out, and caught an attitude.

We headed toward the New England Thruway. I remained quiet and just went along with the ride. It was late in the evening. The sun was setting and we were traveling north. I soon looked up and saw that we were in Co-op

City. Rico lit a cigarette and asked if I wanted a smoke. Hells, yeah, I needed some nicotine in my system. I was stressed. I needed something to ease my mind.

They pulled into the parking lot of Co-op City, the largest cooperative housing development in the world, located in the Baychester section. I stepped out the car, taking a few pulls, and looked around. I had calmed down. Maybe Rico had saved me from some terrible fate, because I wasn't thinking straight and was ready to kill that bitch and her crew. I was ready to put that snub-nosed to work and light muthafuckas up, real talk. My temper was dangerous and it took me places that were mostly hard to come back from. And once I didn't give a fuck, I didn't give a fuck. I wasn't even thinking about my music career or the future. Me and Mouse weren't speaking, so I had blacked out with rage and was ready to do the unthinkable: murder. So I left the gun underneath the seat and chilled with Rico.

Co-op City was a place for the middle class. The towering high-rise structure was a marvel to see from the highway. It was never a place for a family like mine. You had to have a decent income, have a decent credit score, pass a background check, and pay taxes every year to even get an apartment in this bitch. It was my first time really seeing the place.

I took one last pull from the cigarette and flicked it away into the street, and then followed Rico and his towering thug into one of the buildings that stood over fifteen, maybe twenty stores stories tall, far exceeding Edenwald.

"Why we here?" I asked Rico.

"Business, baby," he replied coolly.

The place almost looked pristine in my eyes, a far cry from the grimy dungeon I liked to call the projects. When we stepped into the elevator it didn't reek with piss and litter. The floors were cleaned and cameras watched your every move in the lobby. It was fuckin' Disney World out this bitch.

Rico pushed for the fourteenth floor. We quickly ascended; I stood close to Rico and stared at his thug. He was a mountain of silence, looking intimidating like staring down the barrel of a .50-caliber.

"He don't talk?" I asked Rico.

Rico chuckled. "He's a loyal soldier, Sammy. He don't need to talk 'cause he only needs to speak one language: violence and bloodshed if niggas fuck wit' me," Rico proclaimed.

I rolled my eyes. The nigga was scary looking, I admit that: scar across his face, dark skin, bald head, brawny, and tall. But people who are too quiet around me I just don't trust like that. I feel those are the muthafuckas who will set you up quickly, probably a serial killer. Speak ya mind, 'cause when I don't know what you thinking, I become uncomfortable around you.

"What's his name? I mean, he ain't no fuckin' mute, right?"

"Nah, he's not a mute. Fence is good peoples," said Rico.

I still didn't like him or trust him.

We stepped off the elevator and I followed Rico. We approached this apartment that he had the key to. He unlocked the door and I walked into an empty apartment. What was this? I wondered.

Rico walked around the place for a moment. It was a bit spacious with wood floors and a balcony that overlooked the Bronx. It was three bedrooms and it was way better than my cramped and run-down apartment. I went to look out the window and it looked like I was staring at the city from the clouds. Damn, we were high. I looked at Rico. He looked at me.

"You like this?" he asked me.

"It's nice," I replied nonchalantly.

He lit another cigarette and smoked. He was definitely a chain smoker, worse than me. He walked toward the window and gazed out of it. I stood in silence. Fence stood by the door like he was a trained guard dog. The only thing Rico didn't have on him was a leash.

"I want you to be moved in by next week," Rico said to me.

I was shocked. "What the fuck you talkin' about, Rico?"

He came closer to me, taking pulls from his cigarette with his eyes looking methodical. "This is ya place, Sammy."

"My place? Are you serious?"

I didn't want him to mess with my fuckin' head and I didn't want to owe him anything. I wasn't about to become some in-house pussy like Mouse, where he could come and go as pleased right after fucking me.

"You like it, right?"

I did. It was a castle compare to my current residence. I was never anyone to hold my tongue, so I frankly asked, "And what I gotta do to keep staying in this apartment? If you think I'm about to become some in-house pussy, then you fuckin' must be mistaken, Rico. I ain't the one."

He looked at his thug by the door and said, "Fence, give us a minute, step outside, a'ight?"

Fence nodded and did what he was told. The door closed behind him. Rico said to me, "Fuckin' listen, Sammy, you always so fuckin' harsh wit' the tongue. I don't need to keep hearing this attitude from you. I'm gonna be about business wit' you."

"Just business?" I asked with a slight smile. Damn. I thought about how good the dick was and lost myself for a moment when I came at him with that insinuating remark.

"You are crazy, Sammy."

"I am, and don't you forget that," I replied lightly.

"I hope that's not a threat."

It wasn't.

He remained stoic.

Rico stood near me. He continued with, "I'm moving my operation from Edenwald to over here. And what I mean by moving is my stash house and where my keys are going to be shipped to from now on until further changes. I'm permanently shutting down the two apartments there. Shit is too hot in Edenwald and ya one of the reasons why, Sammy."

"I'm the reason! Are you serious?" I exclaimed.

"Sometimes you can be a live wire."

"And that's the pot trying to call the kettle black," I spat back.

"Your beef wit' Angie and the YGB, it's bad for business. You bring attention wit' that bullshit. And if I didn't stop you today, you would either be locked up or dead," he stated.

"Rico, are you seriously tryin' to preach to me?"

"I've been in this game for a long time."

"And what's that supposed to mean?"

"It means I have fifteen keys arriving next week, and I need a new place to put them. I have an arrangement with the building's supervisor here. He's lookin' out for me, for a small fee of course. But this is the floor with less tenants on it, so not too many people gonna be in our business. And I want you to run things for me."

"What?"

"What you got in ya life right now, Sammy? You always broke, you stay in drama and beef wit' these bitches and niggas in the street, and ya mama is sick. You need the money. Ya music career, it ain't takin' off like that. But wit' my help, you and me, we can build an empire from the streets to the studio. We can make it happen, Sammy. Think about it, you can do whatever the fuck you want wit' money not being an issue. You wouldn't need Search, fuck that *puta,* and you wouldn't need to be stressing 'bout anything."

Oh, it sounded so tempting. I was thinking about it.

"This is all you. You get ya strong clique to play ball wit' you and you can see a whole lot of money comin' in. It ain't like you never hustle before," said Rico with some persuasion. "It'll be like old times, Sammy, but even better and stronger. And the best thing about, it'll be only you and me."

I truly needed the money and I needed a change.

"And what about Mouse?" I asked.

"What about her?"

"So, you just gonna play us both. She's pregnant wit' ya baby, and she's in love wit' you. Are you in love wit' her?"

"Listen, this is business, Sammy. Mouse is cool, and I got love for her, but honestly, I'm not in love wit' her. I just felt sorry for her and wanted to help her out. I'm in love wit' you. Mouse ain't smart like you and me. We're different. We can make millions if we do this right. I can invest into your music and you can invest into a better lifestyle for yourself. *Hacerse rico ahora o morir en el intento.*"

Get rich now, or die trying.

Usually, I would defend my friend, or ex-friend, but I didn't say a word. I asked, "So did you kill her father?"

I found out about her father's death through the grapevine. It didn't disturb me; he was an asshole and even Stevie Wonder saw that murder coming.

"You don't need to know that shit, what's done is done," he replied coolly.

He had Hector killed. But it wasn't my business.

I looked at Rico and went looking around the apartment once more. I really wanted it. It would definitely be a step up from my harsh living conditions. I went into the kitchen and admired the stainless fridge. Rico was behind me. He was quiet, waiting for my decision. I needed to get away and this was my escape. Shit, he did Mouse like this, so why couldn't he do me the same way?

Rico came closer. He slid his arms around my waist and embraced me strongly, his breath against my neck. "You can't say no, Sammy. I need you like you need me," he whispered in my ear.

I took a deep breath. I closed my eyes and thought about the good, the bad, and the ugly, and the consequences. In this game, there were always the ugly and the consequences.

"I'll do it," I said faintly.

"That's my girl," he replied and started to plant kisses on my neck. "We gonna make so much money together."

His embrace became stronger around me. I could feel his touch reaching underneath my clothing, gently caressing my skin. He cupped my breasts and pushed me against the sink. He then moved his hand between my thighs and rubbed my pussy through my jeans. I felt him becoming hard against me. He fondled me.

"Tell me somethin', Sammy."

"What's that?" I asked.

"I love you, and I need to know, who disrespected you in New Jersey?"

He continued to rub my pussy. I wondered why he asked me that, but Rico always had respect for me and whoever disrespected me he was damn sure going to disrespect on a whole new level.

"Just give me his name."

I didn't.

He curved me over the sink and started to undress me slowly, pulling my zipper down and squeezing my breasts like they were pieces of juicy fruit. His tongue tasted my skin and his breath was cool to my soul. He was pressed tightly behind me, engulfing me with his heated passion for me.

"I want you, Sammy. You drive me so fuckin' crazy," he said to me, rubbing on my booty and touching my thighs.

He pulled down my jeans and I stepped out of them; next I came out of my panties and he curved me back into the doggie-style position. My legs spread like a downward V and my sweet pussy became exposed to him like the sun beaming in the sky. It was ready to give him warmth and pleasure. I wanted to feel every inch of him inside of me. I no longer felt guilty about my down-low affair with Rico behind Mouse's back. Fuck it, she had him her way and I had him my way. She was living good and now it was my turn to live good.

He undid his jeans and pulled out his dick. As he grabbed my hips, leaning over me, and getting ready to penetrate me, he said, "Give me his name, Sammy. I can't go on knowing what that muthafucka did to you and he ain't been got yet, still breathing like everything all good."

I felt him slide into me, pushing through my sensuous walls that gripped, and then tangled every hard piece of him like a sexual web. He thrust, I moaned. He thrust harder and I closed my eyes and clenched the sink firmly. He was fucking me like a warrior.

"Oh, baby, the dick feels so good," I cried out.

"Give me his name, Sammy. Give me his damn name," Rico cried out as he fucked me.

His hard flesh pounding in me was gonna make me surrender to his questioning. He palmed my ass, cupped and squeezed my tits, and Supermaned my pussy like he had an S across his chest.

"What's his fuckin' name, Sammy?" he growled.

He pulled my hair and seized my thick hips. I panted. I felt him cemented in my stomach. I shuddered from the dick ramming into me and when I was about to come from the dick and sensation, I helplessly cried out, "It was Macky!"

Rico stopped suddenly and growled, "What? That producer muthafucka put his hands on you and disrespected you! Is he fuckin' crazy?"

"Baby, please don't stop."

Rico's attention completely diverted from me and was hooked on Macky. *Why did I tell him?* I wanted him to finish his business with me and make me come.

"And that's Search's people, right. Stay away from that *puta* muthafucka, Sammy. Fo' real," he warned me.

"I will, Rico. Just fuck me, baby," I cried out.

I turned and saw the look on Rico's face and I hated that his attention wasn't completely on me; it was on the streets.

"Baby, why you stoppin'?"

I wanted him inside of me. I didn't want him to think about anything else but to be inside of me and fucking the shit out of me.

"He's a dead man, Sammy. You on my team now, and anybody that fucks wit' you, will pay wit' their life," he said assertively.

He slid his machine back into my pink folds and continued with his sexual onslaught. He balls slammed against my ass as he fucked me vigorously. It was becoming more intense. I was sure Fence could hear my loud cries and moans from the hallway.

"Ugh! Ugh! Ugh! Shit, shit, you gonna make me cum, baby. Ugh! Ugh!" I panted.

Rico seemed to be in a trance. His body was with me, fucking me and pleasuring me, but his mind was somewhere else. I didn't care, I just wanted to cum. He pounded and pounded and I squirted like a fountain. My head dropped into the sink. My legs felt wobbly.

"Cum for me, Rico. Ugh! Yes! Ugh, yes," I chanted.

I could feel him stiffening inside me. I could feel him ready to explode. And then I felt his release inside of me. He quivered against me like he was having a seizure. He grunted and pushed his fingers into my side as his ejection saturated my pussy. It felt so good. He pulled out my womanly wound with his dick dripping. I looked at Rico and he had a frown on his face.

I thought pussy was supposed to make niggas happy. Rico looked like he had just sucked on a really sour lemon.

He pulled up his jeans and got himself decent and said to me, "I told you Search is no fuckin' good; you stay away from him, Sammy. I got you in this music business now. And his friend, he's dead man. That mama *huevo!*"

Chapter Fourteen

Sammy

July: Summer Madness

It was amazing how your life could change in almost a month. I went from the bottom to the top in no time. I had no more concerns about unpaid bills and not being able to afford things. I was living like a queen and very proud of it. I still was in love with music, but hustling with Rico was paving the way.

I rode in the passenger seat in silence with Rico. It was a dark night and hot like hell. It seemed like it always turned out to be hotter in mid July and moving an inch made you sweat like you were dipped into a pool. I kept cool by letting the wind hit me with force as Rico hit sixty-five mph on the thruway heading north toward New Rochelle.

Since I agreed to be on Rico's team and get this money, my life and respect had upgraded. I wasn't that same young teenager moving crack vials in the stairway. I was older and mature. Rico had me around some serious weight. Fifteen keys and more a week to move was nothing to sneeze at for him. It was some major potent product and major paper that had me living lavishly. Rico was wholesaling most of the keys out of state: New Jersey, Connecticut, Pennsylvania, and DC. Rico had some serious clientele out there who were paying up to $18,000 or more a key. He was becoming the talk of the town. And Rico was on his way to becoming a serious kingpin in this city.

I was right behind him; he trusted me, somewhat anyway. He gave me the first few keys on consignment and I flipped them birds like they had wings and made them fly. Setting up shop was easy; I had the reputation and street credibility not to be fucked with. Drug dealing was putting EBV in a totally different ballgame and bitches were getting paid. Our status in the Bronx was elevated to something supreme.

Rico understood I was quick-witted, smart, motivated, and had more heart than majority of these niggas in the game. I wasn't scared to shoot my gun, and I wasn't scared to get at anyone who made any problems for us. Rico and I were still fucking our brains out regularly. It was coming to a point that he was spending more of his time with me than Mouse. And Mouse and I were in two different worlds. She was trying to become his housewife and I was becoming his ride or die bitch on the street who was getting this money.

I turned the apartment in Co-op City into a cash cow with money-counting machines, guns, and drug paraphernalia, moving about five bricks a week into the streets, from the Bronx to Long Island. Chyna and La-La were on my team, and they became my mules and workers. With Rico, I had the muscle and I had the product.

I was still focused on my music; the main reason why I got down with Rico was to invest into myself. I didn't want to keep depending on anybody to pay for studio time, touring, and promotional items. I wanted the best of both worlds, and I was getting it.

I had heard that Search was back in town through the grapevine and he had been asking around about me. The muthafucka had been gone for almost two months, and not a phone call or any kind of contact from him. He had completely dissed me. So why was he asking around about me? My life had changed dramatically. How could Search mentor me when he could so easily leave me behind? So I left him behind. I thought I would never say this about Search, because he was always there for me, but I was starting to have so many doubts about him.

I ran into Search, or should I say Search ran into me on the block a week ago. I was chilling with my clique on the set, smoking Newports and sipping Cîroc. I had rented a Dodge Intrepid for the week via a friend's credit card and information. I needed something to style in and get around with while handling my business. Search had pulled up in his green Durango. He was alone. He stepped out looking fresh in a gray suit, wingtip shoes, and a long tie, looking like he was trying to be P. Diddy and whatnot. I had sucked my teeth and rolled my eyes at him. I wasn't in the mood to see him at all.

He had approached like everything was okay with us. "Hey, Sammy, can we talk?" he had asked.

Me and my bitches looked at this nigga angrily. They already knew the deal with him and me. How he had left me when he was supposed to be managing me.

"What you want, Search?" I had said pointedly.

"Can we talk alone, Sammy?"

"Fuck that! You dissed me, Search. You went off to ATL and didn't bring me wit' you, fuck you. You didn't even tell me about it. I had to find out through ya fuckin' neighbor," I had barked.

"Can I explain?"

"Fuck outta here, nigga! I trusted you and Macky." His name had slipped out of my mouth.

"Macky? What he got to do with you and me?"

"He ain't got shit to do wit' it. I trusted you, Search! Why you do me like that? You gone almost two months now and you don't holla at a bitch!" I had retorted.

"Sammy, I can explain. Let's just talk about it," he had said coolly.

But I was already heated. I didn't want to hear anything that he had to say to me. The incident with Macky and Search leaving for several weeks had been rooted into me and caused me to become bitter with him. I wanted to fuck him up, or get him fucked up, but Search had history with me and a few other people from the hood, so I let him be.

He looked at me sadly. He was reluctant to tell me his side of the story, but there was no side of the story.

"Sammy, ya better than this, believe me, it's going to happen. I left for a reason. A reason I care not to tell everyone right now. But I'm still on your team if you just let me explain," he had pleaded, coming closer to me.

He was becoming a nuisance and I wasn't the only one who thought so. La-La came in between him and me and jumped into his face. "Search, you heard what the fuck she said; step the fuck off, nigga! She ain't tryin' to hear or see you right now," she had shouted with her finger pointed in his face. "Don't get fucked up, nigga! We don't care how long we been cool wit' you." La-La was a beast and he definitely didn't want to test her.

But Search wasn't intimidated by La-La, who only stood five feet six inches, and weighed no more than 124 pounds. He towered over my homegirl like a sky scraper and smirked at her threats.

"Sammy!" he had continued.

"Oh, you think I'm a joke, Search?" La-La had exclaimed.

He had looked past her and stared at me. It was the ultimate disrespect. Search was pushing his luck, but he was determined to have a word with me. I was being adamant with him. He wasn't my business anymore. I had moved on from dealing with him. You disrespect me and diss me once, there ain't any second chances with you. He should have been real and upfront. I felt he went behind my back on some sneaky-ass shit and now he was exposed. I still didn't know what exactly he did, but I felt Rico was right: there was more to Search than met the eyes. And I wasn't getting rich with Search, but I was getting rich dealing with Rico.

Search had pushed La-La to the side and stepped around her to get to me. Why he had done that, I don't know, but you don't push anyone of my girls away, disrespect them, and expect there wasn't going to be any repercussions. Before Search could take another step closer to me, the baseball bat went across his back like "Wham!" He had stumbled and turned around. La-La was clutching the bat tightly, frowning and cursing. She had hit him again; this time she caught the nigga in his chest, and he folded over like a chair and fell against the pavement.

Before I knew it, he was getting jumped by four of my homegirls and one nigga. He was squirming in the fetal position and trying to protect all his vitals. He cried out. I watched for a minute. I saw blood; they tore his suit and rushed into his pocket. They had his wallet, car keys, and cell phone. His dignity was crushed.

"I told you, nigga, don't fuck wit' us!" La-La had shouted.

She was ready to hit him with the baseball bat again. Search was hurt though.

"La-La, chill the fuck out," I had instructed her.

She knew not to go against me. She had fallen back, still scowling and itching to hurt him some more.

Search was beaten badly, but he wasn't unconscious. He stood up and looked at me. His suit was ruined and blood trickled from the cuts and wounds on his face.

"So it's like that between us, Sammy?" he had asked despondently.

"Yeah, it's like that," I had replied harshly.

He groaned and looked crushed. "You don't know what went down, Sammy. But someone's been in your ear about me and telling you the wrong things. Yes, I left town and went to Atlanta, but the truth isn't what you've been hearing."

"Yo, just leave, Search. I got other things goin' on fo' me right now. I don't need you," I had said.

He took a deep breath, licked his wounds, and had finally gotten the hint. With the little sympathy I had for him, I had said to my clique, "Yo, give him back his shit and let him go."

They were reluctant, but they did it. They had tossed Search everything they took out of his pockets. He had picked up his things from the ground and stumbled back to his truck in worse condition than he came. I fixated my eyes on him. He didn't even turn around to look back at me. He climbed into his truck and drove away. I had strongly made my point.

Fuck him!

I gazed up at the stars in the sky not knowing where Rico was taking me. He said it was a surprise. I didn't ask any questions. It was only us two, riding north on the New England Thruway. We were about fifty miles outside the city and what seemed to be in the mountains, removing ourselves further from civilization.

Rico turned onto a remote road where pavement gradually turned into a dirt road. The thick trees and shrubbery around us shielded us from any traffic that was nearby. With the dark and the woods, it brought about an eerie feeling inside of me. I was getting nervous. The only time you saw a road like this is with serial killers or mobsters, meaning whatever happened, it was hard for anyone to hear you scream and they could easily bury your body, never to be seen again.

I looked around. I noticed what looked like a pair of headlights up the narrow road. We were meeting someone, but who? Rico was calm, smoking his cigarette like usual, and didn't say a word to me.

"Why we comin' way out this way for, Rico?" I asked again.

"Ya see," he replied.

We approached the car that was already parked in the cut. It was a cream-colored Lexus. Two men waited for us to arrive. They lingered outside the vehicle, smoking a cigarette and chatting in the dark. The only light around came from the headlights and interior of the car. They were waiting for Rico.

We stopped; I got out right behind Rico. I was there reluctantly, thinking about this surprise he had for me. I didn't know if I wanted it. Rico walked up to them and greeted them with dap. The two harrowing figures were tall and looked like they were always up to no good.

"It went well, I assume," Rico said to them.

"No trouble at all, Rico," said one of his thugs.

The men moved to the back of the car and stood near the trunk. I followed them. I was silent and curious. Rico looked at me. I returned the stare. He continued to smoke.

"Open the trunk," he instructed, flicking his cigarette away.

They did. From where I stood, I couldn't see what was inside the trunk. Rico looked into the trunk and smirked. I wasn't a fool; I had a hint to what was going on. In this world, you had to expect the unexpected. You had to know there was someone in that trunk. Who? I thought about one person, but truthfully, had no idea.

"Sammy, come over here, let me show you something," Rico said.

I walked over and looked into the trunk. I wasn't shocked to see Macky inside. I knew it was someone in the trunk; it was a plus to see him though. It had been over a month since I told Rico about him, but Rico never forgot. He always held grudges.

Macky was tied up, beaten, and gagged, lying in the fetal position. He looked up at me and pleaded with his eyes. He knew his fate. He knew he'd fucked up.

"This nigga done pissed twice on himself, he so scared," said one of Rico's thugs.

"You like it, Sammy? *Puta* muthafucka," said Rico.

Macky squirmed and grunted. The gag in his mouth made his speech incoherent. He was an infamous music producer in the industry, but in this world, he was nobody to us. However, he would definitely be missed in the music industry.

Rico pulled out a 9 mm and glared at Macky. He then turned his attention to me. He handed me the gun and said, "You do the honors, Sammy. He tried to rape and kill you, so you pop two into this muthafucka."

I took the gun from his hand. I frowned and stepped closer to the trunk. I aimed the gun at Macky's head. I could hear him mumbling and pleading for his life. He squirmed in his restraints. He knew he fucked up. He fucked with the wrong bitch and this was the consequence. I shot people before, but they lived, and I did a lot of grimy shit, but I never killed anyone, even though I was ready to take Angie's life awhile back.

Everyone's eyes were fixated on me. They waited for me to do the deed. The darkness and shrubbery surrounding us cloaked any criminal action. This was the game. This was me taking it to the next level. I wanted to continue to play and get this money. I couldn't look weak in front of Rico or anybody else. If I showed any kind of weakness then the wolves would sniff me out and try to tear me apart.

I locked eyes with Macky. He continued to plead with his eyes. He grunted and squirmed harder. But there wasn't any escape from the inevitable. I frowned harder and thought about what he did to me and what he tried to do to me. This was a monster in sheep's skin. He was a fake muthafucka and a friend of Search, and I wasn't sure that Search was still a friend of mine with bitch-ass niggas like this in his circle.

Fuck it!

Bam! Bam!

I put two into him, one in his head and the second shot tore into his chest. He lay slumped in death, the crimson blood pooling underneath him. I exhaled.

"Damn!" Rico uttered. "That's my girl."

I stood staring at the body with the smoking gun in my hand. Now, there was no turning back. I was in this deep. I was officially a murderer. I definitely proved I was about that life now.

"You see, Sammy, when you kill someone, you do it discreetly, not impulsive, like you was about to do Angie, and then you get rid of the body. No fuckin' body, no fuckin' crime scene," Rico coolly explained to me.

Rico turned his attention to his goons and instructed, "Y'all niggas know what to do wit' this piece of shit. I don't want him found."

They nodded. The trunk was closed and I stood there silently. I still had the gun in my hand. I wanted him dead, and I wanted him gone. Funny thing, I didn't feel any remorse about it. It all felt natural to me, like murdering someone was inevitable. The lifestyle I was living, yeah, it was going to happen sooner or later, with or without Rico's influence. And the one thing I was proud of was that my first victim was Macky. He deserved death more than anything. I felt relieved. I knew this was a pivotal moment in my life.

Music, sex, murder: it was all the making of a plati-num-selling album.

Chapter Fifteen

Mouse

I didn't want to believe it at first, but why would my homegirls lie to me? The tears that fell from my eyes were more like a waterfall staining my face. The truth hurt. But the betrayal was devastating and unbelievable.

"I'm not telling you this to hurt you, Mouse, but you needed to know the truth. They playing you, things done changed a lot in the hood," Tina said to me.

I knew she didn't want to be the one to tell me the news, because she was a true friend to the both of us. But she knew Sammy was wrong and she confided to me. My best friend was smiling in my face while stabbing me in the fuckin' back. It felt like out of sight, out of mind. I was now three months pregnant with Rico's baby and I hear this shit.

Tina sat in front of me in my home, the place where I felt protected and had some comfort, the place where I wanted to raise my family. But there was no comfort with my heart and feelings. The profound agony I felt was making me sick. They might as well have put a gun to my head and pulled the trigger. Yes, it hurt that much.

My belly was growing more and more. I was carrying this muthafucka's baby, changing my ways and trying to make a decent home for him, and he had the audacity to fuck my best friend. I didn't care if we weren't speaking at the moment; she was still a friend of mine.

And Sammy, that snake-fuckin', two-faced bitch. How dare she contradict herself, preaching to me about how Rico wasn't any good, I was rushing into things with him, and she fucked him too, knowing how much I loved him?

"How long has this shit been goin' on, Tina?" I asked in grief.

"For too long, Mouse. I'm so sorry, it ain't supposed to be like this, but Sammy's changing. They jumped Search the other day, beat him up pretty badly," Tina continued.

"Search?"

"Her and Rico are in business together too," Meme chimed. "He got her moving drugs all over the city."

Meme was with her too, also confirming the bad news to me. I couldn't hold my composure. I started to cry heavily. My heart was crushed. I gasped and held on to a piece of furniture for balance. I wanted to react, break things, and fight someone. Fuck that, I wanted to kill this bitch and shoot Rico.

Rico had me pregnant and locked up in this spacious Mount Vernon home, miles away from my hood, and he was out there doing me dirty. It was a lie to me. He was a lie and Sammy was the ultimate lie. All these years of having each other's back, the bond, the sisterhood, and she threw it down the drain for some fuckin' dick. She could have messed with anyone in the neighborhood, but instead, she went after my fuckin' man.

"What you wanna do, Mouse?" Meme asked me. She never did like Sammy, but she loved me. This incident gave her a chance to finally go at Sammy.

"I wanna go see that fuckin' bitch!" I cursed.

I was tired of being in the dark. Now that I saw the light, it was time to fuck things up. I couldn't sit around this house any longer and wait. I was tired of waiting for Rico to come home, only to show me partial loving, fuck me, and then leave for hours, maybe a day or two at times. I was losing my fuckin' mind.

Tina didn't want any serious drama, she just felt sorry that I was getting played by Rico and wanted me to know what was going on with him. He was in the streets doing him, and Sammy wasn't the only bitch he was fucking cheating on me with. She dropped names: Caroline, Desire, Pink, and Tammy. He was a ho and he was nasty. The muthafucka had swag and the gift of gab. He got Sammy to hustle for him again; I always thought she was done with selling drugs.

Meme, she was ready to have my back and fight both these betraying assholes right beside me. She was hyped. She was ready to cut bitches. I was with it. I quickly got dressed and got one of Rico's guns from the bedroom. When Tina saw me with it, she stood and worriedly asked, "Mouse, what you gonna do wit' that?"

"Fuck that, Tina, I'm 'bout to go see that bitch and Rico," I hollered.

"C'mon, Mouse, just chill fo' a minute."

"Nah, fuck that shit, Tina, I ain't fuckin' chillin'. That bitch gonna disrespect me like that, I'ma see her ass!" I shouted frantically.

Meme had her car parked outside, a Maxima. I wanted to jump in it and rush to Edenwald and raise hell, three months pregnant or not. I was still Mouse, one of the baddest bitches in this gang.

"Let's go then," said Meme.

Tina was outnumbered. With or without her, I was going to Edenwald to raise hell. I hurried toward the door. Meme was right behind me. She had her car keys in her hand. Tina looked reluctant. But she didn't have any choice but to come with us. I was thankful that she had my back telling me the news, because she didn't have to say anything to me. Where I stayed at in Mount Vernon, it was about a twenty-minute drive from Edenwald, and for a bitch who rarely traveled outside the hood, Mount Vernon felt like I was on the other side of the world.

I climbed into the front seat of Meme's Maxima. I had the .380 on me and it was fully loaded. There was no calming me down. I was so pissed that I felt sick to my stomach and I couldn't stop shaking. My eyes were red from rage and crying and my sanity didn't exist.

When we got to Edenwald, it seemed like everybody in the neighborhood was outside. It was early evening and hot. It made me wish for a quicker fall and winter. It was a burden being pregnant in the heat. But summer seemed to be flying by like a bullet. I kept a vigilant eye out for Rico or Sammy. Meme informed me that she was driving around in a silver rented Intrepid. She got her money up and now the bitch thought she was the shit.

She wanna fuck my man and talk shit about me. Okay. Bitch, I always kept a job and had money in my pockets, you didn't. Bitch, Rico came at me and he was treating me like his queen, the nigga moved me into a three-bedroom home in Mount Vernon. You, he has you hustling for him, might as well said he was putting you on the track. I don't have to do a damn thing for him but be his woman. Bitch, I am pregnant with his baby and his main bitch, you is the side bitch. Bitch, I've been rhyming since I was twelve, you hitched a ride on my talent and followed my lead and now you think you're better than me? Fuck out here, dumb bitch!

Meme continued to drive around. I was itching to find Sammy and confront her. She had everyone in the hood scared of her; I was far from scared of this bitch. I was ready to show Sammy the true gangster side of me. Tina was trying to calm me down, but it wasn't doing me any good. The more she talked, the more furious I turned out to be.

I finally saw Sammy exiting out of the bodega on Laconia Avenue and walked to her rented Intrepid. She was with Chyna and La-La. I was ready to leap from the car and smash that bitch's head into concrete. Meme sped up to them and before the car came to a complete stop, I jumped out and rushed toward Sammy. Pregnant or not, I was ready to throw down like a prize fighter in a boxing ring. I heard the sound of the bell in my head.

"Sammy, can I talk to you fo' a minute?" I asked roughly.

She looked at me kind of dumbfounded and stopped walking. It was obvious that there was tension between us. Meme and Tina exited the car and hurried behind me.

"What's good, Mouse? How you been?" she asked halfheartedly.

Her little smile toward me was fake and I knew she didn't expect to see me. She probably didn't know I knew about her and Rico. I glared at her. I couldn't hold it in any longer. I was a time bomb ready to go off. The fuse was already lit and it was reaching the TNT.

"You a fake bitch, Sammy," I shouted. I went up to her face, shocking everyone.

"What, bitch?" Sammy retorted.

"You fuckin' Rico? Stay away from my fuckin' man, bitch! You fuckin' hypocrite," I screamed out. "You a nasty-ass ho, Sammy! *Conyo Sucio*." I had my fist clenched and was ready to spit in her face.

Sammy screamed, "Mouse, who the fuck is you, bitch? *Besa mi culo, puto,* fo' real. You ain't shit wit'out me! Get the fuck out my face, Mouse. Back the fuck up. You don't know who ya fuckin' dealin' wit! *Estupido*."

We were in each other's faces heatedly; I could feel her breath and spit on me. She wanted to punch me and I wanted to attack her. I wanted to rip her fuckin' head off. Chyna, La-La, Tina, and Meme, they were there looking speechless. We were all a clique, EBV, supposedly tight like a sisterhood, but everything between all of us was falling apart. It was becoming civil war within our crew.

Chyna and La-La were backing Sammy, and Meme and Tina were backing me. But it was going to be a one-on-one fight with Sammy and me. We had that type of respect on the streets. Anybody else, they would have been torn apart like meat at a butcher's shop between all of us.

Sammy glared at me and she shouted at me in Spanish, "*No me jodas,*" which meant "don't fuck with me," and followed up with a harsh, "*Vete a chingar a tu madre.*" Telling me to go fuck my mother, I went ham on this bitch. I swung and punched her in the face so fast and hard, I thought she went flying across the street. Sammy counterattacked and tackled me and started hitting me.

"Yo, y'all chill, she's pregnant! She's fuckin' pregnant, Sammy!" I heard Tina scream.

"I don't give a fuck!" Sammy shouted.

Sammy didn't care; it was all-out war between us. I grabbed a fistful of that bitch's hair and tried to pull it all out by her roots. She came at me and punched me in the stomach repeatedly. I cried out from the pain. And this angered the fuck out of me, knowing I was pregnant and intentionally trying to harm my unborn. I went berserk on this bitch; I caught her with hard right and then another right to her face, spewing blood from her mouth. She grabbed me to support herself from collapsing. We locked into each other's arms and she brought me down with her. We both hit the concrete like a large tree falling.

There were throngs of people around us, hollering, cheering, and shocked that I was fighting Sammy. She had the advantage at first, outweighing me. I caught a few blows to the face, having the ability to absorb her punishment, and then I bit the bitch and punched back. I was small, but I was strong and a beast. I kept hearing a few people scream out, "Yo, she's pregnant. Stop it! Stop it!"

I wasn't thinking about my baby when I was fucking this bitch up. But someone cared enough to roughly pull us apart and separate us from each other.

"Bitch!" Sammy screamed. "You dead, bitch!"

"Stay the fuck away from, Rico, bitch! Fuckin' slut!"

"*Vete al infierno,*" she shouted.

"You first, bitch!"

"Yo, ain't y'all friends?" someone shouted.

"Fuck her!"

"Fuck you, bitch," I retorted.

Edenwald had just seen the clash of titans. The streets were howling about us. Tina was trying to pull me back to the car. I resisted so heavily that I was ready to fight her. I didn't want the fight to end, but it did. Meme helped with Tina trying to drag me to the car with me cursing and carrying on like some lunatic. I grabbed my stomach all of a sudden and folded over. I suddenly felt hurt; a sharp pain in my side felt like a thousand needles were digging into my skin. I cried out. Tina and Meme pushed me into the car. I wasn't giving birth at three months, but I became substantially worried about my unborn child.

As Meme rushed me to the local hospital, I started to cry. Not from the pain in my stomach and side, but the pain I felt from the betrayal and then having my whole world collapse around me. There weren't any words to describe what I was feeling, but it was the end of the world for me.

I was rushed to Jacobi hospital in Meme's car and quickly seen by doctors in the emergency room. They ran some tests on me, took blood, and treated me carefully because of my condition. They said I was okay, that it was probably stress or an anxiety attack. I was told to rest and drink plenty of fluids.

I was going through a lot and a girl in my condition didn't need the added stress in my life. But besides that, me and my baby was okay. He or she was a trooper like me. However, yes, I was okay on the outside, physically healthy and still ticking, but mentally I was sick and fucked up. I couldn't stop thinking about my fight with Sammy. The fight between us was the final blow to our already shaky friendship. The betrayal from her had me not wanting to trust anyone ever again, and it had me feeling suicidal. That feeling hurt so bad I would get these pains in my chest and become so emotional.

Tina and Meme didn't leave my side the entire time. They were with me through every step and every way. They did their best to comfort me. But I was just too upset. The nurse who was taking my blood pressure in the room would look at me, seeing my minor bruises on my face from the fight, and the tears staining my face. She said to me, "Chile, he's not worth it. Take care of yourself and that baby. It is the only thing that matters."

I was ready to curse this bitch out. Who was she to fuckin' judge me and be in my business? She didn't know me at all. I glared at her, holding my composure and tongue for some reason.

She continued with, "You are a very beautiful young woman, chile. God has blessed you with life developing inside of you. You are going to become a young mother. I can see the pain in your eyes and the hurt in your soul. Let it go and only be concerned for your unborn."

The woman gazed at me with genuine concern. She was black, maybe with West Indies roots. She looked to be in her early forties and was beautiful with long black hair and gray streaks. She seemed to really love her job and truly care for the patients she was treating.

"What is your name?" she asked me.

I didn't answer her. I frowned; she continued to smile.

"It's okay, my name is Gail. And I'm your friend."

"I don't need any friends," I spat. "So fuck you!"

She continued to smile and was warm and friendly with me. I wanted her to do her job and leave me the fuck alone.

"It's always good to have a friend, especially when you are going through hard times. I know the world you come from and I can see the mistrust in your eyes, chile."

"You don't know shit about me, bitch, so stop faking like you really care about me. You don't know the shit I been through and where I'm fuckin' from!" I shouted.

The bitch didn't even seem startled by my outburst. She continued to treat me and talk to me so warmly. I didn't know her angle or motive. What did she have to gain from being nice to me? It felt like she wanted me to open up and confess something.

"Well, if you don't want me to know a little about you, then I'm going to tell you something about me." She smiled heavily.

I didn't want to know, but she was going to tell it to me anyway.

"I don't know you, but I love you," she said.

I was thinking this bitch was weird, a freak or a lesbian and I didn't swing that way. I scowled at her and clenched my fists. If she moved the wrong way toward me, then I was ready to go ham on this weird bitch.

She went on with, "I love you, because God loves me and He loves you."

Oh my God, she was a bible-thumping fool. I didn't want to hear any more, especially about God. But she added, "I know your life, chile."

"I'm not ya fuckin chile!" I exclaimed.

"Then what is your name?"

"They call me Mouse."

"It's a beautiful name."

"Whatever!" I rolled my eyes.

"Mouse, let me tell you something: sometimes life doesn't get easier, we only become stronger. And God is telling me that a dangerous storm is coming your way."

"What? You a psychic or somethin'?"

She chuckled. "No, I'm not a psychic, but God is. He knows our comings and goings, and I see something very special in you, Mouse."

"You see somethin' special in me?"

"I was you at one point in my life. Pregnant when I was seventeen, and in the streets doing everything and anything to survive. The baby's father wasn't around. So I sold dope and I sold myself on these streets just to provide for and feed my oldest son. It was hard for me, Mouse. I was so young and scared, and my friends were against me."

Now she was becoming interesting.

"Where are you from?" I asked.

"I'm from the Bronx too. I grew up in Soundview. This was way before your time, Mouse. I used to be on drugs so bad when I was around your age. But a few years ago, I gave my life over to Christ and He led the way for me."

I wasn't trying to hear about Christ or any of that other religious nonsense. But I admit, this nurse did become a lot more interesting to me.

She looked at me, like she was reading me, or saw something that I didn't see.

"It's gonna get harder for you, Mouse. I know. But you have to remain strong and have faith. You must forgive whoever hurt and did you wrong, and move on."

"Fuck that bitch!" I spat.

She continued talking and preaching to me. She was trying to get through to me, preach to me about love and Christ, but I was being too stubborn. But I admit she did have a way of calming me down. I didn't want to be calmed down. I wanted revenge.

Before the nurse left my room, she gave me her phone number and said if I ever needed to talk or wanted to attend church with her, then to give her a call anytime. She promised that she would never be too busy for me. I took her number, and before she left the room, she said a prayer for me and my unborn child. I never had anyone pray for me before. It was weird. But it was nice.

"I don't know you, Mouse, but I love you. You are special. God has something special planned for you, and when that storm comes your way, you anchor yourself to faith and Him, and you stay there and fight. And if you ever need me, you have my number," she proclaimed warmly.

What storm was she talking about?

I exhaled and felt something strange inside of me. I'd been through many storms in life and I was still here, surviving and doing me. I wasn't weak. Gail's words did linger in my mind for a moment after she left. Her advice and words to me did have me thinking, but when Tina and Meme walked back into my room, that nurse's talk went out the door and reality hit me. I didn't know that bitch and chances were I would probably never see her again.

I was being discharged from the hospital that same day. I stood outside the emergency room with Tina. We were waiting for Meme to get the car and pull up. They didn't want me to walk the three blocks where she was parked.

But I didn't want to go back home. I didn't want to see Rico's cheating face, because if I did, I would kill him and someone would end up killing me. But I had nowhere else to go. It was a heartbreaking moment for me. Meme said I could stay with her, but she lived in Edenwald, in the building next to Sammy's, and I didn't want to see that bitch again, even though they said that she was now living in Co-op City. I was ready to kill her.

When Meme pulled up, I climbed into the front seat. Meme looked at me and asked, "Where you wanna go, Mouse? I'll drive you anywhere. And you already know you can stay wit' me for how long. I got ya back."

I was flattered. I huffed and said to her, "Just take me home."

"Mount Vernon?"

I nodded.

Mount Vernon was my home now. I had nowhere else to go. It was comfortable and it was away from the bullshit. The only flaw was it was Rico's place and I had to share it with him. And even though he made me sick to my stomach, I was carrying his baby and he was still my man.

Meme drove off. I sat back in my chair and closed my eyes. I wanted to be alone for a moment. I didn't feel like talking. I only wanted to rest. I wanted to go into my book of rhymes and write. Like always, I wanted to escape.

Meme arrived at my Mount Vernon address thirty-five minutes later. It was late. I didn't see Rico's car in the driveway or parked anywhere on the block. I got out. Tina and Meme wanted to come inside with me, but I told them no. I didn't want any company. I walked inside to a dark and lonely house, just like my heart. I didn't know what to do with myself. Like usual, Rico wasn't home and I wasn't going to call his cell phone. He never answered anyway. I went into the bedroom and undressed, and went to bed, but I wasn't tired. I only wanted to lie down and dream I was somewhere else.

I lay in bed for forty minutes with my eyes open and gazing at the ceiling in tears. I thought about a rhyme I wanted to write. I needed to express myself. *If you love me, you sure don't act like you do. If you desire me, then why the fuck do I feel so used? I'm ya boo, but nigga you don't have a clue, you have a woman that's true to you, but you fuck my bitch like that shit is cool, I'm ride or die fo' ya fuckin' lies, I'm in love, these tears that fall is my life, nigga I should cut off ya dick and string it around my neck, bitch nigga, now I'm the one wearin' the family jewels, sportin' this bitch like he can exist.*

As I was working on my rhyme I heard the front door open. It was Rico coming home. I wasn't going to rush to confront him. I really didn't want to see him. How was he going to explain his infidelity to me? How the fuck was he going to explain fuckin' my best friend? How the fuck was he going to explain his lies to me, the way he was dogging me? There was no way to explain it.

I heard him coming my way. I dried my tears but more continued to fall. He had to have heard about the fight. The streets were always talking and Rico was always listening. Rico came into the bedroom. I was propped up, sitting Indian style with my back against the headboard. I glared at him. He looked at me with this deadpan expression, like he wasn't sorry for everything he'd done.

"You just gonna look at me, or you gonna say somethin'?" I shouted.

"What you wanna know? I fucked up, a'ight? *Lo siento.*"

He said he was sorry. I didn't believe him. "That's it! Rico, do you fuckin' love me?" I dried my tears once again.

"Yeah, I love you," he replied coolly. "But what you gonna do, you gonna leave me?" It was a very bold statement coming from him.

He stepped closer to me. His apologetic look turned into a sinister stare at me. "Sammy and I got history. Yeah, I fucked her. But you got my seed and you ain't goin' anywhere. I got you livin' comfortable, Mouse. *Como una reina maldito,* and you owe me for all of this," he said gruffly.

"What?"

"Bitch, you heard me!"

I got up from the bed. I was ready to leave him. "Fuck you!"

He charged at me and smacked me across the face and I went flying across the bed. He stood over me with his fists clenched. He had changed drastically.

"You ain't goin' any-fuckin'-where, Mouse. Ya my woman and you stay here!"

I cried out. He attacked me again. And just like that, I went from the frying pan and into the fire. This wasn't my life. This couldn't be my life. I went from an abusive father to an abusive boyfriend. And Rico didn't have any problems putting his hands on a pregnant woman—his woman. He beat me and then raped me for what felt like an eternity. He shoved his dick into me forcefully. I tried to fight, but the more I resisted, the more aggressive he became. He punched me and punched me while he was on top of me fucking me. He thrust inside of me with his hand around my neck and the tears streaming down my face.

"Rico! Stop it! Stop it!" I cried out.

My cries for him to stop fell on deaf ears. He seemed in some kind of trance. It was hurting. It was painful. He fucked me roughly and then came inside of me. It felt like he just used the toilet on me. This wasn't the man I fell in love with a few months back. This was a stranger in my home.

When he was done, I was black and blue all over, and sore. He finally got off of me and pulled up his jeans. He stared at me with this smug look, and he looked proud of his work.

"Bitch, you ain't goin' anywhere. You in my home now and I own you. You live good here, so get used to it. You leave when I say so. And if you ever fuckin' leave me, then I'll find you and I'll kill you, pregnant or not," he said brusquely.

I just cried and cried. When he left the bedroom, I was in agony and tears. I was so sore in many areas of my body and I was blinded by my watery eyes. I wanted to go home. But I had no home. Gail warned me that a storm was coming, but I didn't believe her and I didn't know it was coming this fast. I still had her number in my jeans pocket. I was tempted to call, but for some reason, I didn't. I think I was embarrassed because she was right about everything. I had brushed her off and was a complete bitch to her. I could only stare at her number and sob. This was hell on earth for me. When was my pain and suffering going to end? When was I going to find happiness?

Sammy

Four months later: November

The morning sickness was killing me; I didn't understand how women could do it, be pregnant all of the time and deal with the changes your body gradually goes through. I spent almost the entire morning in the bathroom feeling nauseated and throwing up. I had business to take care of and couldn't afford to be pregnant. However, it was confirmed from my doctor. I was six weeks pregnant with Rico's child. Which meant the nigga had to knock me up sometime in October. It wasn't a shock to me; I never once used protection with him and we were fucking all the time. I was hooked on that dick and I was in love with him.

Rico knew about the pregnancy, and he must have felt proud about himself. He got two best friends pregnant at the same time. He accomplished something that niggas in the hood been trying to do for a very long time: lock down two of the finest bitches with his seed. I couldn't believe I was carrying his baby, too. He didn't want me to get an abortion. He was so adamant about it that I thought he would kill me if I tried to.

"You ain't killin' my baby, Sammy," he had said to me.

So I was stuck carrying either a boy or girl inside my belly. But I was still in the streets; pregnant or not, getting that money wasn't going to ever stop. I had an organization to run and a career to pop off. I hadn't spoken or seen Mouse in months, actually since our fight in July. We weren't best friends anymore and the bitch was out of sight, out of mind. We made sure to stay separate from each other. The last I heard about her, she was still shacking up with my man, pregnant, looking like a house and trying to be the best housewife she could be. Dumb bitch! I was getting money and she was Mrs. Brady. I had to laugh.

I wiped my mouth and got myself right. I walked into the living room. Saint and Romeo were bagging the last of the kilos on the table. It was a large shipment of cocaine from our Colombian connect in Washington Heights: twenty kilos. I oversaw the entire operation. I was making money by the boatload and I was that bitch on the streets. The past five months had been very profitable. I still had the apartment in Co-op City, another place in Edenwald, and a stash house that was an hour upstate from here. I didn't want to be poor anymore. My wardrobe changed considerably: Gucci, Donna Karan, Chanel, Fendi. I was wearing it all and loving it. I drove around in a dark blue Mercedes-Benz, and the best thing about hustling was I was able to invest heavily into my music. I was a solo artist and spending numerous hours in the recording studio and doing my own promotion. I had money to burn and I invested into my music career. I wanted to become the female P. Diddy or Russell Simmons in the game. I had an army backing me.

I sat in the apartment counting money and watching the news, and when I heard them mention something about Macky, it caught my attention. It had been months since I put two bullets into that muthafucka, and Rico's goons took care of disposing the body. The media had announced that he'd been missing for almost four months now and everybody was looking for him. He was a prominent music producer who suddenly disappeared from his upstate home and his family and friends were extremely worried. Even Search was asking around about him.

I took a pull from my Newport and smirked. They wasn't going to find him. From my understanding, the two men Rico had with him that night were good at getting rid of bodies. I wasn't concerned about it. There was no connection to me.

"Y'all niggas almost done wit' that work?" I asked Saint.

"Yeah, we almost done," he replied.

I wanted to hurry up and get rid of this shipment. I was uncomfortable having too much weight in one place. Once we got the product from the Heights, the majority of the keys went across state lines for wholesale prices, and the remainder we cut and bagged up for street distribution.

I was satisfied with the way things were turning out. I walked to the window and gazed outside. It was a brisk November evening with Thanksgiving right around the corner. I was never too big on celebrating holidays. I never had a family to celebrate with and I damn sure didn't have anything to celebrate about. It was just another day to me. I continued to smoke my cigarette and stared at the Bronx from fourteen floors up. This was where I was supposed to be: on top of the world.

I lingered by the window for a moment, hearing the counting machine go off in the background. It was always good to hear them count thousands of dollars that most times added up to hundreds of thousands of dollars. I smiled. A bitch came a long way; look at me now. I was running things, almost second in charge. I became a hustler, a businesswoman overnight, and was ready to open up my own record label if the money kept pouring in like this.

I exhaled and heard my cell phone ringing. I looked at the caller ID and saw it was Paco calling, one of Rico's henchman. I answered and before I could say a word, Paco hollered, "Sammy, Rico just got knocked by the feds. Hurry up and shut down shop!"

"What?" I uttered.

"Shut everything the fuck down, now!" he shouted.

I didn't have time to ask questions. I hung up and ordered Saint and Romeo to shut down everything, letting them know that Rico just got caught up with the feds. They jumped from their chairs and knew the routine. Everything went to the bathroom and we had to flush seven kilos of cocaine, pills, and weed, and dump everything down the trash chute. We erased any criminal files or evidence from the computers by pouring bleach and acid on the equipment. We all went scrambling around the apartment like chickens with their heads cut off. We didn't know if the feds were coming for us, and if so, how soon they'd be showing up.

I ran to the window and gazed outside. I didn't see anything outside, but it was hard to see anything from fourteen floors up. We had to hurry and make our exit. I didn't want to see jail. I ran to the bedroom and collected cash, over $100,000, and a few important items and ran out. The apartment was in chaos, everything destroyed, and the entire product flushed and gone. It was heart-breaking to lose that kind of money, but we had to. We got rid of automatic weapons and wiped the place down in record time and we left like we were never there in the first place, taking the stairs instead of the elevator.

I separated myself from Saint and Romeo and hurried to my Benz parked on the corner. I jumped inside, started the ignition, and took a deep breath. Rico was locked up, so I wondered who else the feds were coming for next. I sped away to my spot a few miles away from here. It was time to lay low and see what was going down. Just like that, everything was gone and I didn't know what to do at the moment. I was pregnant and really nervous.

I walked into the visiting area of Rikers Island with my heart beating rapidly. It'd been one month since Rico's incarceration. He was remanded, bail denied because of his long criminal record, and the DA was trying to take his head and hit him with so many indictments that I lost count. They labeled Rico as a murderous and dangerous kingpin and he was going to be charged with the RICO act. I was heartbroken. They didn't come for me, not yet anyway. The feds had been investigating Rico for over a year now and a snitch and an informant helped put him away. Their identities were still a mystery. The feds made sure to keep their identification a secret, because whoever they were, they were dead men.

I followed a half dozen women into the large and grungy visiting area, where there were about two dozen women and inmates socializing under the watchful eyes of a half dozen corrections officers strategically positioned everywhere in the room. I had to see Rico. He was asking for me. The DA was trying to give him life in prison, but if he took a plea then he was looking at twenty-five years. It was a hard pill to swallow, but Rico was hardcore and he knew the risks. He wasn't bitching out and trying to snitch on anyone else.

I sat down where the CO pointed, at a small, round table that looked fit for a kindergarten class, with two chairs and nothing in between us but space and air. I was dressed regular in a T-shirt and jeans and black Nikes, and my hair was pulled back into a long ponytail. I didn't want to stand out. I was nervous that they were going to know everything about me and keep me. I knew I wasn't off the feds' radar yet; they were still investigating his crew and still making arrests. I just had to keep cool and keep a low profile. With it being December, and Christmas approaching, I was two months pregnant and showing.

I sat and waited for Rico to emerge into the room. Next to me was this black couple holding hands across the table and touching, and fondling each other discreetly. They kissed until the guard had to warn them that there was no excessive affection during visits. He had to warn them numerous times until he threatened the visit was going to be cut short if it happened again.

I waited. The streets were talking, people were hungry, and it was becoming ugly out there. With Rico locked up there was a void in the drug game that was sparking up a war. Everybody wanted to get paid and bullets were flying and bodies were dropping. I stayed away from Edenwald for several weeks, getting my mind right. It was so scary out there that even hardcore killers were walking around like there were eggshells on the ground. Every step taken could be someone's last.

Rico finally made his way into the room with an expressionless look. He was clad in an orange jumpsuit with DOC printed on the back in black, bold letters, and he was still looking good. His cornrows were longer and freshly done and he moved through the visiting room with a sense of power about him. He had respect and his reputation preceded him. He focused his attention on me and didn't even smile.

I stood up and gave him a strong and passionate hug. I didn't want to let him go, but there wasn't any long and affectionate contact like that. I released my arms from around him and pulled away.

"You look good, Sammy," he said.

"You look good too," I replied.

We took our seats opposite each other. Rico leaned over and started talking. It wasn't a long visit and he didn't want to waste any time with nonsense like casual talk.

"I'm hearing things, Sammy," he said.

"What you hearing?" I asked.

"Things are falling apart out there, getting ugly. I leave you in charge and they say you ain't been around to handle things. What's goin' on?"

I was kind of upset that he didn't acknowledge the baby that was growing in my stomach. He acted like he didn't care; the streets were more important than his unborn child growing inside of me.

"Things been too hot for anyone to do anything, Rico," I replied. "What I'm supposed to do?"

"You supposed to be out there representin' fo' me, Sammy, not hiding and being a fuckin' bitch," he spat. "I'm the one locked up, so you do whatever to keep this organization going."

"Are you serious?"

"You made a lot of money because of me. You invested in your music career, got shit off the ground for yourself, and now you wanna give up and run. I made you!"

"And I have other important things to think about, like our baby inside of me. I don't want our child to be born in a fuckin' prison, and I don't wanna get shot down while I'm pregnant," I hissed. "Do you fuckin' care, Rico?"

He leaned in closer to me and scowled. "You tryin' to abandon me, Sammy?"

"I'm not leaving you, Rico. I just need time to think about things," I told him.

"You better think right and fast, and you better not fuckin' leave me, Sammy. I might be locked down in here, but I own you," he threatened. "*Esto no es un juego.*"

"Own me?" I frowned heavily. "Nobody fuckin' owns me, Rico."

"You think I don't? I'm nobody to fuck around wit'. I'm as dangerous in here as I was out there. And I'm not gonna be forgotten, Sammy," he growled without due consideration for me.

"You crazy, Rico. I'm nobody's slave. And you got the fuckin' audacity to come at me when I'm carrying your baby inside of me. The doctors say I'm havin' ya son," I chided. "Even though it's too early to tell right now."

"My son." He smirked.

"Yes." I tried to keep the tears from falling. I quickly wiped my eyes. Being pregnant made me emotional, and I hated being emotional and going through these different conditions.

"They found Macky's body the other day," he said to me in a low voice, changing the subject.

"I thought you took care of that."

"I thought so too, but the Thompson brothers didn't do that good of a job as I thought they would. But guess what, you fuckin' cross me and you'll be in here wit' me. Remember, you were the one who killed him, ya fingerprints are still on the gun. It only takes one phone call and ya life is over," he threatened me.

I was speechless. I didn't know what to say or do. He was blackmailing me. I was tricked, bamboozled, and he had this planned all along.

"Why?"

"'Cause I can and I will. I don't give a fuck, Sammy. I'ma let you have my son, but when the time comes and I need somethin' from you, you better jump and fuckin' do it. You understand?"

I didn't respond. I was just shocked and stupid. This muthafucka didn't change one damn bit. He was selfish and still about business.

"I'm talkin' to you, bitch!"

"I understand," I replied faintly. The tears fell from my eyes and I wanted to disappear.

"And another thing, you have a contract on ya head," he mentioned.

"What?"

"That bitch Angie, she's fuckin' gangsta, and she really wants you dead. They green-lighted the hit on you, but I used my influence to stop it. Ya gonna be the mother of my son, and I can't be havin' that shit happening, so thank me," he said smugly.

"Thank you?" I said incredulously.

"Ya fuckin' welcome."

I wanted to rush out that room and throw up. Rico locked eyes with me and I was sitting in front of the devil himself. The muthafucka was devious and evil. I hated him. I couldn't say anything else to him. This visit was over. I removed myself from the chair, indicating to the guard that I was done. I hurried to the exit. Once I was outside in the open, I dropped to my knees in tears and started to throw up. I felt trapped and fuckin' angry. I had nowhere to go and Rico had a leash around my neck with this murder.

Epilogue

Mouse

January 22

I lay spent in the hospital bed after giving birth to a baby girl, who was seven pounds and eleven ounces. She was so beautiful and the most precious thing I ever held in my life. I was a proud mother. I spent fifteen hours in labor pushing out my daughter and it was the most agonizing and unbearable pain that I ever felt in my life. But it was all worth it in the end. I named my daughter Eliza and she was going to be somebody special, my angel, because I needed an angel in my life when shit was turning out to be fuckin' hell for me.

The feds raided Rico's house early in the morning with me inside. They took me in for questioning, and the feds didn't have anything on me and with my condition, I was released, but the damage had already been done. They seized everything, cars, money, the house, and I was left homeless and scared. I had to go move in with Meme; she had room for me in her two-bedroom apartment.

Rico found out where I was staying and he would send his goons to visit me, or intimidate me. He was incarcerated hundreds of miles away and still was dangerous. He had taken a plea deal a few months back, receiving twenty-five years in a federal prison. He wanted me to bring him his daughter, but she was still a newborn and that trip upstate was just too much for me too soon. I was scared of him. It seemed like he always had eyes on me. He knew where I was staying or going. I wanted him out of my life, I didn't care if I did have his daughter. He was bad news and dangerous. I never went to go see him while he was in Rikers Island. I didn't want anything to do with him, but he wanted everything to do with me.

My life was different and becoming harder. The money and the luxury was all gone, like yesterday. I felt it was never coming back. I was stuck staying from one friend's place to another, now with a baby attached to my hips. I was nineteen and becoming my worst nightmare: a single Latino mother with no job, no schooling, and broke. I thought my life was going to be better when I got with Rico, but it only got worse. He was a fraudulent mutha-fucka. He brought me down so far that I couldn't even see the top anymore. I cried almost every night after giving birth, and if it weren't for the precious angle I held in my arms I probably would have committed suicide. The dreams I once had about having a family, living like the Cosbys, it didn't come true for people like me. We seemed to always be stuck with hell and lies. And my music career was gone. Who wanted to sign a single, fat Latino mother with a troubling past and having more baggage than a grocery store? I always made wrong choices growing up, but dealing with a monster and having his seed, it was a painful feeling. I loved my daughter to death, don't get it twisted, but I loathed her father. I wished I could have seen clearly last year like I did now. I would have acted so differently and wouldn't be stuck under the thumb of Rico and maybe have gotten a record deal. But I was blinded by his fraudulent charisma, the big dick and sex, along with the luxury he was giving me. Now my life was a nightmare. But the worst of it all was I didn't have

Sammy in my life anymore. I didn't have my best friend to have my back and help me through difficult situations like she always did. Now I was completely alone, and thinking, *where the fuck do I go from here?*

Sammy

July 16

I gave birth to Rico's son at five in the morning. It was nineteen hours of pain and agony. I just wanted this fuckin' baby out of me so badly that I started crying like a baby myself. I was hurting and shit felt so uncomfortable and awkward for me with my legs spread, I was cursing and crying, the doctors and nurses gathered around me and watching my pussy stretch like it was a rubber band. I pushed and pushed until I finally gave birth to my son. He was six pounds and eleven ounces. He was a healthy and beautiful baby boy. When they placed him into my arms, I already felt the connection. I already felt like a mother to him. He had the biggest and brightest brown eyes. He was so small, fragile, and innocent. I loved him already, despite who his fuckin' father was.

Rico had received a twenty-five year prison sentence in January and he was locked away in Attica. I reluctantly went to see him a few times after his threats against me. I still had money in accounts and the feds didn't come after me, which was a blessing. But I was still trapped in a prison. I had to make sure Rico's commissary was well taken care of and when he was sent upstate, I would send him clothes, magazines, books, and other things. My music was put on hold, and everything just stopped for me.

I still had Macky's murder lingering over my head. The hip-hop world was stunned by his gruesome death. When they found the body it was so badly decomposed that he needed a closed-casket funeral. The family put out an award for any information and arrests about his death. It was haunting me. The man was a fuckin' monster and he was still taunting me from the fuckin' grave. I wanted to leave town with my baby, but I didn't know anywhere else but the Bronx. And with Rico being the devil muthafucka he was, he wanted me to stay in the Bronx and be his eyes and ears on the streets. Everything went from sugar to shit for me so fast that within the blink of an eye I was changing into something I hated: his personal bitch under his command. And if he could fuck me whenever he wanted, he would be taking the pussy. But his incarceration prevented that from happening.

But what hurt the most was seeing Search on TV, doing his thing, doing it big. He was attending music awards ceremonies, was on the radio a few times, doing interviews in magazines and whatnot. He was managing this new female rap group who called themselves Promise. They were from the Bronx too, and they weren't as good as Mouse and me. But they were shining, taking over where we left off, and I wanted to cry. It was supposed to be us out there on stage, being on MTV, doing articles in *Vibe* and *The Source* magazine. I was starting to hate my life, and if it weren't for my son, I think I would have killed myself.

I regretted every decision I made last year, from my fight with Mouse to fucking Rico and hustling for him again. Everything that glittered damn sure wasn't gold, and I learned that the hard way. I wasn't thinking. I was caught up in the hype and now look at me becoming another statistic: a single Latino mother with her child's father incarcerated. I wasn't meant to live this way. I was on my way into becoming a superstar, I was so close, making the right connections, and now I was under Rico's thumb. He wasn't the only one in a prison.

Now I didn't know what to believe anymore. Search always proclaimed that he had a reason for his sudden departure to ATL, and why he couldn't take me. But Rico was brainwashing me, putting shit into my head about Search, and then with Macky attacking me, it all fell perfectly into place. I treated Search like shit and never apologized for it. I never got to hear his side of the story and being in the position that I was, I regretted it with every bone in my body. He was always good to me. He always believed in me. Now I looked at his life and mines, and I went in the wrong direction while he went soaring in the right direction without me. The gangs, the violence, Rico, the money, it caused a devastating detour in my life and the only thing I could do was cry and cry. The decisions you make in the past can definitely affect your future. And I let easy money seduce me and a smooth talker persuade me. I felt alone. And the worst of it was I didn't have Mouse to talk to and have my back.

But now if I was to get a second chance with Search, my music, and being a better woman, I wasn't going to make the same mistakes twice, best believe that. But I didn't know what my future looked like. It seemed dark. I felt so defeated and used. I felt angry and betrayed. I wanted everything and now I ended up with almost nothing but a beautiful son I had to nurse.

I sat in my room nursing my baby boy with the milk coming from my breast. I was being discharged from the hospital with him today and I wanted to go home and be alone. I was staying back at my mother's apartment. She was getting worse every day and I felt she didn't have that much time left on this earth. She was so skinny and frail, like a broomstick. I knew she was going to be proud to see her grandson and hold him in her last days. It was the only thing I could do for her, my one gift or blessing she could receive from me.

I heard a knock at the room door. I looked up and saw Fence staring at me. He was still creepy and ugly. I quickly covered up my breast and my son, and asked roughly, "What the fuck you doin' here, Fence?"

He remained deadpan, stepped farther into the room, and said to me, "Rico wants to see his son."

I groaned and felt it was the beginning of it becoming hell on earth for me.